Praise For

more . . .

Also by Larry Brown

FACING THE MUSIC

Stories

DIRTY WORK

A Novel

BIG BAD LOVE

Stories

J O E

LARRY BROWN

WARNER BOOKS

A Time Warner Company

for my big bad bro,

Paul Hipp

This is a work of fiction. All names, characters, places, and incidents are either the products of the author's imagination or are used fictitiously. No reference to any real person is intended or should be inferred.

Warner Books Edition
Copyright © 1991 by Larry Brown
All rights reserved.

This Warner Books edition is published by arrangement with Algonquin Books of Chapel Hill, North Carolina.

Warner Books, Inc., 1271 Avenue of the Americas, New York, NY 10020

W A Time Warner Company

Printed in the United States of America

First Warner Books Printing: October 1992
10 9 8 7 6 5 4 3

Library of Congress Cataloging in Publication Data

Brown, Larry,
    Joe / Larry Brown. — Warner Books ed.
        p.   cm.
    ISBN 0-446-39438-6
    I. Title.
    [PS3552.R6927J64   1991]
    813'.54—dc20   92-13730
                                                                            CIP

Cover design by Louise Fili
Cover illustration by Anthony Russo

The road lay long and black ahead of them and the heat was coming now through the thin soles of their shoes. There were young beans pushing up from the dry brown fields, tiny rows of green sprigs that stretched away in the distance. They trudged on beneath the burning sun, but anyone watching could have seen that they were almost beaten. They passed over a bridge spanning a creek that held no water as their feet sounded weak drumbeats, erratic and small in the silence that surrounded them. No cars passed these potential hitchhikers. The few rotting houses perched on the hillsides of snarled vegetation were broken-backed and listing, discarded dwellings where dwelled only field mice and owls. It was as if no one lived in this land or ever would again, but they could see a red tractor toiling in a field far off, silently, a small dust cloud following.

The two girls and the woman had weakened in the heat. Sweat beaded the black down on their upper lips. They each carried paper sacks containing their possessions, all except the old man, who was known as Wade, and who carried nothing but the ragged red bandanna that he mopped against his neck and head to staunch the flow of sweat that had turned his light blue shirt a darker hue. Half of his right shoe sole was off, and it flopped and folded beneath his foot so that he managed a sliding, shuffling movement with that leg, picking it up high in a queer manner before the sole flopped again.

The boy's name was Gary. He was small but he carried the most. His arms were laden with shapeless clothes, rusted cooking utensils, mildewed quilts and blankets. He had to look over the top of them as he walked, just to be able to see where he was going.

The old man faltered momentarily, did a drunken two-step, and collapsed slowly on the melted tar with a small grunt, easing down so as not to hurt himself. He lay with one forearm shielding his face from the eye of the sun. His family went on without him. He watched them growing smaller in the distance, advancing through the mirrored heat waves that shimmied in the road, unfocused wavering shapes with long legs and little heads.

"Hold up," he called. Silence answered. "Boy," he said. No head turned to hear him. If his cries fell on their ears they seemed not to care. Their heads were bent with purpose and their steps grew softer as they went on down the road.

He cursed them all viciously for a few moments and then he pushed himself up off the road and went after them, his shoe sole keeping a weird time. He hurried enough to catch up with them and they marched on through the stifling afternoon without speaking, as if they all knew where they were heading, as if there was no need for conversation. The road before them wound up into dark green hills. Maybe some hope of deep shade and cool water beckoned. They passed through a crossroads with fields and woods and cattle and a swamp, and they eyed the countryside with expressions bleak and harried. The sun had started its slow burning run down the sky.

The old man could see beer cans lying in the ditches, where a thin green scum nourished the tan sagegrass that grew there. He was very thirsty, but there was no prospect of any kind of drink within sight. He who rarely drank water was almost ready to cry out for some now.

He had his head down, plodding along like a mule in harness, and he walked very slowly into the back of his wife where she had stopped in the middle of the road.

"Why, yonder's some beer," she said, pointing.

He started to raise some curse against her without even looking, but then he looked. She was still pointing.

"Where?" he said. His eyes moved wildly in his head.

"Right yonder."

He looked where she was pointing and saw three or four bright red-and-white cans nestled among the grasses like Easter eggs. He stepped carefully down into the ditch, watchful for snakes. He stepped closer and stopped.

"Why, good God," he said. He bent and picked up a full can of Budweiser that was slathered with mud and slightly dented, unopened and still drinkable. A little joyous smile briefly creased his face. He put the beer in a pocket of his overalls and turned slowly in the weeds. He picked up two more, both full, and stood there for a while, searching for more, but three were all this wonderful ditch would yield. He climbed back out and put one of the beers in another pocket.

———

"Somebody done throwed this beer away," he said, looking at it. His family watched him.

"I guess you going to drink it," the woman said.

"Finders keepers. They ain't a fuckin thing wrong with it."

"How come em to throw it away then?"

"I don't know."

"Well," she said. "Just don't you give him none of it."

"I ain't about to give him none of it."

The woman turned and started walking away. The boy waited. He stood mute and patient with his armload of things. His father opened the can and foam exploded from it. It ran down over the sides and over his hand and he sucked at the thick white suds with a delicate slobbering noise and trembling pursed lips. He tilted the can and poured the hot beer down his throat, leaning his head back with his eyes closed and one rough red hand hanging loose by his side. A lump of gristle in his neck pumped up and down until he trailed the can away from his mouth with his face still turned up, one drop of beer falling away from the can before it was flung, spinning, backward into the ditch. He started walking again.

The boy shifted his gear higher and stepped off after him.

"What's beer taste like?" he said, as the old man wiped his mouth.

"Beer."

"I know that. But what's it *taste* like?"

"I don't know. Shit. It just tastes like beer. Don't ask so many fuckin questions. I need to hire somebody full time just to answer your questions."

The woman and the girls had gone ahead by two hundred feet. The old man and the boy had not gone more than a hundred feet before he opened the second beer. He drank it more slowly, walking, making four or five drinks of it. By the time they got to the foot of the first hill he had drunk all three.

It was that part of evening when the sun has gone but daylight still remains. The whippoorwills called to each other and moved about, and the choirs of frogs had assembled in the ditches to sing their melancholy songs. Bats scurried overhead, swift and gone in the gathering dusk. The boy didn't know where he and his family were, other than one name: Mississippi.

In the cooling evening light they turned off onto a gravel road, their reasons unspoken or merely obscure. Wilder country here, also unpeopled, with snagged wire and rotten posts encompassing regions of Johnsongrass and bitterweed, the grim woods holding secrets on each side. They walked up the road, the dust falling over their footprints. A coyote lifted one thin broken scream down in the bottom; somewhere beyond the stands of cane they could see a faint green at the end of the plowed ground. They turned in on a field road at the base of a soapstone hill and followed it, stepping around washed-out places in the ground, past pine trees standing like lonely sentinels, where doves flew out singing on gray-feathered wings, and by patches of bracken where unseen things scurried off noisily through the brush.

"You know where you at?" said the woman.

The old man didn't even look at her. "Do you?"

"I'm just followin you."

"Well, shut up then."

She did. They went over the last hill and here the whole bottom was open before them, the weak light that remained stretching far down across an immense expanse of land that had been plowed but not yet planted. They could see all the way to the river, where the trees stood black and solid.

"It's a river bottom," said the boy.

"Well shit," said the old man.

"Can't cross no river," the woman said.

"I know it."

"Not in the dark."

The old man glanced at her in the falling light and she looked away. He looked around.

"Well hell," he said. "It's bout dark. Y'all see if you can find us some wood and we'll build us a fire."

The boy and the two girls put everything they had on the ground. The girls found some dead pine tops next to an old fence and they pulled them whole into the road and began breaking them into pieces small enough to burn.

"See if you can find us a pine knot," he told the boy. The boy left and they could hear him breaking through the brush up the hill. When he came back he was dragging a gray hunk of wood with one hand and carrying in the other arm some dead branches. He threw all this down and started off for more. The old man squatted in the dust of the road and began to roll a cigarette, his attention focused finely, aware of nothing but the little task at hand. The woman was still standing with her arms clutched about her, hearing something out there in the dark that maybe spoke to no ear but her own.

6

The boy came back with another load and said, "Let me see your knife."

The old man fished out a broken-bladed Case and the boy fell to shaving thin orange peelings of wood away from the pine knot. He drew the blade down, breaking the chips off close to the base. When he had a good handful whittled, he arranged them in some unseen formation of his own devising in the powdered gray dust.

"Let me see some of them little sticks," he told his little sister. She passed across a bundle of brittle tinder and he set this around and above the pine chips. He drew a box of matches from his pocket and struck one. In the little fire that flared, his face loomed out of the dark, curiously intense and dirty, his hands needlessly cupping the small flame. He touched it to one of the chips and a tiny yellow blade curled up, a tendril of black smoke above it like a thick waving hair.

"That stuff's rich as six foot up a bull's ass," the old man said. The little scrap of wood began sizzling and the resin boiled out in black bubbles, the flames eating their way up. The boy picked up another one from the pile and held it over the fire, got it caught, and added it to the fire. One of the sticks popped and burst into flame.

"Give me some of them a little bigger," he said. She handed them. They smiled at each other, he and little sister. Now they began to be drawn out of the coming dark, the five of them hunched around the fire with their arms on their knees. He fed the sticks one by one into the fire, and soon it was crackling and growing and red embers were breaking off and falling into the little bed of coals already forming.

He kept feeding it, jostling and poking it. He got down on his knees and lowered his face sideways to the fire and began to blow on it. Like a bellows he gave it air and it responded. The fire rushed over the sticks, burned higher in the night.

"Y'all go on and put some of them big ones on it," he said, getting up. "I'll go up here and get some more."

The girls hauled limbs and piled them on the fire. Soon there were red sparks launching up into the smoke. The stars came out and enveloped them in their makeshift camp. They sat under a black skyscape beside woods alive with noise. The bullfrogs on the creeks that fed the river were hoarse and they spoke from the clay banks up into the darkness with a sound the ear loves.

The woman was digging among her sparse duffel, pawing aside unusable items at the top of the sack. She pulled out a blackened iron skillet and a pint can of green beans. She set these down and looked some more.

"Where's them sardines?" she said.

"They in here, Mama," the oldest girl said. The youngest one said nothing.

"Well, give em here, honey."

The boy came crashing down through the bushes and laid another armload of wood by the fire and went away again. They could hear him casting about like an enormous hound. The woman had the knife up and she was stabbing at the can of beans with it. She managed to open it and with careful fingers she pried the jagged edge up and turned the can over, shaking the beans into the skillet. She set it close to the coals and started in on the sardines. After she got the can open she rummaged around in her sack and pulled out a package of paper plates partially wrapped in cellophane and set them down, took out five. There were five of the little fish in the can. She put one in each plate.

The old man immediately reached over with grimed fingers and picked up a sardine daintily and bit it once and bit it twice and it was gone.

"That was his," she said.

"He ort to been down here," he said, chewing, wiping.

The boy had moved far back in the brush. They listened to him while the beans warmed.

"How much longer?"

The woman stared into the fire with a face sullen and orange.

"It'll be ready when it gets ready."

She looked off suddenly into the dark as if she'd heard something out there, her face grained like leather, trying to smile.

"Calvin?" she called. "Calvin. Is that you?"

"Hush," he said, looking with her. "Shut that shit up."

She fixed him with a look of grim desperation, a face she wore at night.

"I think it's Calvin," she said. "Done found us."

She lurched up onto her knees and looked wildly about, as if searching for a weapon to fend off the night, and she called out to the screaming dark: "Honey, come on in here it's almost ready Mama's got biscuits fixed."

She gathered her breath to say more, but he got up and went to her and shook her by the shoulders, bending over her with the ragged legs of his overalls flopping before the fire and the girls silent and not watching this at all. The little one got up on one knee and put another stick on the fire.

———

"Now, just hush," the old man said. "Hush."

She turned to the oldest girl.

"You water's not broke, is it?"

"I ain't pregnant, Mama." Her head was bowed, dark hair falling down around her face. "I done told you."

"Lord God, child, if you water's broke it ain't nothin nobody can do about it. I knowed this nigger woman one time her water broke and they wasn't nobody around for a mile to help her. I tried helpin her and she wouldn't have me."

"I'm fixin to slap you," he said.

"She wasn't about to have me. I's standing out yonder by the pumphouse and they come in there three or four and tied her down and she had the biggest blackest thing stickin out butt first . . ."

He hit her. Laid her out with one lick. She didn't even groan. She fell over on her back in the dirt and lay with her arms outspread like a witness for Christ stricken with the power of the Blood.

The girls looked at her and then they looked at the beans. They were almost ready. The old man was crouched beside their mother, his hands moving and working.

The boy was running back down through the brush and the woods, the wire singing one high shrieking note when he hit it. He stumbled panting and on all fours to the fire and noted his mother lying stretched out on her back and his father bent over her in an attitude of supplication and saw his two sisters watching the fire with hungry looks and yelled out, over the noise of the bullfrogs and the maddening crickets screaming and the murmur of the water running low in the creek: "They's a *house* up here!"

oe rose early from a sleep filled with nightmares of shooting guns and swinging pool cues launched up in his face and stealthy blacks with knives who lurked around corners with their eyes walled white in the darkness or slipped up behind him on cat feet to take his life for money. At four-thirty he made some instant coffee and drank about half a cup. He put a load of clothes in to wash, moving through the brightly lit rooms while all around him outside the community slept. He turned on the television to see if there was anything on, but there wasn't anything but snow.

The dog was standing in the yard with his head up when he pushed open the door.

"Here, dog," he said. "Hey, dog."

He bent with the two opened cans of dog food in his hands and spooned the meat onto a concrete block at the foot of the steps. He moved out of the way when the dog moved in and stepped back up into the open door to watch him eat. Just a few grunting noises, the jerking of his scarred head up and down.

The coffee was cold in the cup when he sat back down at the

table. He pitched it into the sink and made another, then sat sipping it slowly with his arm laid out to rest on the cheap metal table, a Winston smoking between his fingers. It was five o'clock by then. He had some numbers written down on a piece of notebook paper that had been folded and rained on, and he spread it out before him on the table, smoothing it, silently rehearsing the numbers with his lips. The phone was on the table in front of him. He lifted the receiver and dialed.

"You goin to work this mornin?" he said. He listened. "What about Junior? He get drunk last night?" He listened, grinned, then coughed into the phone. "All right," he said. "I'll be up there in thirty minutes. Y'all be ready, hear?"

He hung up on a babbling voice. He listened to the clothes chugging in the machine and he listened to the silence he lived in now, which was broken most times only by the dog whining at the back step. He got up and went to the icebox and brought the fifth of whiskey that was in there back to the table. He held it in his hand for a minute, studying it, reading the label, where it was made, how long it was aged. Then he opened it and took a good drink. There was a canned Coke on the table, half empty, flat and hot. He made sure nobody had thumped any cigarette ashes in it before he took a drink. Coke, then whiskey, Coke and then whiskey. He wiped his mouth and capped the bottle and lit another cigarette.

He turned off the lights at five-fifteen and went down the steps and across the wet grass of the tiny yard and no one saw him leave. The stars had gone in but dawn had not yet paled the sky. The dog whined and nuzzled around his legs as if he'd go, too, but Joe pushed him away gently with his foot and told him to move, then got in the truck.

"Stay here," he said. The dog went back under the house. The whiskey went under the seat. He cranked the truck with the door still open, found the wiper switch and watched the blades slap against the dew on the windshield. The truck was old and rusty and it had a wrecked camper hull bolted over the bed, where the poison guns and jugs lay in wreaths of dust and where the scraps of baby pines left from the past winter had dried into kindling. Spare tires and flat ones, empty beer cans and whiskey bottles. He sat revving it until it would idle and then he shut the door and turned on the lights and backed out of the driveway. It coughed up the road, missing and lurching, the one red eye in the back slowly fading toward the dawn.

There were five of them standing beside the road with their hands in their pockets and the orange tips of their cigarettes winking in their lips. He pulled up beside them and stopped and they climbed into the back, the truck shaking and jarring as they sat. He stopped twice more before he got to town, taking on one rider at each halt. It was getting daylight when he drove into the city limits. He eased under the red light at the top of the hill and turned onto the project road with the back end sagging. The blue lights of the police cars that were gathered in the parking lot washed the gray brick walls in sporadic sapphire, while the strobes flashed and illuminated the junked autos and spilled trash and overflowing Dumpsters. He pulled up short and stopped and sat watching. There were three patrol cars and he could see at least five cops. He stuck his head out the window and said: "Hey, Shorty."

One of them climbed down from the back and walked up beside the cab to stand next to him. A thin youth in a red T-shirt.

"What's goin on, Shorty? Where's Junior at?"

The boy shook his head. "Somebody fucked up."

"Well, go see if you can find him right quick. I don't need to be around these damn cops. They'll think I did it."

"I'll go get him," the boy said, and he moved off toward the nearest building.

"Hurry up, now," he said after him, and the boy broke into a jog. Fifteen or twenty black people were standing in a group on the sidewalk, watching. Most of them were wearing undershorts or nightgowns. One cop was keeping the crowd herded back.

As he sat looking at them, the police led a man in a pair of white jeans to one of the cars. His hands were cuffed behind his naked back. They opened a rear door and one of them put his hand on top of the man's head in an oddly gentle act and kept him from bumping his head as he got in. Some of the workhands in the back end of the truck started out but Joe called for them to stay put, that they didn't have time. He lit a cigarette and saw a red glow moving through the pines behind them. He swiveled his head to see an ambulance coming slowly with the siren off. Somebody dead, no urgency, had to be. Then he saw the foot. Just one, turned with the toes up, sticking out past the left side of a patrol car. A black foot with a pale bottom unmoving on the asphalt. If he hadn't been in such a hurry he would have gotten out to take a better look. But the ambulance had pulled up now and the attendants were unloading a stretcher from the back. They wheeled it around, two men in white jackets. They bent over the body and then the foot was gone.

"We ready now," the boy said beside him. There was another boy with him.

"That you, Junior?"

White teeth gleamed in the dying night. "It's me. You let me have a cigarette, Joe?"

He pulled a pack off the dash and shook one out for him.

"Hell. I thought that might be you laid out yonder, Junior. What's done happened?"

He lit the cigarette for him and Junior stood there a moment. He smoked and yawned and scratched the side of his jaw with the fingers that held his smoke.

"Aw, Noony been drunk and talkin his old shit again. Bobby's boy shot him, Mama said."

"Just get up front with me, Junior. Let's go, Shorty. We got to haul ass."

He put it up in reverse and waited for Junior to come around. Junior got in and then he couldn't get the door to stay shut.

"Slam it hard," Joe said. "They all in back there?"

"I reckon. Shoot. I was still in the bed."

He backed the truck around quickly and pulled it down into low. He took off, but the gears crashed when he tried to shove it up into second. He pushed in the clutch hard and tried again. It finally caught, but the valves rattled as it struggled up the hill.

"I got to buy me a new truck," he said. The black boy beside him giggled like a girl. "Where's your hat, Junior?"

"Run off and left it. Shorty say you's fixin to leave me if I didn't come on."

"Hell, we late. Be daylight before we ever get out there. I guess ever one of y'all needs to stop at the store."

"I got to get somethin to eat," he said. "What you take for this old truck if you buy you a new one?"

"This truck ain't old. It's just got some minor stuff wrong with it."

They stopped under the red light and waited for it to turn green. Another cruiser came up the hill and turned in with its blue lights flashing. He pulled the shift down into low and took off again, clashed the gears and dropped it into third. The truck sputtered, lurched violently and died. He cranked on it and the lights dimmed until he pushed them off.

"Ragged son of a bitch," he said. It cranked finally and he wound the hell out of it in low, up to almost twenty-five before he dropped it into high gear. It rattled a loud complaint but it went on.

"Linkage messed up," said Junior.

"Let's see if we can fix it at dinner."

"All right."

They turned at the intersection and took the road that led out of town. The stores were just opening.

"Say you was still in the bed, Junior?"

"Yessir. I got off with Dooley and them last night. Don't even know what time we got in. It was late."

"I guess y'all was drinking some whiskey."

"Shoot. Whiskey and beer both. I won me a little money and then got drunk and lost it."

Joe looked out at the coming morning. It was coming fast.

"Shit," he said. "We got to hurry. Y'all can't stay with it in this heat. Gonna be ninety somethin today."

"You done got the ice?"

He started to touch the brake and then he shook his head, mashing the gas harder instead.

"Why, hell naw. We ain't got time to go back for it now. There's probably still some left in the cooler. Freddy may have some. We'll get some out there if he does."

"Let me get one more of them cigarettes off you."

"Up there on the dash, son. I'm gonna have to start takin cigarettes and beer out of you boys' pay. I went out to the truck other evening after we quit and it was one beer in the cooler. Y'all drink it up fast as I can buy it."

"Them old cold beers good when you get off," said Junior.

"Well I guess so when it's free."

They rode in silence for a few miles, the dark trees whipping past on both sides and the lights beginning to come on in the houses along the road. Once in a while they had to straddle a smashed possum.

"And say that was Noony that got shot? Was he the one that used to work for me? Little short guy?"

"Naw. That's his brother. Duwight. Noony the one been in all that trouble with the law. I think he spent about three years in the pen."

"He did? When was he down there?"

"I don't know. He been out I guess three or four years."

"I just wondered was he the one I used to know one time. What did he get put in the pen for?"

"I think he cut somebody. He just got to where he stayed in jail all the time. He's on probation right now."

"He is?"

"He was. Motherfucker dead now."

Joe got the last cigarette and crumpled the pack and threw it out the window. He leaned over the steering wheel with both arms as the old truck rushed along. He could hear faint cries coming from the back and he grinned.

"Goin too fast for them boys," he said. "How come that boy to shoot him? What? Did he come over there fuckin with him?"

"I imagine. Aw, I know he did. He always think he have to be fuckin with somebody. I knocked him in the head with a speaker one day."

"You did?"

"I sure did. He come over at Mama's one day, said I owed him some money. I told him he better get his ass out I didn't owe him shit. Told him he want some money get out and work for it. What I have to do."

"Then you knocked him in the head."

"Knocked a durn hole in his head. Mama said he got shot about three o'clock. Been out there till the garbagemen found him."

"You don't know what time y'all got in?"

"Naw. It was late."

"He wasn't out there when y'all got in?"

"I don't reckon. He mighta been."

Joe cracked the vent wider and flicked the ashes off his smoke.

"Well, I'll tell you," he said. "Folks lookin for trouble can find more than they want."

Junior nodded and crossed his legs.

"You right," he said. "You exactly right about that."

They unloaded from the back end at Dogtown like a pack of hounds themselves and went into the store talking and laughing and opening the doors on the coolers, reaching for milk and Cokes and orange juice. Joe watched them milling around inside while he pumped gas into the truck. Cars were coming along the road with their lights on, carrying people headed to work in the factories who had to be on the job by seven. He had done that and he was glad he wasn't doing it now. He shut off the pump and hung up the nozzle and looked at his watch as he went in.

"Y'all hurry up, now," he said. They were getting Moon Pies and crackers and sardines and cans of Vienna sausage.

At the counter Freddy looked up at him with a sick smile as the men lined up in front of him with their lunches. Freddy charged their food and drinks and smokes to them each day and was paid off on Friday when Joe brought them by. He kept their tickets in little pads beneath the counter.

"Hey, Joe," he said. He stopped writing, sighed deeply and put down his pen. "You want some coffee?"

"I can get it." He found a Styrofoam cup and poured it full, then dumped in a whole lot of sugar and stirred it well.

"Let's see now," Freddy said. He was examining Shorty carefully. "You're Hilliard, right?"

"Shorty," Shorty said, and pointed to another man. "He Hilliard."

Freddy shook his head and looked at Shorty's groceries.

"Y'all gonna have to start wearin name tags. I can't keep you straight from one day to the next."

"Y'all gonna have to hurry up," Joe said. "It's almost six-thirty. Where you got Jimmy at today?"

"All right," Freddy said. "That's got you. Who's next? You want a sack for that?"

"Yessir. Please."

He pulled out a small bag and started putting the items inside.

"Gone fishin," he said. "I'm fixin to fire that boy."

"He told me you'd done fired him three times."

"I'm gonna fire him for good if he don't start helpin me out some."

"Where did they go? Sardis?"

"Naw. I don't know. Off on some goddamn river somewhere. Him and Icky. They'll probably come in drunk today and won't have no money or no fish either, more than likely."

"You gonna see if he got any ice?" said Junior.

Joe set his coffee on the counter. "Yeah. Freddy, you got any ice?"

"I don't know. He didn't run yesterday but you can look in the freezer and see. There may be some left."

"Go see if he's got any, Junior." He looked at his watch again. "Y'all gonna have to get the lead out, now. It's almost daylight right now."

"They two bags back here," Junior called out.

"Well, go put it in the cooler, then. Put some more water in there, too."

He picked up his coffee and stood sipping it until the last hand had gone out the door with his little sack. Then he set it on the counter again and waited for the storekeeper to open the till. Freddy didn't look happy when he looked up from his money, and spoke to Joe.

"You couldn't wait a little while on this, could you?"

"What's the matter? You ain't got it?"

"Aw, I got it. I got it right here. My gas man's due today, though. If I can't buy gas I might as well not even keep the door open."

"When you gonna learn not to bet money you can't afford to lose, Freddy?"

"I never thought Duran would beat him."

"So you said."

"Would you let me give you half this week and half next week? She's gonna notice this as it is."

He thought about it for a moment, about winners and losers and high rollers and those who aspired to be. Finally he said: "All right. Give it here."

Freddy reached in quickly and took out three hundred dollars and handed it over, shaking his head with relief.

"I sure appreciate it, Joe. Business ain't been good lately."

"Looks pretty good to me," said Joe.

They were trying to finish up a tract of a hundred and seventeen acres close to Toccopola that they'd been on for eight days. He'd started with a crew of eleven, but he'd fired two and one had quit the second day. He stopped the truck on a bulldozed road deep in the woods, a slash of red dirt high in the green hills of timber. He sat on the tailgate with the file in his hand, while Shorty and Dooley held the blades across his leg for sharpening, a small pocket of bright filings growing in a crease in his jeans. When he had five ready, he told Junior to get the men started. Shorty had climbed into the back and wrestled the thirty-gallon drum of poison over on its side and he and Dooley were filling the plastic milk jugs with the thick brown fluid.

Joe raised his head and looked far down the tract to the dying trees they'd injected three days before. It was as if a blight had grown across the emerald tops of the forest and was trying to catch up to where they stood.

"Y'all won't need no water yet," he said. "Go on down there to where we quit yesterday and start in before it gets too hot."

"It ain't gonna rain, is it?" one said hopefully.

Joe looked up to a sky gray and overcast, with rumblings of thunder in the distance.

"It ain't gonna rain," he said. "Not till dinner anyway."

He finished with the last blade and tried to hurry the hands as much as he could while they in turn tried to prolong the beginning of their labor by filling their guns and priming the tubes.

"All right, let's hit it," he said. "Y'all done fucked around long enough. We got to finish by tomorrow if it takes all day."

The man who carried their water and poison took up a jug of each and followed behind them and they all went off down into the hollow to find their marks and begin. Joe got in the cab and pulled the whiskey out from under the seat and opened a hot Coke and sat there. He lit a cigarette and coughed long and slow, spacing the spasms out, clearing his throat and finally spitting something onto the ground and wiping his mouth. He took a couple of drinks and then capped the bottle. The wind was coming up a little. Faint flashes of lightning speared the earth miles away. He lay down on the seat with his cap over his eyes and his feet out the door. Before many minutes had passed he was asleep.

Soft droplets on his face woke him. He opened his eyes and looked at the cab roof over his head. He'd knocked his cap off and water was running down the inside of the door on him. His feet were wet. The windshield was blurred by rain and he could see only bleary forms of greenery through it. It was ten minutes after nine. He put his cap on and slid out the open door, put his feet into the mud already forming. The new ground was soft and he was under a hill, so he got in and cranked the truck and backed sliding and fishtailing through the red muck until he could wheel it onto a turnaround and point it out. He left it there and went down into the woods to see if he could find the hands.

It was a fine rain, a fragile mist that paled everything in the distance to a thin gray obscurity. The green woods, the dead red hills. He had to watch his balance going down into the hollow, catching at saplings on the steepest parts and easing himself down like an older man, the thousands of days of cigarettes wheezing in his chest.

At the bottom of the hill there was a small creek with tiny young cane and rocks and dewberries that he jumped in stride, landing heavily on the wet leaves and looking and finding the pink plastic ribbon tied to the tree. He walked around and found the fresh cuts on the live timber and stood looking at them for a minute. They'd never get the tract finished by the next day if the rain drove them out now. He knew they'd want to quit, even though the rain wasn't going to hurt them. He watched the sky, leaden and

23

heavy with clouds. It wasn't going to clear off. It looked ready to set in for the day. He got in under a big tree and lit a cigarette and squatted, smoking, the smoke hanging in a small drifting cloud in front of him. It seemed as if the air itself had thickened.

He picked up a little stick and idly began breaking it into pieces, looking out at the woods from under the bill of his cap. At once the rain came harder and he made up his mind. He got up and went back toward the hill, across the creek again, bending to get through the underbrush, getting his cap snatched off once by a brier and picking it up and brushing the dirt from it before carefully setting it back on his head.

He leaned on the horn for two minutes, until he was sure they'd heard it. He gave them ten more minutes and then blew it again to let them get their direction and cut off the distance by coming straight to him. It took them almost twenty minutes to get back. They arrived in a herd, laughing, wet, their clothes sticking to them, large red overshoes of mud encasing their feet. They stomped and kicked their shoes against the tires and the bumper, scraped them with sticks.

"Let's get in and go before it gets any worse," he said. "This road's slick as owl shit now."

They loaded up and settled in the back. They were happy and laughing, able to get by on two hours' pay. He heard somebody yelling just as he cranked the motor, and Shorty came around in a hurry, stepping high and wild in the mud, grinning.

"Let us get our stuff," he said.

The sacks were piled up on the seat and he handed them out the window. Shorty went back with them stacked up in his arms. The rain was coming harder now and the wipers beat against the streaming water as he eased out on the clutch and felt the tires trying to spin in the clay. The red ground was bleeding, little torrents of muddy water already eating into the hillsides and funneling down the road. Missiles of mud bombarded the fenderwells with hollow detonations. He had to keep it in low and not risk missing second all the way up the hill. The truck slid and almost bogged down and tried to swap ends, but he kept cutting the wheel and finally they crested over the top and trundled away peacefully toward the highway, another day gone and wasted.

When he could steer with one hand, he reached and got the bottle from beneath the seat and set it between his legs. He twisted off the cap and searched on the seat for a Coke. It started raining harder.

He had them all home by ten-thirty and he was back at the house by noon. The dog met him, stood looking at him from behind the steps, his broad white head lumpy with masses of scar tissue and the yellow eyes peaceful and strangely human in their expression of wistfulness. He spoke to the dog and went on in with his two sacks. The house felt empty now, always. Loud and hollow. He looked at the mud he was tracking over the carpet and sat down on the floor beside the door, unlacing his boots and standing them together beside the refrigerator. There was a pack of hot dogs and a bag of buns and a dozen eggs and two six-packs of Bud in one sack and he put it all in the icebox. He poured some Coke in a glass and dropped in three ice cubes and filled the rest of it with whiskey, then sat down at the table with a pencil and some paper to do his figuring. Days and time and hours where he saw his profit coming through. Even with the bad weather he was making over two hundred dollars a day. He figured up what he would owe the hands if they didn't work the next day and drew it all up into individual columns and figured their Social Security and subtracted it and wrote down all their names and the amounts he owed them and then he was through.

There was a little watery stuff left in the glass, and he rattled the thin cubes around and drank it off. The rain was coming down hard on the roof and he thought about the dog in the mud, trying to find a dry spot in this sudden world of water. He got up and opened the back door and looked at the shed. The dog raised his head from his forepaws and regarded him solemnly from his bed of rotten quilts. Then he settled, whining slightly, watching the dripping trees and flattened grass with his eyes blinking once or twice before they closed.

He closed the door and thought about making another drink, but then he went into the living room and turned on the television and sat on the couch. Somebody was giving the farm report. He got up and changed channels. News and weather. The soap operas hadn't come on yet. There was a pale pink bedspread on the floor and he picked it up and pulled it over himself like a shroud and lay on his side watching the news. After a while he turned over on his back and adjusted his head on the pillow that stayed there. He closed his eyes and breathed in the stillness with his hands crossed on his chest like a man laid out in a coffin, his toes sticking out from under the edge of the bedspread. He thought about her and what she'd said that morning.

She was on the front desk now and that was better because he could go in like anybody else and talk to her if he didn't talk too long. He'd gotten at the end of the line and waited, watching her deal with other people, watching her smile. She looked better than he remembered, each time he saw her, as if leaving him had made her more beautiful.

The line moved slowly and he didn't know what he would buy. Stamps and more stamps, a drawer full of them at home already. Finally he stood before her, smiling slightly, averting his whiskey breath.

"You lookin good today," he said. "They keep you busy."

She kept her eyes on slips of paper in front of her, kept her hands busy with things on the counter. She looked up. Pain was marked in those eyes so deep it was like a color, old love unrequited, a glad sadness on seeing him this close.

"Hi, Joe." She didn't smile, this thin girl with brown hair and skin like an Indian who'd born his children.

"How you been gettin along? You all right?"

"I'm okay. How are you?" She still didn't smile, only folded her little hands together on the marble slab, her painted nails red as blood. He looked at her hands and then he looked at her face.

"I'm all right. We got rained out today and I done took everbody back home. What time you get off for lunch?"

"I don't know today," she said. Her eyes wandered, then came back to rest uneasily on him. "Jean's sick and Sheila's having her baby. I don't know when I'll get to go."

He coughed. He started to reach for a cigarette and then stayed his hand.

"I thought I'd see if you wanted to eat some lunch. Thought you might want to go out to the Beacon or somewhere."

"I don't think there's any need in that. Do you?"

"It wouldn't hurt. I'd just like to buy you some lunch."

She pulled a pencil from beside her ear and opened a drawer at her waist. But she closed the drawer and laid down the pencil.

"I'm not going out with you if that's what you want."

"I ain't said that. Why you want to do me like this?"

"Like what?"

"Won't talk to me. Won't even see me."

"This is not the place to talk about it. You're not gonna come in here like you did that other time. Mr. Harper'll call the police if you ever do that again." She leaned toward him and whispered: "How do you think that made me feel? Everybody in here saw you. I've got a good job here."

"I know you do. I'm proud you do."

"Then let me do it."

He raised his hands a little. "Hell, calm down. I just wanted to see you a minute."

"Well, this is not the place to see me. I've got to work."

"Where is?"

"I don't know. You want to buy something?"

"Yeah. Gimme a book of stamps."

She shook her head and reached under the counter.

"You use more stamps than anybody I know."

"I got me some pen pals now," he said.

She rolled her eyes and smiled a little. "Sure."

He pulled out his billfold. "How much is that?"

"Two-fifty for ten or five dollars for twenty."

"Give me twenty. You need any money?"

"Nope."

"I can let you have some if you need it."

"I'm doing fine. I got a promotion and a raise last week."

"Oh yeah?"

"Yeah."

"You been out with anybody?"

"None of your business. I wouldn't tell you if I had. There you are." She put the little booklet on the counter. He gave her a five dollar bill.

"Let me give you some money," he said. He had three fifties folded between his fingers and he put them on the counter.

She looked around to see who was watching.

"I'm not taking that. You'd think I owed you something then."

"You don't owe me nothin, Charlotte. I'd rather you have it as me. I won't do nothin but blow it. You don't want to go eat lunch?"

He had drawn his hands back and the money lay between them. He went ahead and lit a cigarette, turned his head and coughed.

"I can't right now," she said. Somebody had moved up behind him. An old woman, he saw, smiling and digging in her purse, shaking her head.

"I been doin real good," he said. "I ain't been out in about two weeks."

"That's good, Joe. But you can do whatever you want to now."

"Only thing I want is to see you."

"I've got to get to work now. Take this money," she said, and she held it out to him.

"I'll see you," he said, and he turned and walked out.

On the couch he turned his face to one side and saw the things happening on the television screen without seeing them and heard the words the actors were saying without hearing them. They were like dreams, real but not real. He closed his eyes and it all passed away.

T hey entered over a rotting threshold, their steps soft on the dry dusty boards, their voices loud in the hushed ruins. The floor was carpeted beautifully with vines, thick creepers with red stalks matted and green leaves flourishing up through the cracks. An ancient tricycle sat before the dead ashes of a fireplace whose old rough bricks, ill spaced and losing their homemade mortar, chip by sandy chip, seemed bonded only by the dirt dauber nests that lined the inside.

"Looky yonder," the old woman said, pointing to the tricycle. "Reckon how old that is."

In the vault of rafters overhead a screech owl swiveled its head downward like something on greased bearings to better see his invaders, then spread his small brown wings to glide soundlessly through the gable and out into the spring brightness.

They moved through the house with red wasps droning above them, to a back room where a nest anchored to the top log spanned sixteen inches, a mass of dull bodies with black wings crawling there like maggots, poised and vibrating. They backed away into the front room, quietly, carefully.

"Ain't nobody lived here in a long time," the boy said. He reached down and pushed the tricycle, which rolled woodenly across the floor, the pedals turning perhaps with weak remembrance from the feet of a long-dead child. He stood at a glassless window and touched two logs notched to within the thickness of a sheet of paper and wondered at what it had taken to raise hewed timbers a foot square and set them in place with such precision.

"We'll have to get somethin over them windows," the old man said. "And these vines got to be cleaned out."

"We better get that wasp nest down first," the woman said. The two girls had settled in a far corner with their sacks. They studied their father with a sullen recalcitrance.

"This old house is awful," the oldest one said. Her name was Fay and the little one was Dorothy.

"It's bettern a culvert," Wade said.

The old man stopped before a wooden safe weathered of varnish and blistered from a fire survived in some other household. He opened one of the doors and it protested with a thin yawning. On the dusty shelves inside were mice pills, the dry hollow husks of insects, tiny colored bottles with rusted caps.

The boy was fascinated by the logs. He touched their axed surfaces, felt the dried mud chinked in the cracks. He thought he would have liked living in times when men built houses like this one.

"Mules," he said. "I bet them people used mules."

The old man was picking up bottles from inside the safe, small blue ones and tall green ones of strange and flawed glass with bubbles of air trapped within the wavey walls.

"These old bottles liable to be worth some money," he said.

There was a little room attached to the side of the house. The ceiling joists were only six feet above a floor littered with leaves, scraps of newspaper yellowed and brittle, rotted bits of discolored fabric. The boy toed among the refuse, searching. He glanced at his father and mother. They were examining the bottles and arguing quietly over them. With his shoe he scraped twigs and dust away from the floor. The mold of untold years. He bent and picked up a shotgun shell soft with ruin, green with tarnish. He touched the crimped and swollen end and the faded paper flaked away in his hand. Small gray shot was packed loosely within, almost white now. He turned it up and poured over his shoes an almost soundless rain of lead. They were murmuring in the other room, talking. There was no furniture other than the safe, not even a chair. He looked out a window and saw a small shed tumbled down, windrowed with leaves, composed of green boards and cancerous wooden shingles. He saw a caved-in outhouse. And just beyond, a wall of pine woods was already gathering the day's coming heat. He looked around in the room. Whoever had lived here had been gone for a long time. He went back up front and joined his parents.

"Y'all can start pullin these weeds up," his daddy said.

Gary bent immediately and began tearing handfuls of them up through the floor, carrying them to the window and throwing them out.

"I wish I had a broom," his mother said.

"What we gonna do for water?" Fay said. "We ain't got no water."

"I imagine they's a creek around here if you'd look," Wade said. "Why don't you get up off your ass and see if you can find it?"

"Why don't you go find it your own self?"

The boy stopped what he was doing and looked at his sister. The old man was standing over her, the woman turning now and watching them. The girl got up slowly.

"They ain't even no bathroom in this place. Look at it. It's full of wasp nests, and weeds is growin right up through the floor. You don't even know who it belongs to."

The old man slapped her. A sound like a pistol shot, his hand suddenly exploding on her cheek, the dark hair flying around her head as her face was slapped sideways. The old woman moved and froze at once, sank down to the floor with her legs crossed and her hands in her hair. The girl doubled up her fist.

"Don't double that fist up at me," Wade said. "I'll slap the hell out of you."

She swung at his nose but missed by a good six inches. He caught her arm and twisted it up behind her back. He was trying to whip her with his open hand and she was trying to kick him. They danced in a demented little circle in the dust. The youngest girl watched with her hands caught at her mouth.

He tried to push her against the wall, but she whirled and kicked him hard in the balls. He went down with his teeth bared. She picked up a stick from the floor and commenced pounding him over the head with it, whipped him to the floor where he lay curled and groaning and trying to fend off the blows she was laying on him like someone beating a rug, him screaming for her to *Quit* it, that *Goddamn*, that *hurts*.

34

"How you like it?" she asked him. But Gary took the stick away from her and threw it out the window.

"That's enough," he said.

"You taking up for him now? What you taking up for him for?"

"Cause," he said. "All you gonna do's make him mad."

"I wish he'd die," she said. She bent over her father. "You hear me? I hate your guts and I wish you'd die. So we wouldn't have to put up with you."

The old man moaned on the floor with his eyes tightly closed. Through gritted teeth he said: "I'm goin to beat your ass till you can't sit down."

"You ain't nothing," she said. "I wish you's dead and in hell right now."

"You gonna wish you was somewhere when I get through with you," he told her.

"Y'all stop it," Gary said. "Here. Help him up."

He took hold of Wade's arm and pulled him to a sitting position. The hat had come off his head and his sparse gray hair was in disarray, coated with dust. He sat rocking back and forth, holding his belly. The girl was still circling him, looking for another opening.

"Get away from him, Fay," Gary said.

"You better get outa here," Wade said.

"If I had any other place to go I would."

"Get up off the floor, Mama." The boy bent to his mother and helped her up, one knee at a time. She was dazed and trembling, was pawing at her hair with her fingers as if she meant to comb it. The old man had one knee up and was forcing one of his hands against it in an attempt to rise. He showed his rotten teeth and struggled, finally made it up, and stood panting in the center of the room. He bent over and picked up his hat and dusted it off.

"I want this place cleaned up fore dark," he told Fay.

"You kiss my ass," she said. He lunged and got her by the throat. She didn't scream. She just closed her eyes and tried to force his hands away from her throat, the two of them stumbling against the logs. The boy tried to get between them, and the little girl and the woman joined in, all of them tugging at the hands clenched so tightly on her. She gagged and coughed and her face started turning purple until she said: "All *right*. Damn," and he turned her loose. She rubbed her throat and coughed some more. He weaved in front of her, raised one finger and put it in her face.

"You gonna do what I tell you," he said.

She didn't answer. The marks of his fingers were red spots on her neck.

"You hear me?"

Gary watched them and didn't move away. He could hear them heaving like runners after a race.

"One day," she said.

"One day?" The old man stepped closer. "One day what?"

"Nothin."

"All right, then. I don't want to hear no more of your smart shit. I'm tired of it. You hear?"

"I hear."

"Well, go on and do like I told you."

"What?" she said.

He gestured wildly with his hands. "Go on and start pickin this shit up. Get some of these sticks and leaves outa here."

They began picking up the leaves and trash that had blown in through the broken windows and carrying it all to the door and throwing it out. The old woman found a scrap of broom somewhere and they were soon obscured in the dust she raised attacking the floor. Wade started to say something, but then coughed and sagged against a wall. He leaned there coughing and then bent over gagging. His tongue came out. He was fanning at the dust with his hands. She swept harder, whipping the dust into a rolling cloud of brown smoke. The old man had both hands around his throat as if he might strangle himself. The dust plumed out the windows and rose to the rafters. Wade retched like a victim of tear gas, going to his knees on the wide boards. Gary helped him to his feet and led him outside, the old man hacking ferociously now, all but being carried by the boy. He allowed himself to be led to a fallen tree in the yard and he sat down on it, putting his head between his legs with his tongue hanging out.

"You gonna be all right?" Gary said. His father didn't answer, couldn't. He sat there choking, his shoulders moving in great spastic jerks.

"Maybe you need to get up and walk around," he said. He turned and looked at the dust billowing out into the yard. The dim figure of his mother inside was moving methodically through the room, the shaft in her hands sweeping back and forth. Fay stepped down from the house, coughing, and held onto the doorjamb with one hand.

"Hell fire," she said.

"Where's Dorothy?"

"I don't know. I guess she went out the other side if she ain't done choked to death. I don't see how Mama can stand it her ownself."

They went around to the other side of the house and the younger girl was there, beating the dust from her clothes.

"You okay?" he said. She nodded her head that she was. They stood together and watched the dust swirl and settle in the grass.

"She's crazy as hell," said Fay.

"Don't say that."

"Well, she is."

"You don't have to say it," he said. "If you don't quit smartin off to him . . ."

"I ain't scared of him."

"Ain't nobody said you were. It just don't do no good to aggravate him. All it does is just make it worse."

"He ain't worth killin," she said.

"Hush." He nodded with his chin toward the little girl. "She's listenin to you."

"I don't care if she is. How you think we gonna live out here? They ain't no water. Ain't even no windows in that old house."

"I'll fix em," he said.

"Horseshit. You can't fix up that old house. We don't even know who it belongs to. What we gonna do if whoever owns it comes up here and catches us?"

He thought about it for a minute. "Well, maybe we can find us someplace else."

"Where?"

"I don't know. He's sposed to know some people around here.

Maybe they know of a place. A place a little closer to a store or somethin. We got to have some way to get somethin to eat. Have we got anything left?"

"I doubt it. I don't think she's got nothin left. I don't know what we had to leave Texas for. At least we had a garden out there. There ain't nothin here." She looked around in disgust. "Back off in the woods. Poison ivy all over the place. I bet you couldn't find nobody in his right mind would live up in here."

"I wonder if he's got any money," Gary said.

"What do you think?"

"Naw."

"You know he ain't. If he did he'd of done found him a liquor store somewhere and spent it."

"Well, what we gonna do?"

She just looked at him.

"I don't know."

By noon they had most of the trash cleaned out but they were having to stay out of the room where the wasp nest hung. They were sitting under the shade of some trees in a yard that honeysuckle vines had taken over. Like foraging cows they had trampled them down and flattened them.

"Now how much money have we got?" the old man said to them. He looked hopeful.

"I ain't got none," Gary said.

"Don't look at me," said Fay.

"Where's your purse?" Wade asked her.

"I said I ain't got none," she told him. "What, you think I'm lyin?"

"I just want to check."

"I done told you I'm broke."

"Well, I just want to see."

"Well, you can just jump up my ass." She got up and started to pick up her purse, but he caught her by the arm. They fought briefly over it until he broke the strap and snatched it away from her. He upended it and dumped the contents on the ground while she cursed at him. A comb, a mirror, two sticks of gum, hair clips, lipstick. He shook it but nothing else came out.

"Now. You satisfied?" She knelt and started putting her things back in it, muttering under her breath.

"We got to have somethin to eat," he said.

"You oughta thought of that before you got us out here."

"You want me to slap you?" he said. She didn't answer.

"We gonna have to do somethin," Gary said. "Find us a job."

"Where you gonna find one at?" the old man said.

"I don't know. I guess I'll have to go look for one. How far is it to town?"

The old man looked around at the woods as if the trees bore road signs that marked the route to civilization.

"It's about ten mile, I guess."

"Ain't there a store no closer than that?"

"They's one over here at London Hill. Or used to be."

"Reckon they'd give us some credit?"

"They might. You could ask. They might give us credit."

"Well, why don't we walk over there and see? We got to do somethin. We can't set around here all day."

"You go. My legs is hurtin s'bad I can't hardly get up."

The old woman had not spoken but she was unfolding limp green paper in her hands. Each of them realized it gradually, turning one by one to look at her as she sat with her head down, her fingers trembling slightly as she fumbled with the wrinkled bills. She smoothed each one on her knee as she drew it from the wad.

"Where'd you find that, Mama?" Gary said.

"I had it," she said. Her hair was coated with dust and it hung limply around the sides of her head so that her ears stuck through.

"How much you got?" the old man said. He was taking it off her knee and counting it. "Eight dollars? You got any more?" She shook her head.

He got up immediately, his leg forgotten, and put the bills in his pocket.

"I'll go on over to the store," he said. "See what I can buy."

Gary got up. "Let me go with you," he said.

"Ain't no need for you to go. I can do it."

"Go with him, Gary," Fay said, nudging him.

"Just stay here. I'll be back after while."

"You gonna get some gas?" Gary said.

"Gas? What for?"

"For that wasp nest."

Wade shook his head, already starting off. "I ain't got nothin to carry it in."

"We gonna have to rob that wasp nest before we can stay in there."

"Well, if I find a jar to bring it back in I'll buy some." They stood and watched him stagger away through the hot woods. When he was out of hearing Fay turned on her mother.

"What'd you give him all that money for? He ain't gonna do nothin but catch a ride to town and buy whiskey with it."

"Leave her alone," Gary said. "She don't need you fussin at her."

At nine that night they were gathered around a small fire in the middle of the yard, mute in the thunderous din of crickets. The grasses and weeds were beginning to look like a bedding ground. They were cooking a meal of pork and beans in opened cans, and the old man was halfway through a bottle of Old Crow. They had foraged for firewood and had a pile nearby.

The faces around the fire were pinched, the eyes a little big, a little dazed with hunger. They sat and watched the blaze burn the paper off the cans. When the beans began to sizzle, the woman stooped painfully on her bad hip and reached for the cans with a rag wrapped around her hand. Clotted strings of hair hung from her head. She took five paper plates, set them out on the ground, and dumped the beans onto them, shaking them as she went, the way a person might put out dog food for a pet. She dumped the largest portion into the plate intended for the old man.

The breadwinner was sitting crosslegged on the ravaged grass, the whiskey upright in the hole his legs formed. He was weaving a home-rolled cigarette back and forth from his lips, eyes bleary, red as fire. He was more than a little drunk. His head and chest would slump forward, then he'd jerk erect, his eyes sleepy. Grimed and furtive hands reached out for the plates quietly, took them back and drew away from the fire into darker regions of the yard. The old woman took two small bites and then rose and scraped the rest of her food into the boy's plate.

The fire grew dimmer. The plate of beans before the old man steamed but he didn't notice. A candlefly bored crazily in out of the night and landed in the hot sauce, struggled briefly and was still. The old man's head went lower and lower onto his chest until the only thing they could see was the stained gray hat over the bib of his overalls. He snuffled, made some noise. His chest rose and fell. They watched him like wolves. The fire cracked and popped and white bits of ash fell away from the tree limbs burning in the coals. Sparks rose fragile and dying, orange as coon eyes in the gloom. The ash crumbled and the fading light threw darker shadows still. The old man toppled over slowly, a bit at a time like a rotten tree giving way, until the whiskey lay spilling between his legs. They watched him for a few minutes and then they got up and went to the fire and took his plate and carried it away into the dark.

Noon. The field bordering the road lay baking beneath a white sun, pale green rows of little plants that merged far away. The earth seemed to be smoking and it had no color, so dry was it, as if it had never known rain. It seemed dead as old bones. Down at the south end of the bean patch a tiny blue tractor was turning and coming back. It struggled against the immense flat landscape, crawling at what seemed an inch at a time, the dry soil not folding but merely breaking into dust across the plows. The old man scowled up at the blistering sky.

"Throw the rest of em out," he said.

The green metal Dumpster he stood beside was positioned off the blacktop on a bed of pit-run gravel as hard as concrete. The county workmen had bolstered up the shoulder of the highway and widened it, and bits of ground glass lay everywhere.

The boy was standing inside the rusty iron bin. He picked up another black garbage sack and slit it open with a knife; then, leaning toward the open door, mired to the knees in refuse, he dumped it out. A rain of cast-off matter cascaded: wet beer cans, egg shells, a half-pint whiskey bottle, cigarette butts and blowing ash. Unidentifiable bits of ruined fruit and fly-specked vegetables. Here a half-chewed weiner that a dog or a small child had worked over. All of it covered with wet coffee grounds. The old man bent over, pawing through it. He lifted three Diet Coke cans and fourteen Old Milwaukee cans from the rubble and put them into his tow sack.

"Ain't you gonna mash em?" the boy said.

Wade made a dismissive gesture with his hand. The boy bent to the piles of sacks behind him. He picked up another one and said, "If you'd mash em it'd make more room."

The old man just grunted. Each time he bent over, the boy could see a patch of loose belly flesh, pink and soft, in the gap where his overalls buttoned on the side. He tottered light-headed and delirious with hunger over mounds of garbage inside the smoked-up walls. He moved a newspaper. Green bottleflies swarmed up off a stringer of bream that somebody had thrown into the Dumpster. The fish were bloated, their eyes solid white. Their bellies were pale and their scales were gray. His stomach heaved but there was nothing to come up.

"Hurry up," the old man said.

The boy bent once more to his work. He knew his father was wanting to finish and get away from the road quickly, but before they had the tow sack half full, a pickup appeared far down the road. He raised himself up.

"Who is it?" he said.

"I don't know. You got any more in there?"

He didn't answer, only stood watching apprehensively as the

vehicle grew nearer and slowed. They looked at each other and Wade said: "Get outa there."

Gary climbed down from the Dumpster, holding onto the door. The pickup had slowed to a crawl and now a shield emblazoned on the door appeared, a county emblem like a Maltese cross. The truck stopped and the driver shut the motor off. They waited. A tall man with brown hair and khaki clothes got out. He didn't say anything at first, only studied them as if they were errant children whose unacceptable behavior he had suffered far past reason.

"Hidy," Wade said. "How you?"

The man put his hands on his hips and walked over to the Dumpster. He looked inside and shook his head.

"You don't care for us gettin these cans, do you? We didn't figger nobody wanted em."

The man kicked at the piles of trash they'd thrown on the ground, nudging at the mess with his toe as if he'd lost something in that stinking heap of offal. Then he looked up.

"You people are unbelievable," he said. "You really are." He kicked at the stuff again. "What do you think this Dumpster's for?"

"We ain't hurtin nothin," the old man said. "We just after these cans. Who are you, anyway?"

The man stared hard at him. "By God, I'm Don Shelby. I'm the supervisor of this beat. Who in the fuck are you?"

Wade Jones toed among the mosaic of ground glass and said nothing.

"Look at this mess," the man said. "Who do you think's going to clean it up? When we had a dump here and kept it bulldozed you wouldn't even drive down to the end to throw it out. And now I'll be goddamned if you're not throwing it out of the Dumpsters." He looked at Gary. "Do you know you can get put in jail for this?"

"Nosir," he said. He was wondering if he should run for it. The woods were pretty close.

"Well, by God, you can. It's a five-hundred-dollar fine for littering. Have you got five hundred dollars?"

"Nosir. I ain't."

"Well, that's what it would cost you. It's a state law." He looked at the pile of trash again as if he couldn't believe it was still there. "My hands can't run over here every fifteen minutes and pick this stuff up. They've got other things to do. Now you two pick up every bit of this mess and put it back where you got it. And I'm gonna stand here and watch you."

"Say you the supervisor?" said Wade.

"Damn right."

"But you ain't the law," he said doubtfully.

Shelby stepped up until he was in the old man's face. "Naw, I ain't the law. Smart son of a bitch. But I got a radio in that truck. And if you don't pick this shit up in the next five minutes I'll call the law out here and you can smart off to them."

Wade blinked. "Come on, boy." He nudged him. "Get down here and start pickin this stuff up. I told you not to make all this mess."

Gary bent and picked up an armload. "Ain't you gonna help me?" he said.

"I'm helpin," Wade said, tossing in a soup can, a rag, an empty potato chip bag. Nothing too heavy. A cereal box, a paper, an egg carton.

"I want it just as clean as it was before," Shelby said. He watched Gary for a bit, watched him bending over trying to pick up the myriad scattered lumps of trash. "Wait a minute," he said. He walked back to his truck and reached into the bed and brought out a new shovel with the price tag still attached. "Here," he said. "Use this."

"Yessir," Gary said. He started scooping. Wade stopped and raised one side of his hat, scratching at his head. He leaned back on the hood of the truck, the limp sack of cans tinkling faintly. He drew a handkerchief from his pocket and mopped his face. The man on the tractor was coming alongside them in the field and he had his head bent to see the wheel in the row. He and his machine were engulfed in dust, the thin silt rolling up on the tires and pouring like water off the cleats. They watched him pass, and as he came by he lifted a hand in greeting. The blades of the plow where they cut the earth were polished bright as chrome, rising and falling in the lifeless dust and the steady chug of the tractor echoing endlessly over the silence against the scrape of the shovel.

"He wants it clean, now," the old man said.

Gary nodded and kept at it. Shelby looked at his watch. The boy was pushing small piles of rubbish together, pushing them up against the wall of the Dumpster and using his hand to get it all in the shovel.

"I guess that'll do," Shelby said. Gary straightened and looked at him and then looked at this father. Wade nodded. The supervisor held out his hand for the shovel and the boy gave it to him.

"I don't want to see this happen any more," he said. He tossed the shovel into the bed of the truck and it hit with a loud bong. He waited for Wade to unlean himself from his hood.

"My hands has got enough to do as it is. If you want cans you better get out and pick em up off the side of the road. That's where most of em's at anyway."

"Yessir," Gary said. Wade had his hands on his hips and was looking around like somebody deaf.

Shelby opened his door and stood with one hand on it, fixing them with a cold stare, each in turn. "I keep my eye on these things," he said. "I come by here just about every day."

Wade wouldn't even look at him.

"All right," he said. "You been told."

He got into the truck and cranked it and pulled away. They stood beside the Dumpster and watched him go up the road slowly, then pull off to the side and turn around. He was doing forty by the time he came by them again. They waved. He didn't. He went down the highway out of sight and finally even the sound of his tires vanished. It was hot and still where they stood, and the trac-tor was turning to make another pass.

"All right," Wade said. "He's gone. Get back up in there."

"What if he comes back?"

"He ain't comin back. It's dinnertime."

"He might, though. He might come back after while to see if we still here."

"You hear what I said?"

"Yeah."

"Then do like I told you."

"We done got just about all the cans," he said, but he was already climbing back up through the door.

A pattern emerged, one they discovered by employing a system of regular reconnaissance. The Dumpsters were emptied on Tuesdays and Fridays, which left the other five days of the week for harvesting the depths of them. They changed their salvage operations to night, covered safely by the cloak of darkness. Parts of each day were given over to walking along the sides of the highways, the boy down in the ditches throwing the cans up onto the road, the old man shuffling along and stuffing the sack. Often he would have to sit down and rest, and the boy would range far ahead and come back with his arms laden and his own sack full. They dumped the cans in a pile beside the house, and they would stand sometimes and quietly contemplate their growing wealth.

The old man made a trip to town one day, hitching a ride with a farmer who was going to the feed mill in a pickup. The farmer had a load of shelled corn, big sacks of it that swirled chaff into the face of the rider where he sat nodding in the back end.

When the truck stopped, he roused himself and got out in front of a barnlike building, its walls patched over with roofing tin and Purina signs. A rutted parking lot of gravel was littered with rusted farm implements, their moving parts frozen solid with corrosion and decorated with ten or fifteen cats. He climbed down from the back as the farmer came around.

"I sure thank you for the ride," he said. "Is it much further to town?"

The farmer was a man in denim pants and a T-shirt, a busy man hurrying toward his feed. "It's bout a mile," he said, pointing up the road with his chin.

Wade nodded. He looked, his eyes taking in the searing strip of asphalt lined with trees standing still under no breath of air and the sun overhead like a white coin in the sky. The farmer started lifting the sacks out and handing them across to a black man who had come silently from the depths of the shadows inside the building pushing a heavy two-wheeled cart.

"Well, listen," Wade said. He put a somber look on his face. The farmer in the truck stopped with both hands on the sewn ears of a sack and regarded him, the muscles in his forearms standing up like little ropes.

"You couldn't loan me a dollar or two, could you? I got a sick youngun at home and I done called about the medicine. They said it was five dollars and somethin and I ain't got but four dollars."

"A dollar?"

"Yessir. A dollar or two. I hate to ask you after I done caught a ride and all with you but she sure needs that medicine." He had one hand on the sideboards of the truck and his upturned face looked weak and ashamed.

"Why, hell," the farmer said, and looked ashamed himself. "Feller, I don't even know you."

"That's all right," the old man said quickly. "That's okay. I thank you for the ride anyway." He turned away and had taken but three steps when the farmer called out to him.

"Hey. Wait a minute."

He turned. "Yessir," he said. Waiting.

"Hell. Come back here a minute. You didn't say nothin about you had a sick youngun."

Wade scuffed his shoes among the little stones.

"I just hated to," he said. "You's good enough to give me a ride and all. I hated to ask you for anything else."

The farmer in the truck and the black man on the dock were watching him. The black man pulled the cart back and turned it and pushed it away into the dim stacks of feed and disappeared. The farmer got down from the truck and dusted his hands off. He approached his rider with a hurt look, his eyes downcast.

"Is she bad sick?" he said.

"Well. She stays sick pretty much. Been sick all her life."

The farmer nodded and rubbed his chin with a finger.

"How old is she?"

"She's four years old. Course the doctor's always sayin he's surprised she's lived this long. They said at first she would never live this long." He lifted his head and looked off into the distance, shaking his head slightly in awe. "She don't never complain, though. Just to look at her you'd never think they's nothin wrong with her."

"Well, Lord," the farmer said softly. "I got a granddaughter four years old." He had one hand in his back pocket and one hand rubbing his lower lip in indecision. It didn't take him long. He pulled out his billfold and opened it. He took some money out and thrust it at the old man as if it were burning his fingers.

"Take this," he said. "She might need somethin else."

Wade didn't look at the money but shook his head firmly. "I couldn't take that," he said. "I *can't* take that."

The farmer shook the money at him. "Go on," he said. "Hell fire. Take it."

"I sure hate to, mister. You done been so good already."

The farmer walked close and stuffed the money down in the old man's pocket. Wade stood with his head down, shaking it. He did that for about a minute. Then he turned and took five steps and stopped and looked back. The farmer was standing in the gravel watching him, his face touched with compassion or maybe something else.

"I got a bunch of stuff to do here or I'd carry you on into town," he said, and he seemed still ashamed. "But if I'm here when you come back by I'll be proud to give you a ride back home."

"I thank you," Wade said. "I reckon I better get on uptown and see about that medicine."

"Well. I hope your youngun gets all right," the farmer said softly.

The old man nodded and walked away.

In the air-conditioned cool of the supermarket he plucked a small bunch of grapes from the produce stand and had them all in his mouth by the time he got to the peanut butter. Squatting against the shining jars of jelly, he worked his mouth stealthily, firing the seeds down between his feet into a razored-open carton that he pulled from beneath the shelves. He went up front and got a cart and loaded the little section in the rear with dented cans of Vienna sausage and purple hull peas from a crate of damaged goods marked down to quarter price. He was a careful shopper, a bargain hunter adding figures in his head, carrying the ones. Like a blank-eyed countryman, he stopped in the middle of the aisle with his face up, as if the computations he performed so swiftly in his mind were written on the ceiling panels. He paused beside the dairy case, idly inspecting the merchandise, noting with disbelief the price of real butter. When no one was looking he opened a plastic half-pint of grape juice from the shelf and poured it down his throat, placing the empty carton behind the full ones. A few feet away, a boy in a green apron came pushing out from the double metal doors that led to the back. He got a quick glimpse of baled flour tiered to the roof, dog food on skids, block walls against which pallets of beer and soft drinks were neatly arrayed. He pushed his cart down to the meat case and examined the chickens and pork chops. Leg quarters were on sale for twenty-nine cents a pound but he passed them by. He picked up a package of sliced smoked picnic ham, the meat so brown and delicately marbled, the cooked hub of sawn bone in the middle. It was $6.97 for eight slices. He dropped it in his cart. Through the glass he could see a great hanging side of beef on a hook and butchers at work around tables. There was a button to summon the meatcutters set into the front of the case, and he pushed his cart down to it and pressed it with his finger, watching them. Heads looked up, looked back down. A young black man with a white paper cap on his head stared at him with thinly veiled disgust and wiped his hands on a paper towel before coming out to the front. He bent over the meat case and rearranged sirloin steaks and chuck roasts as he worked his way down to this customer.

"Can I help you," the butcher said, when he stopped in front of Wade.

"Y'all got any meat scraps?" Wade said.

"Meat scraps?" He looked out from under his cap, his hands moving busily and with trained efficiency over his goods. He stopped and rested his forearms over the back of the case and looked up the aisle.

"Yeah. Just some old bones or meat scraps for dogs. You got scraps to throw out, don't you?"

The butcher shook his head and he didn't look happy. "I don't know how much we got. Have to go back in the back and see. Ain't cut much today."

"I want some if you got some," Wade said. "I got some dogs at home."

"Well, we kinda busy," the butcher said. "I can go look when I get through with what I'm doin." Then while he shuffled the meat he mumbled about his own dogs and his daddy and his daddy's dogs, the full meaning of which Wade couldn't understand.

"Well, where's the manager?" Wade said. "I'll go ask him." He started looking around wildly.

The black man stood erect quickly. "Naw," he said. "Naw, don't go ask him. Hell, I'll go get it." He turned away and started toward the back.

"Y'all got a bathroom around here?"

The butcher pushed open one of the doors and jerked his thumb to the right. "Round back."

"Y'all care for me usin it?"

"Help yourself." He banged the doors when he went through.

The old man left his cart in the detergent aisle and stepped quietly through the swinging doors. He didn't see anybody back there among the cardboard boxes of ruined lettuce and black bananas, wet mops, sacks of potatoes, spilled cat litter. There were two massive white doors on the left. He walked all the way to the back of the room and looked to the right. He saw the door marked *Men*. The door was open and the light was off. He jerked his head left as the butcher came through with a box on his shoulder and went into the rear of the meat market, saying soft motherfuckers to himself. Wade went to the double doors and looked back out, toward the front. There was nobody out there. He knelt by the second freezer door and felt of the Miller tallboys stacked next to the white frost that oozed from the bad gasket at the lower corner of the door and crept across the floor, up the sides of the cans like a fungus. They were cold as ice, sweating thin beads of condensation. He took two from the plastic template that bound them and put in each pocket the champagne of bottled beer, then rose and made his way to the bathroom, where he turned on the light and locked the door.

When he emerged, belching, ten minutes later, he'd smoked two cigarettes in utter comfort and buried the empty cans in the trash bucket beneath wads of toilet paper he'd taken off the roll and stuffed in there. He retrieved his cart from the aisle and went down to the meat case. The same butcher looked up and saw him before he could press the button again. He came out of the meat market with a large cardboard box, marked on the side in heavy pencil NO CHARGE.

"Here," he said, and handed it across. It was a heavy box, the sides bulging. Wade just barely got it in his cart. He opened the flaps and looked inside. Bonemeal and bad briskets and the pink tails of pigs. He nodded.

"All right," he said, but the butcher had gone back inside. He glared as Wade pushed his cart away, then swung his meat cleaver down to the block with a vengeance.

Pork and beans were on sale, four cans for a dollar. A dozen went into his cart, along with two loaves of the cheapest bread. When he turned into the beer aisle he'd spent all he was going to on food.

He stopped and mentally added up his purchases. He considered the weight of his goods. Displays of beer were lined up on both sides of the aisle, the shelves stacked with many different brands. He ignored the imported and went straight for the domestic. Budweiser was $3.19 a six-pack for twelve ounce. Shit, he thought. He looked at a twelver to see if he could cut the cost. It was $5.99.

"Thirty-nine cents," he said, and a woman standing next to him jerked and looked at him and moved away. Busch was a little better at $2.98 but still he shook his head. The Old Milwaukee in cans was the best comparable buy he could see at $2.49 for fourteen ounces. But then he saw twelve-ounce bottles for $2.09. He stood there in a dilemma for three or four minutes trying to figure. For a fleeting moment he considered putting some of the bread back. Then he thought about the pork and beans. He was looking back and forth from his cart to the beer. And then he realized that he hadn't even considered cigarettes.

"*Shit*," he whispered. A boy sweeping the aisle was trying to sweep around him.

"What's the cheapest beer y'all got?" Wade asked him. The boy stopped and scratched his head. He looked around as if seeing it for the first time, since, in fact, he was.

"I don't know," he said.

"Well, see if you can help me. You got anything cheapern this Old Milwaukee? It's two forty-nine."

The boy went from display to display, checking prices.

"I guess we got this here," he said, tapping a stack of quarts. "It's sixty-nine cents."

Wade eyed it doubtfully. "What's that shit?" he said.

"Says. Misterbrow. Somethin."

"What'd that be for a case? Ten and two. Six ninety and . . . one thirty-eight. Be . . ." He looked at the boy.

"I don't know," the boy said.

"Be eight twenty-eight."

"Plus tax," said the boy.

"Plus tax. Which is . . . what? A nickel?"

"Six cents now."

"Six cents. Six eights forty-eight." He was wagging his head slightly from side to side. "Almost nine dollars."

The boy didn't say anything.

"But that's three gallons of beer," Wade told him. "Ain't that right? Twelve quarts to the case?"

"I guess."

"But I still got to get some cigarettes. And tax on all that . . ."

"I got to sweep this floor," the boy said.

"What'd I say while ago? Nine dollars. So a half a case'd be bout four and a half. Gallon and a half of beer. And this other . . ." He turned his head and looked back to the Old Milwaukee. "Two six-packs five dollars. Fourteen times twelve . . . ten's a hunnerd and forty . . . and twenty-eight . . . that ain't but a little over a gallon," he said. The boy had dropped all pretense of trying to sweep. He was just listening to him.

"Half a case of that's what I need," Wade said. "How bout takin six of them out for me?"

In the end he ditched six cans of pork and beans into the freezer section along with one of the loaves of bread, and wound up with five packs of generic cigarettes instead of a whole carton of Camels. He shoved into line and waited for the girl to set his things on the counter. He moved his head from his goods to the register like a tennis spectator as she rang it all up. He winced when she added the sales tax.

"Goddamn," he said. "Y'all the highest place in town, ain't you?"

She just leaned on one arm and tapped her nails on the counter and gave him a shitty look while he pulled out his money. A boy sacked the groceries and started to push the cart out the door.

"I got it," Wade told him, and went out onto the sidewalk. He had all his groceries in one sack, but the meat scraps alone were almost more than he could carry. He looked out over the parking lot as the sweat leaped out of him. He saw a parked cab and he pushed his cart down the ramp and went over to it. There was a ponytailed young white man sitting at the wheel.

"You got a fare?"

The man glanced up from his paper and flipped some ashes off his cigarette down the door. He looked at his newspaper again and turned a page.

"I's supposed to had one but if she don't bring her black ass out here in about two minutes I'm fixin to go eat dinner."

"What'll you charge me to carry me out to London Hill?"

The driver looked up.

"London Hill? Hell, that's way out in the country." He shook his head a little. "I don't know."

"What'll you take?" Wade said.

"How far is it?"

"It's bout ten mile."

He looked at his watch. "Let's see," he said. He looked up and squinted from the sun. "I'll cut the meter off and run you out there for ten dollars."

"All right."

The driver got out in a hurry and opened the back door, saying, "Hurry up and get your stuff in fore that nigger woman gets out here."

When the passenger was settled comfortably in the back seat with his groceries around him, he dug into the sack and found one of the hot quarts on the bottom. He pulled it out and twisted the cap off, then turned the bottle straight up.

"Put that bottle down, damn. These cops in town see you they'll have my ass."

He took it down. "What?" He was talking to the cab driver's eyes in the rearview mirror.

"Hell, feller. You can't be drinking beer in my cab in town. Don't you know that?"

"Well, you got a cup or anything?"

"Naw, I ain't got no cup. Just wait'll we get out of town." He picked up his mike. "Wait'll we get up on the bypass at least. I'm fixin to check out for dinner there, Ethel."

He pulled out into the street.

"You get that woman at Midtown?" said the radio.

"Did not there. I waited on her thirty minutes."

He went down the hill and turned east.

"Well, she called back there and said she's ready. Swing around and take her home before you go to dinner."

He put his knee up and clenched the mike, steering with one hand.

"I'm heading to the service station right now with one goin down. This thing's hot as a two dollar pistol, too. I might be able to get her in about a hour there. Maybe. Ten four?"

He stopped at an intersection and looked both ways, then pulled out. The radio sputtered, making the sound of frying bacon. He cut down the squelch and swung up onto the ramp and mashed the gas pedal to the floor. He met Wade with his eyes in the mirror.

"All right," he said. "You can get happy now if you want to."

He drove swiftly on the country road. Wade swayed slightly in the curves with his beer in one hand and a piece of the picnic ham in the other. Things were much changed from what he remembered from years ago. New houses, fields where woods once stood, a new county high school. Even the road was new.

"Say you live out there at London Hill?" the driver said. He didn't look around.

"Right the other side of it."

"You don't know old Joe Ransom, do you?"

The old man thought about it a while. He'd known some Ransoms at one time, back when he was much younger. Thirty or forty years before.

"I don't know," he said finally. "I used to know a bunch of folks out there. I been gone a long time, though. What's his daddy's name?"

"I don't know. You ain't never heard of him?"

"I don't reckon."

"I just wondered. He's supposed to live out there somewhere. I just thought you might know him."

"I don't guess I do," Wade said. He dug into the sack for another piece of meat.

He was halfway finished with the second quart when he told the driver where to turn off.

"How much further?" the driver wanted to know.

"It ain't much further."

"I got twelve miles on this thing already," he said, and he looked over his shoulder when he said it.

"I'll pay you."

Tractors were toiling their way through heavy clouds of dust. Trucks were parked in the fields with their loads of fertilizer and seed. The taxi sped by and left them behind.

"Bunch of farmers out here," the driver said.

"It's about another mile up here where you turn off. Big dirt road to the left and you go up this hill."

He slowed the driver down, and as they turned onto the dirt

road he pitched the second bottle out the window. The track was rough and the car bellied and bumped over the ruts.

"I ain't gonna get stuck up in here, am I?" the driver said.

"Naw. It ain't much further."

They went across a wooden bridge where a creek lay shallow within the banks, an eddy sluggish and brown and studded with stones showing their moss-grown faces, stepping stones for the coons and foxes and possums whose tracks dotted the sandy silt and went up the slopes of young cane, thick and nearly impenetrable, over the slides of beavers crusted with sun and broken open into jigsaw puzzles of hardened mud. Through fields of unnamed bushes and sagging wire, between oaks leaning to form a tunnel of shade, the dusty cab sped rocking and jarring, rocks flying.

"Damned if you don't live back in the sticks," the driver said.

"Here it is," Wade said, pointing. "Just drive right up in there."

The driver stopped and eyed the iron ruts left by tractors. He shook his head.

"This is far as I'm goin," he said. "I done come fourteen miles and you said it wasn't but ten."

"Hell, you can get up in there."

"Not in this car."

He shoved the shift into parking gear and got out. Wade climbed out on the other side and slid his box of scraps and his sack onto the ground. The beer bottles clinked.

"Owe me fourteen dollars," the driver said. Wade looked at him for a little while and then took the money out of his pocket and counted it. He had four dollars left after he paid his fare. He bent and stuck it into a sock and straightened. There was a cloud of dust far down in the field traveling along the rows. The driver put the money in his pocket and got back into the car. The old man had already started walking off with his hands empty when he leaned out and said: "You not goin to take this stuff with you?"

Wade turned around and looked at him. "I got somebody can carry it," he said.

urt Fowler was on his front porch taking the last sip from his last beer. He pitched the can into the aluminum boat that sat beside the porch just as a pickup with a camper bed came over the hill, the tires sucking gently in the mud. The truck slewed slightly as it swung into the yard and came to a lurching halt beside the single tree, where a rope hung. The door slammed and Joe got out and came around the front of the truck with five beers in his hand.

"What say, Curt."

He walked up to the porch and sat on the step.

"I knew somebody'd bring me a beer if I set out here long enough," Curt said. He helped himself to a beer and opened it and started pouring it down his throat.

"You ain't fishin today, Curt?"

"Naw, hell, water's too fuckin muddy, it rained like a sumbitch over here last night. You ain't workin today?"

Joe had on his sunglasses and a pair of knit slacks the color of cream and a new green velour shirt with tan piping around the collar. His shiny black loafers had mud on them.

"My niggers can't work in the rain. Afraid they gonna melt, I reckon. We's in a bad place, anyway, and I was afraid we wouldn't get out so we just come on to the house. It's been like that near every day. Where's that sorry-ass brother of yours?"

Curt shook his head. "I ain't seen him in about two weeks. I reckon he's gone back to Texas to hang sheetrock. Melba said she don't even know where he is."

"I wish to hell I knowed where he is. He owes me some damn money."

"He ain't never paid you that yet? Damn. I figured he'd done paid you by now."

Joe drained the can of beer in his hand and tossed it into the boat, which was fourteen feet long and already three-quarters full of cans. "I can't catch up with him," he said. "If you see him, tell him I want to see him."

"I'll tell him. What you fixin to do?"

"I don't know. Reckon Henry and them's got a game tonight?"

"I don't know. The sumbitch won't never tell me when they gonna have one no more. After I took a bunch of money off him he won't. Bastard's gonna make me mad sometime and I'm gonna whip his ass is what I'm gonna do."

"He might shoot your ass, too. George'll shoot you in a goddamn minute."

"They ain't gonna shoot nobody. They ain't gonna shoot me."

Joe got himself another beer and opened it. He pulled out his cigarettes.

"Let me get one of them off you," Curt said immediately.

"You the bumminest little fucker I ever seen," said Joe, but he gave him one.

"I just ain't had no way to get to the store."

"You just too lazy to walk, Curt. Where's Bobby?"

"Still in jail, I reckon. I heard you got into it with Willie Russell other night."

"Naw. He kept fuckin with me and I just slapped the shit out of him was all. He was drunk. Runnin his mouth. You know how he is."

"I'm surprised somebody ain't done killed him by now."

"Somebody will."

Curt sipped his beer and looked out across the yard.

"You know, though, I don't think he's been right at all since he mashed his balls off."

"Shit. I don't believe he mashed em off."

"You don't?"

"I don't. I've heard he's got one ball and I've heard he mashed em both off, but I don't know."

"Satch said he believes he's queer."

"I don't believe he's queer neither. I just think he's too fucked up for anybody to have him. That's why you don't never see him with a woman. Ain't no woman'll have him."

"I had a cousin one time like to lost his dick," Curt said. "Zipped it up in his zipper. You know how you'll do that when you're little."

"Oh, hell yes. It'll just about make you shit on yourself."

"He was grown, though. Zipped it up too fast and got some of the skin caught in it. And messed around and let it get infected

---

before he went to the doctor. He like to went crazy over it. Thought they's gonna have to amputate his dick. They had to take him down to Whitfield for a while. His dick like to rotted off."

"Well, what'd they do?"

"His daddy told me they did a skin graft on it. Said they took some skin off his leg and sewed that on it."

Joe leaned back and sipped his beer and crossed his legs, gave off a little shiver.

"Off his leg? Why hell, it don't look like that would work. I don't believe I'd want no skin off my leg on my dick."

"You might if they's fixin to amputate it."

"They could amputate mine right now for all the good it does me," he said. He got up suddenly. "Reckon when Franklin'll be back?"

Curt was eyeing the three remaining beers mournfully.

"It ain't no tellin about him," he said.

"He probably don't even remember me letting him have it. Was drunk when he got it. I hate to have to chase down somebody that owes me money."

"I know it," said Curt. He started drinking faster. "When you seen old Van House?" he said, stalling for time.

"I ain't seen him," Joe said, and stepped down into the yard. "You tell Franklin when he comes back I want my money. I have to work for it just like everybody else and I ain't rich."

"I'll tell him. Let me get another one of these beers off you before you go."

Joe barely glanced at them. "Hell, get all of em. I got some more in the truck. Only reason I'm drinking beer's cause it's so hot."

He was almost to the truck when Curt came down the steps, two of the beers in one hand and another freshly opened in the other.

"You ain't fixin to go to town, are you?"

"I don't know," he said. He went on around and got in the truck. "I don't know where I'm fixin to go." He hated now that he'd stopped.

Unshaven, his hair wild, his clothes rumpled from sleeping in them, the man in the yard leaned in the open window of the truck to further detain this visitor, this rare company. "Let me ride up town with you," he said.

Joe looked at him, his eyes unreadable behind the dark glasses, his hand on the key and his foot on the clutch.

"You got any money? I ain't gonna buy your damn beer all night long."

"Oh, I got some money," he said. "I got a check I can cash."

He was already opening the truck door and sliding in. There were three packs of cigarettes on the dash and a little cooler in the floor. He slammed the door and sat there, ready for takeoff.

"Let's see it," Joe said.

"What?"

"Sumbitch, if you ain't got no money you ain't goin with me."

Curt set his beer in the floor and did a quick frisk of his pockets, grabbing himself all over with spread fingers.

"It's in the house," he said. "Let me run get it." He got out and started across the yard. "Wait on me!" he yelled back.

Joe sat shaking his head, thinking: Fuckass around here all evening waiting for him to get ready to go.

After a minute, Curt stuck his head out the screen door and said: "You got time for me to shave right quick?"

"Hell naw. You come get your ass in if you're goin. I'm fixing to leave."

He mashed the clutch and cranked the truck and revved the engine. Curt came flying out the door with a fresh shirt flapping around him, an envelope in his hand.

"I got it," he panted. He got back in and said: "I'm ready now. I got to stop somewhere and cash it, though." He picked up his beer and reached into his shirt pocket. "Goddamn. Left my fuckin cigarettes in the house. Wait on me just a minute."

He opened the door and Joe let out on the clutch. They went rolling through the yard.

"Wait a minute. I got to get my cigarettes."

"Just smoke some of mine. They's some up on the dash."

Curt grabbed a pack and closed the door as they moved through the yard and down the driveway and out onto the road. Joe looked at his watch.

"Don't start no shit and expect me to finish it, now. What kind of a check you got?"

"It's a goverment check," said Curt. "I can get it cashed anywhere. Grocery stores'll cash em."

"What you doin with a government check? What are you drawin from the government?"

"Aw, it's Mama's. I always cash hers for her."

"How much is it?"

"A hundred and thirty dollars. It's a pension check."

"Pension."

"Yeah."

"Your mama draws a hundred and thirty dollars a month?"

"Yeah. Plus, she draws Social Security and welfare, too."

"What's she doin lettin you have it?"

"She don't know I got it."

Joe shook his head. They went up the gravel road with the rich red mud squishing under the tires. Curt kept up a running commentary, expansive now with the promise of more beer and a night on the town. The woods thinned and opened up into green hills dotted with horses and cows and cultivated land gleaming wetly under the weak sun trying to break through the clouds. Tarpaper shacks and shabby mobile homes, actually no more than campers, lined the road, the yards full of junked autos and stacked firewood overgrown with weeds and pulpwood trucks with the windows smashed out and the rear ends jacked up and propped on oil drums, El Dorados with mud halfway up the sides parked before porches of rough sawmill lumber. Here and there were school buses fixed up with furniture and beds on the inside, the awnings made of splintered fiberglass, and new brick homes within sight of firetraps where carports were cluttered with dogs and three-wheelers and washing machines.

They turned onto the blacktop, and mud began slapping off the tires onto the undersides of the wheelwells. The bottomland lay untilled and dark with water, the brown rows of the past year's crop still standing in the new grass threatening to bury it. Stumps the size of Volkswagens had been bulldozed into piles in the corners of the fields.

"They gonna plant any of this this year?" said Joe.

Curt tossed his can out the window and reached for another

one. He felt of it. He looked at Joe. "You got any cold beers in that cooler?"

"They's a six-pack iced down in there. Goddamn, you done drank all them?"

"Naw. I'm gonna swap one out with you." He put the lukewarm beer in the cooler and took out a cold one and popped the top. "Hell, it's been too wet," he said. "It's rained on it just about ever week. They tried cuttin part of it about three weeks ago and mired the tractor and brought a dozer over to pull it out and mired it. I reckon it's still settin there if somebody ain't done stole it."

They turned at a crossroads and headed back up into the hills.

"I thought you's goin to town," Curt said.

"I am. I got to stop and see Henry first and see if they've got a game up tonight. I need to win me a little money if I can."

They crossed the bottomland, the long rows whipping past and wheeling by like spokes. Butterflies wafted and flitted through the lush growth at the roadsides, snake doctors hovered like gunships. The road brightened and the shadow of a cloud stood immense and dark and held part of the land in shade, a line of demarcation halfway across the fields.

"Look at that," Joe said. "We got to try and work tomorrow if we can. It's costin the shit out of me to lay out."

"Shit. If I had your money I'd throw mine away."

Joe grunted. He steered the truck between the holes in the road and tried to find some music on the radio. He'd been meaning to get a tape deck but he'd never gotten around to it. He punched a button and got WDIA.

"Damn it," he said. He twisted the dial around, and the radio snarled and whined while quick-speaking Spaniards exhorted their wares and somebody screamed CASH MONEY and twangy garbled country music flared and diminished amidst roaring and fuzz and static until finally he snapped it off. The road twisted through stands of pine, hills of hardwood timber green as Eden. They went down into a smaller bottom where one old unpainted house sat back from the road, with dead cotton stalks all around it, even in what should have been a yard. They pulled into a short driveway.

"You goin it?" Joe said, after he'd killed the motor.

Curt looked dubiously at the house.

"Naw. I don't want to go in. I'll just set out here."

"Suit yourself," he said, and he got out and slammed the door and went up the steps onto the porch. He knocked on the screen door and stuck his head inside.

"Henry? Hey, Henry." Somebody answered and he stepped into the hall. The house was built with a breezeway through the middle and rooms on each side. The old boards bowed and sagged under his weight. Joe opened a door on the right but there was nobody in there. Somebody said something again and he went to the back of the house. The door he opened belonged to the kitchen, and three men stood in there at a table, hacking and slicing on the carcass of a skinned deer, two holding, one cutting, all of them trying to keep it from sliding onto the floor.

"Now how'd y'all know I wasn't the game warden?" he said.

"Hell, they all out on the lake robbin trotlines," said Henry. "You know anything about cuttin up a deer?"

He looked at the thing doubtfully.

"I've cut up a few. I ain't no expert."

He leaned up against the wall and surveyed the mess on the table. It was covered with cut hair and caked with enormous clots of blood.

"What are y'all tryin to do, cut it up into steaks or what?"

Henry waved his knife. He was an old man with long white hair, overalls, no shirt or shoes.

"We just trying to get it so we can eat it. Thought we might cut it up in some roasts."

"I don't believe I'd cut it all up into roasts," Joe said. "Course you can do it any way you want to. I'd cut most of it up in steaks if it was mine."

"Well, you know how to do it? Stacy said he knowed how to cut it up and like to cut his fuckin arm off a while ago."

A drunk grinned and lifted a beer in a hand swathed with bloodsoaked paper towels. All the men were brothers.

"Hell, let George cut it up," said Joe. "George could cut it up if they give you enough time, couldn't you, George?"

"I could do as good as they doin," said the blind brother.

Joe unleaned himself from the wall and walked over to the table. "I hate to get a bunch of blood on these clothes. I'll cut the loins off for you and show you how to cut up the hams. You can make roasts out of the shoulders if you want to. That's about all they're fit for anyway."

They stepped back.

"Well, go to it," said Henry.

"You got a sharp knife?" he said, and laid his cigarettes down.

"I got a filet knife right here," said Henry.

"Let me see that, then."

He had them turn the deer on its side and then he tested the edge of the blade against his thumb.

"This is the best meat on it right here," he said, and he put the tip of the knife just behind the shoulder and sank it into the meat.

"Just hold it steady, now," he said. He pushed the knife down until he felt it stop against the first rib and drew it down, slicing the backstrap away from the vertebrae all the way down to the hip.

"Where did y'all get this deer?"

"It was hung in a fence up at Mr. Lee's old house a while ago," Stacy said. "Me and Henry was comin back from town and seen it. I come home and got George's pistol and shot it."

"What was it, a buck or a doe?"

"It was a doe. Big old doe."

He cut in deeply just behind the shoulder and just ahead of the hip, then took the knife forward under the meat and sliced toward his belly with the tip until he could grasp a corner of the loin and pull it up. He worked the blade back and forth against the ribs, pulling the meat up in a single strip and keeping the blade close against the bones. It came up smoothly, the white sinew wrinkling over the dark burgundy flesh until he passed the knife all the way down the ribs and held in his hand a thick strip of meat almost two feet long. He laid it on the table.

"That's some good stuff there," he said. "Look here."

He placed the top side down and cut and squared off the end and pushed the scrap aside with the knife. He cut off a loin steak two inches thick, then cut halfway through it again, so that when he spread it with his fingers it had doubled in size.

"That's how you do it. Butterfly steak. That's the best meat on it."

He put the knife down and went over to the sink and started washing his hands.

"Y'all can cut up the rest of it. Just saw the hams off and slice it all up in steak. I got to get on. When you gonna have another crap game?"

"We gonna have one tonight," Henry said.

"What time?"

"I don't know. When everbody gets here. We got to get through with this deer first. We got to get some freezer paper somewhere. Reckon John Coleman's got any at his store?"

"Yeah, he's got some. He keeps it."

"Well, just stick around. Stacy and George can finish this."

Joe picked up his cigarettes and lit one. He leaned against the sink.

"I got to go to town first." He grinned. "I got Curt out in the truck with me."

"What?" Henry said. "He scared to come in?"

"Said you's pissed off at him. Said he took a bunch of money off you other night."

"Why, the son of a bitch is lying."

"I figured he was."

"I'll tell you what he got pissed off about. He got pissed off cause I wouldn't loan him fifty dollars. Comes down here drunk, wantin to borry money off me to gamble with me. If I loaned him

78

fifty he'd owe me a hundred. You ever heard of anything like that?"

Joe picked up his cigarettes and put them in his pocket. "I ain't surprised at nothin Curt would do. He's got his mama's pension check in his pocket right now. Fixin to cash it when he gets to a grocery store."

Henry shook his head.

"Him and Franklin have pissed away every penny that old woman had. When Jim died he owned two thousand acres of land and had way over a hundred head of cows. And I mean by God worked his whole life to get it. I can remember when he didn't have nothin. And now she ain't got nothin. Taxes. It's their own fault, I reckon. When them two boys was coming up they was a gallon churn used to set on the kitchen table. Was full of money, change. Quarters and dimes and nickels. Wasn't no pennies in it. Franklin and Curt would get ready to go to town and they'd go in there and just scoop up a handful. They always had plenty of money but they never had to work for none of it. No sir, I ain't loanin him no money."

"I'm fixin to take him uptown and get him drunk," Joe said. "He knows where Franklin's at, but he won't tell me when he's sober. I'll get about a six-pack in him and get some of them old gals to rub some of that leg on him. He'll tell me then."

"A drunk man tells no lies."

"You got that right. Well, I'll be back after while, Henry. You don't want me to bring Curt back with me?"

"I don't care. Leave him uptown and make him walk home if you want to. You can get you some of this deer meat when you get back if you want to. We ain't got much room in the freezer."

"All right," he said, and he went out the door. He closed it behind him and walked up the hall. He could see Curt sitting on the hood drinking a beer. He had his legs crossed, and was smoking a cigarette.

"Is Henry in there?" he said.

"Yeah. He said if you come in there he's gonna shoot your ass. Come on, get in and let's go." He was going down the steps as he talked, and he stopped beside Curt where he sat on the hood. A truck came around the curve and it started slowing as it neared the house. They turned to watch it come.

"I wonder who that is," Joe said.

"I don't know. Looks like it's comin in here."

It was. It slowed gradually and stopped beside the driveway, a white '78 Ford truck with a smashed fender and a driver screaming strangled curses as he dragged something up from the floorboards. Fried hair and a yelling mouth fifty yards away, a man with blood between his eyes.

"Is he talkin to us?" Joe said.

"God*damn!*" Curt threw one leg off the hood and slammed his beer down and Joe had started around the other side of the truck when the barrel came out the window and smoke erupted. Two concussions back to back sent hot lead flying as they labored with their hands up beside their chests, cartoon characters slipping and losing traction in the loose gravel. They were shot before they could move three feet. Joe fell and covered his head. Another shot went over his back and slammed into the house. Curt sobbed aloud and crawled behind the wheel of the truck, blood running from his shoe. Joe's ears were roaring and he heard the transmission of the truck grinding as the driver tried to shove it up in reverse. He got up and jerked the door open, hitting Curt in the head with it, and felt around among the beer cans under the seat for his pistol. His hand closed over it. He snatched it out and ran to the road. The pickup had backed into the field above the house and the driver was winding the wheel in a panic, looking out the window. Joe ran up the ditch, trying to shorten the range. The truck roared out, skidded, almost went into the ditch on the other side, and he stopped and opened up with the little .25, towtowtow, towtow- towtow! Two small medallions of paint leaped off the tailgate. As the truck pulled away, he threw the tiny gun after it. He slapped a hand up beside his ear and it came away slick with blood. His shirt had three holes in it that he could see, and more blood was coming from his arms and back. He wiped the blood away from his head and walked back to his truck. George and Henry and Stacy were on the porch, Henry with a 9MM Browning automatic in his hand.

"You all right?" Henry said.

"Hell yeah. I reckon. Where's Curt?"

They pointed to the truck. He knelt down and looked under it. Curt lay curled into a ball, his hands over his head.

Joe stood up. The hood and the left front fender had been ventilated. Later, he would count twenty holes in them, little puncture wounds that could have been in him.

"Come out from under there, Curt." He pulled up the sleeve of his shirt and saw the ragged hole in his bicep. "Shit," he said. It didn't hurt.

Henry and Stacy came off the porch. George stood back, both hands on a post.

"Get out from under there, Curt," he said again. "He's gone now. How bad you hurt?"

"Damn, Joe," said Henry. "You bleedin like a stuck pig."

"I'm all right. Little son of a bitch. I'll fix his ass. Get out from under there, Curt."

"I can't," said the small muffled whine in the dirt.

"Why not?"

"Cause," he said. He waited a moment. "I shit in my britches."

Joe looked at Henry and Stacy and grinned. "How you know I didn't shit in mine?" he said.

t happened that the old man and the boy had been walking down a road with their bags of cans.

"I'm bout give out," Wade said.

"You want to stop and rest?"

"Yeah. Let's set down a minute and see if anybody comes by."

They sat and sat and sat.

"I don't believe nobody's gonna come by," Gary said.

"Just shut up. We need to get us a car."

"I'd like to have me a new car. I know what I'd buy, too. I'd buy me one of them SS Chevelles with a automatic transmission and tinted windows. And blackout mags. I'd run everybody around here."

The old man lay on his back and pulled his hat over his face.

"You know what?" the boy said.

"What?"

"If we'd get us a car I could get my driver's license."

The old man grunted and turned on his side.

"You can't get a driver's license. You don't know how to drive."

"If we had us a car I could learn, though. How much you reckon we could buy us a car for?"

"I don't know. It depends."

"Depends on what?"

"Depends on how much they want for it."

The boy pondered this and reamed out his ear with his finger, producing a crescent of brown wax on his nail that he wiped on his leg. He looked around.

"Let's walk on up the road. Ain't nobody gonna come by here. We might catch a ride up at the crossroads."

But the old man was sleepy and did not answer. The boy reached out and jostled his leg. His father moaned and turned in his sleep. He was lying in an ant bed. Ants were crawling over his shoes.

"You better move from there," Gary said.

His father's head collapsed onto an arm. He'd begun snoring.

"All right, then," Gary said. He sat there for a minute. He reached out and shook his father's leg. "You better move," he said. The old man pawed out at him, wheezing muttered words under his breath.

The boy sat and watched him sink deeper and deeper into sleep and fitfully begin a tortured turning and moving, as if his bones lay uneasy in his flesh. He whined once, sharply. His mouth jerked open and his nose twitched. He slapped groggily at his face and missed. The boy grinned. The old man bowed his back on the ground and stuck one hand inside his overalls and scratched. He panted gently, like a dog in labor, his face contorted. He seemed to nod vague agreement to some unspoken truth in his sleep. His limbs stopped moving momentarily and he lay on his side with one hand caught between his knees and the other arm pillowing his head.

It was as if a bolt of electricity suddenly penetrated him. His eyes snapped open and a look of such dread appeared in them that it was no surprise to the boy when he screamed.

"Haaaaaaaaaaaaaa!" he said. He was off the ground like a shot, running, jerking at the straps of his overalls and falling with a foot caught in his hands, trying to get his shoes off. But he couldn't even wait for that. He got one off and jumped up again and began a demented parody of aerobics or teenaged cheerleaders caught up in gymnastic attempts and twitched and hopped one-footed over the asphalt, making strange and meaningless gestures, emitting all manner of oaths, motherfuckers especially, a series of impotent ravings like one crazed with hydrophobia or loosed from a madhouse. He kicked one shoe flying and it sailed into a tree and hung there. The boy stood up and watched him.

"I told you to get up," he said.

The old man shucked clean out of his overalls and stood slapping them against the ground in his dirty shorts and T-shirt. He drew his shorts down to his knees so that his flaccid asscheeks and purple-headed penis were revealed among unbelievable amounts of short gray fur. Tiny red marks were all over his skin, as if he'd been sprinkled with a shotgun.

"Why didn't you tell me I's layin in a ant bed?" he said.

"I told you."

He started putting his clothes on, stepping into his overalls, but then he stopped and drew them back off and turned them inside out and inspected them minutely. He was still looking them over when they heard something up the road and saw a white pickup heading their way, coming across the bridge.

"Yonder comes somebody," said the boy.

"I ain't blind. Get down yonder and get my shoe out from that tree."

He got into his overalls and fastened the galluses and the boy went down into the ditch and picked up a stick and knocked the shoe loose, then tossed it up on the bank. The old man sat down in the road to put it on. The truck slowed and he watched it come. He was tying his shoelace when it pulled up beside him. He got up and looked through the windshield and went past the grille to the other shoe and picked it up and started putting it on. The boy came out of the ditch and stood beside the road. The driver of the truck was looking at them.

"What are y'all doin?" he said. He weaved behind the seat a little and turned up a Busch tallboy, and the old man homed in, going to the passenger window and hanging his arms down inside.

"We just messin around," he said. "You ain't got another one of them beers, have you?"

The man behind the wheel studied him carefully. He opened his mouth and let out an enormous belch, then threw the can out into the road. His face looked as if somebody had been ahold of it with a hatchet in years past.

"Where are y'all goin?" he said. He spoke very slowly and he could hardly speak at all.

"We just pickin up some cans," Wade told him. "You got one of them beers I could borrow off you?"

The man looked at him as if he couldn't figure out what he was.

He turned his head, slowly, steadily, and looked for the first time at the boy.

"What's he?" he said. "What's? Yonder's a can right there you can pick up," he said, pointing to the one he'd just thrown out. "Fuck it," he said. "I'll get it." He opened the door and held on with both hands and moved over to the can with his arms out for balance and bent over ever so slowly in the road and picked up the can.

"Where's you sack?" he said. "Where is your sack."

He leaned against the hood and turned the empty can up to his mouth. He wobbled when his head went back and then he took the can down. He stumbled backwards along the fender, trying to steady himself with his arm on the hood, but he didn't stop until his shoulder touched the windshield.

"Whoa," he said. He was offering the can. "That's one more." He ran his fingers up over his forehead and pushed his hair back. "Whew," he said. He looked owlishly about. He straightened back up and put both arms on the hood. The boy couldn't keep from staring at his face. The man saw him looking and said: "The fuck you lookin at?"

"I ain't lookin at nothin," Gary said.

"What are y'all doin?" he intoned again.

"Let me get one of them cold beers off you if you got another one," Wade said.

The man was trying to find a cigarette in his pocket and he finally found one. He turned it over in his hand a few times and stuck the filter in his mouth and then lit it. He smoked it for a moment, took it out and looked at it, then stuck it back between his lips.

"I tell you what I'll do," he said.

"What's that?" Wade was grinning, his eyes knowing, shining, as if they shared some secret.

"I'll give you a beer if you'll get me one while you in there, but first I got to tell you somethin."

"All right."

"Call him over here too."

"Who?"

"Him." He pointed to Gary.

"C'mere," Wade said.

Gary walked over and stood beside his father. He looked at a place on the man's neck.

"Look at me," the man said.

Gary looked at his face. "What?" he said.

"I said look at me." His eyes were dark and rimmed with redness. Gary looked. Looked deep at the hate burning in there, meanness ingrained but neutered by alcohol, impotent. Nothing to fear but still he feared something. He knew that he and his father would get in with this man and go wherever the road led as long as the beer held out. And he feared that.

"You see my face?" the man said.

"I see it."

"I went through a windshield at four o'clock one mornin and I don't give a fuck."

"Say you got a beer?" said Wade.

"I got a whole fuckin case."

"You want me to get you one?" said Wade, already heading for the cooler in the back end.

"Yeah. Y'all want a ride?"

Wade said that they did.

"Well, hop your fat ass in."

The boy was squeezed up between the two men with his feet on the hump, while Wade was freely smoking Willie Russell's cigarettes. Telling one lie after another. Russell had told them about ten times that he'd gone through a windshield at four o'clock one morning and didn't give a fuck.

"You want a cigarette?" he asked Gary.

"I don't smoke."

"Well hell, try one. You might get started."

"I don't want one," he said.

"Smoke one," Russell said.

"I don't want one."

"What, you a candy ass?"

"Naw."

The boy tried to sleep but he couldn't sleep with them talking. They went over roads he hadn't seen before. They pissed in the road and ran off the road. Russell opened the glove box and pulled out a Remington twelve-gauge shell and showed it to them.

"You see this?"

They saw it.

"I don't give a fuck who it is. He can't stand up to this. That's double-aught buckshot. You believe me?"

Wade was jovial, chuckling with a cigarette hanging out the corner of his mouth. Benevolent. A Samaritan to guide his driver over the sand hills and through the rough dirt roads, down the highways of patched asphalt lined with rusted wire and thickets of blackberries. Dark fat cows with white faces stood knee-deep in grass, their jaws so slowly working their tufts of fescue and their eyes fixed with such blank stares that they seemed stoned on a more potent weed. Willie Russell kept drinking, but he didn't seem to be able to get any drunker. In the watered ice at the bottom of the Igloo, Wade found a fifth of peppermint schnapps and they started passing it back and forth, talking like old friends, the ice water dripping on the boy's legs and soaking through instantly to his skin.

"I don't let no sumbitch slap me," Russell said.

"A sumbitch slaps me better look out. You know it?"

"Well," Wade said.

"Cause I'm fixin to kill him."

"Aw."

"But I ain't scared of the sumbitch and never have been. And I'll whip his ass if he fucks with me. Again. If he ever. Fucks. With me. Again."

Then why don't you do it stead of talking about it? the boy wondered. Drunk talk's all it is.

After an hour or so they turned onto a dirt road, the entrance to it overhung with great leaning trees and vines, the shade deep and strong like a darker world within the outer, a place of cane thickets and coon dens and the lairs of bobcats, where the sun at its highest cast no light over the rotted stumps and stagnant sloughs. The trees that bordered the road and spread out across the land beside it had closed their tops together, so long had they stood there admitting neither light nor shadow of hawk nor the blue smoke of chain saws. Old timber, and magnificent, the bark worn slick on the cypresses from the constant track of coons and the black mud richly marked with the feet of the things that lived there. They went down the road past the posted signs and stopped on a wooden bridge. Russell got out.

"I'm ready to go home," Gary told his daddy.

"Well, I ain't. They ain't a goddamn thing at home."

The boy sat on the seat for a moment and then slid out the open driver's door. He was tired of sitting cramped up and he wanted to stretch his legs. Russell was weaving on the edge of the bridge, waving a stream of his own into the stream below. Gary stepped to the edge and stood looking down. The water was twelve feet below, a thin trickle sliding over holes in the clay bottom where tiny fish hovered. He looked at Russell. He was pissing and holding a beer can straight upside down against his mouth.

Gary didn't know where he was and he was hungry and he knew there was no telling where they would wind up. They'd taken a lot of turns and gone over many roads and this place didn't look familiar. He saw the moccasin, immobile on the bank among the dried sticks and shriveled roots, a phantom appearing out of nothing. Without thinking he reached for the largest rock he saw and heaved it over. It made a great splash. Russell surged back and wavered on the precipice of the single two-by-eight that formed the border of the bridge and then, standing there with arms waving, dropped his beer and fell and caught himself by his arms and chin, hanging off the wood.

Gary went to him and grabbed the back of his shirt. Then he reached lower and caught his belt and heaved up on it.

"You little motherfucker," Russell said. Gary turned him loose and stood up. He looked at the hands clutching so desperately the splintered wood, the fingers so splayed and vulnerable, the nails just begging to be stomped.

"Goddamn, boy, what's the matter with you?" said Wade. He knelt and hauled on the back of Russell's shirt.

"Help me get him up."

"Let him get up by himself." He stood back and watched Wade trying to pull him up over the edge. Russell clawed at the boards, his chest, half-emerged, his eyes wild and his hands waving and slapping hard at the wood. He came shaken and panting onto the bridge and finally lay with his feet hanging out over the empty air but for a moment, and then he got up and took three fast steps and slammed the boy against the truck.

"Boy, I'll slap your face," he said. Wade didn't say anything. Gary looked at his father but he wasn't even looking at them. The boy tried to move, but there wasn't any use. The hands clamped on him were hard and ungiving.

"I ain't done nothin to you," he said. "Turn me loose."

"I seen you laughin at me."

"I wasn't done it."

"You throwed that rock at me."

"I throwed it at a snake. I wasn't throwin it at you."

Gary pushed one hand off him and jerked the other shoulder away. Russell shoved him hard and he fell to the bridge. Wade was drinking a beer and looking off into the trees as if this magnitude of land were his and he was pondering its worth. No help from that quarter, never had been, never would be.

"You a lyin little son of a bitch. I think I'll just throw your ass off in there and see how you like it."

Gary kicked at Russell at first while scooting backwards. But then he turned over and came up and they met beside the truck. Twice he was slammed against the quarter panel. He pushed, blind, striking blindly. Russell laughed at him. He was being slapped and, after the first blow, he couldn't even see where the hands were coming from. He didn't know where his father was and he didn't know why he wasn't helping him and more than anything he was afraid he was going to cry. He did the only thing he could do. He spied a rock between his feet, one about the size of his fist, and he bent over and seized it and drew back and delivered it to Russell's forehead. A steer in the killing pen goes down no sooner. He thought he'd killed him. A little droplet of blood squeezed out of the cut and ran down one side of Russell's nose. Gary stood over him. With his foot he rolled him over to send him for good into the creek. But the old man walked over with a hand up to halt him.

"Here now," he said. He pitched his empty can into the water below. While his son watched he robbed the still figure, turning out the pockets and taking the money. Russell lay on his back breathing raggedly, air and blood snuffling and mixing in his nostrils. The boy stood watching as his own breathing gradually slowed down, as his heart ceased its thumping. He heard the sounds his father was making in the truck after he turned away, but it wasn't until the old man started walking up the road without waiting for him to follow that he looked and saw the pockets of his parent crammed full of beer and the neck of the fifth of schnapps in his hand.

"What we gonna do with him?" he called.

Wade didn't look around when he answered, just kept walking.

"I ain't doin nothin with him."

"We gonna just leave him?"

"You better get the fuck away from him."

He looked down at Russell and saw the wisdom of this. But what of the future and the chance of meeting up with him again? It wouldn't be his father. It would be him.

After a while he went after the old man, keeping his distance, the bag of cans he retrieved from the back end rattling faintly against his leg.

J oe wouldn't let Curt sit on the front seat when he took him home. He made him ride in the back where the hands rode. After he left Curt's house, his arm started to hurt a little more, but he knew that was shock wearing off, knew it was natural because he'd been shot once before, with a .22. It was hurting like hell by the time he pulled up in front of his own house. He took the whiskey inside with him.

With his chest naked and the bloody shirt in the trash, he faced himself in the bathroom mirror and surveyed the damage. Two in the neck, one in each arm. Puckered and swollen craters of flesh, the blood already black deep in the meat. He picked up the whiskey off the vanity and took a drink. His face was unmarked and he couldn't imagine all that missing his head, three loads. The ball in his left arm lay blue against the skin, having come from behind, and it was the size of a pencil eraser and very hard. The two on the outside edges of his neck had passed through. He dabbed alcohol over the wounds, front and back, and stoppered them with Band-Aids.

It was sort of like being shot with an arrow in a Western. Home surgery was required. His knife wasn't sharp enough. He took it out and tested the edge with his thumb and put it back in his pocket. The piece of lead moved around under the skin of his left arm when he put his finger on it. There was a peculiar feeling of fever in both his arms. He felt around on the other arm and couldn't feel anything. There was just the hole in back. He found a hand mirror of Charlotte's and held it over his shoulder, looking at the wound in the mirror. He turned the bottle of alcohol up over it and doused it thoroughly. It burned a little and then quit.

He had to go back to the kitchen to find the tape and he had to look in three drawers before he found it, some half-inch stuff he'd bought a long time ago for masking a car's windows. He wrapped some of it around one side of a new double-edged razor blade and then he held himself still before the mirror. The blood started as soon as he began to cut, and he had to blow it out of the way, to see where to put the blade. The pellet looked to be just under the skin but it was actually in the muscle. He cut with the grain, separating the fibers of his body, tensing his shoulder as much as he could in the hope that it would pop out. But he had to widen the hole and grit his teeth and close his eyes sometimes as he bore down on it, until he felt the steel meet the lead. Then he squeezed it like a pimple, the black ball tearing itself out of the wound and forcing the tissue aside until it slid all slippery and skinned to the surface, where he picked it off with his other hand and held it in his palm. A little piece of lead, badly misshapen. He threw it in the trash.

He stood and let the blood flow for a while, then took up the bottle of alcohol and upended it against his arm, sealing the mouth of the bottle with the muscle of his bicep. Tiny boiling clouds of blood entered the bottle and he watched while the alcohol slowly turned pink. When he'd stood it for as long as he could, he took the bottle down and wetted a washcloth and bathed the blood off his arms and chest. He patted around on the hole with a dry tissue. The flesh around the lips of the wound was puffy. He put Band-Aids front and back.

The whiskey still stood on the sink beside him, and he picked it up and drank some of it, then shivered and shook his head. Blood was seeping out around his bandages. He turned off the light in the bathroom, staggering a little, and took the bottle with him. It wasn't even dark outside yet. There was no way he could go to town, bleeding the way he was. It would ruin another shirt if he put one on. He lit a cigarette and opened the back door and looked out into the woods behind the house where a matted little copse of honeysuckle surrounded the remnants of a treehouse he'd built once, now only rotten boards hanging from rusty nails. If he killed Russell they'd send him back. This time they'd keep him until he was old.

He called the dog a few times but he didn't come. He heard somebody going down the road on a three-wheeler and he looked past the corner of the house to see who it was. Some kid, his hair flying, who lived up the road toward London Hill.

He went into the kitchen and mixed a drink and sat down on the back steps with it. By dark he'd mixed two more.

He was on the couch with some music playing low when he heard the car pull up and stop. He lifted his wrist. Nine-thirty. A car door slammed, then another. He heard the dog growling under the house and he got up stiffly and went to the door. He called to the dog to be quiet when he saw who it was.

"Shut up," he said. "Y'all come on in."

"Will he bite?" one of them said. They were standing in the yard, just beyond the dim light cast by the living room lamp.

"He won't while I'm out here. He better not."

The dog rumbled a low warning in the dark beneath the porch. They didn't come any closer.

"Hold him, Joe."

"He won't do nothin."

"I'm scared of him."

"Why, hell." He went down the steps and squatted on the concrete blocks and whistled at the dog, trying to calm him down. "You better shut up under there. Y'all come on. He ain't gonna bite you, I promise."

As they stepped closer the dog was a white flash rocketing from under the house. They dropped their beer and tried to run but he nailed Connie and she fell. He had her boot in his mouth, but Joe grabbed an ear just as the dog tried to go up her leg. He pulled the ear taut and doubled his fist and gave him a lick on the side of his head. The teeth clicked like a steel trap as Connie snatched her foot away and got up.

"Son of a bitch, what'd I tell you?" he asked the dog. The dog tried to pull away from him toward the girls. They picked up their beer and stepped past him and went into the house and shut the door. The dog had his belly low to the ground, straining, and it was all Joe could do to hold him. He hit him in the head three times. The dog just closed his eyes and took it.

"When I tell you to shut up I mean shut up. You hear me?"

The dog straightened and stood balanced on all fours and looked at him, his gaze clear and level and his eyes untroubled. He licked the hand that whipped him, then turned his head and stood watching the house. Joe turned him loose.

"You go get under the house and you stay there. Go on, now." The dog walked away until he was once again a white blob and disappeared into the gloom by the steps. He settled there, invisible, a pale guardian who never slept.

Connie had her boot off and the leg of her jeans pulled up when he went in. Her friend was on the couch beside her, her face a little strained with fright.

"Did he get you?" he said. She shook her head.

"I think he just bruised it. It didn't break the skin."

"Hell, I should have held him, I guess."

"What if you hadn't been here?" the other girl said.

"If I hadn't been here," he said, looking carefully at her, "you wouldn't have no business in my yard."

"I ain't hurt," Connie said. She pushed down the leg of her jeans and started putting her boot back on. "We come to see if you wanted to drink a beer. What you got those Band-Aids on for? What you been into?"

"Nothin," he said, and got up. "I'll be back in a minute." He walked down the hall to his bedroom and took an old work shirt out of the closet and put it on. They were talking in low voices with their heads together when he went back into the living room, but they pulled apart and smiled at him.

"What are y'all up to?" he said.

"We just been riding around," Connie said. "We didn't know if you'd be home or not."

"I didn't mean to be," he said. "Who's your friend?"

"This is Cathy. She lives down at Batesville. She knows Randy."

He looked at her again. She was thin and had long black hair.

"I don't really know him that well," she said. "I just know who he is. I see him sometimes out at D.J.'s"

"You do? I don't never see him. Tell him his daddy said hi next time you see him."

"Okay. I will."

"Is he still over there in that trailer on old Six with them other boys?"

"I think he is. We was supposed to've gone to a party over there a couple of weekends ago but we didn't go. This girl I was with had a wreck."

"Aw." He got up and took his glass to the kitchen and started mixing another drink. "Anybody get hurt?"

"No sir."

He looked at her and then grinned at Connie.

"I mean, no. She was fixing to drag this boy and run into him. But they got us for dragging. That's why we didn't get to go."

He went back to the chair and sat down again.

"Don't you want one of these beers?" Connie said.

"Naw. I drank some beer this afternoon. I don't want no beer. I was just about asleep when y'all pulled up."

"We didn't mean to wake you up."

"It's all right. It was time for me to get up anyway. I'm glad he didn't hurt you. Usually when he gets ahold of something he won't turn loose."

"What kind of a dog is that, anyway?" the girl Cathy said.

"He's a pit bull, ain't he, Joe?"

"He's half pit bull. Half pit bull and half treeing walker. Why his ears look like they do. I meant to have em trimmed at the vet's when he was a puppy but I never did."

"He's big," the girl said.

He lit a cigarette and Connie opened a beer. He wondered why she'd brought somebody with her and knew she probably wanted something.

"Can I talk to you for a minute?" Connie said.

"Talk."

"I mean . . ." She moved her head slightly toward Cathy.

"Oh. Well, come on back here." He got up and she followed him down the hall to the bedroom. He sat down on the bed and she shut the door.

"What you want?" he said. "A quickie?"

She smiled and slid down over him, pushing him back on the bed, running her hands over the mat of hair on his belly. She kissed him, but he turned his head away suddenly and coughed.

"Damn," he said. He put his fist over his mouth and coughed and coughed. "Shit." He wiped his mouth and sat up and took a drink of her beer. "I got choked for a second. I got to quit smoking one of these days."

"You all right?"

"Yeah." But he could feel the blood running under the Band-Aids, and when he looked, he could see it. He got up and stripped off the shirt and wadded it and threw it on the floor. The Band-Aids were peeling loose.

"What happened to you?" she said.

"Don't worry about it. I'm just gonna get a bath cloth and wash it off. I'll be right back."

He stepped into the bathroom and took a washcloth from the clean pile of towels in a chair and soaked it in hot water and washed the blood off again. It looked as if the wounds had scabbed over lightly once, but he'd torn them loose messing with the dog and with her. Now they bled freely, clear fluid seeping with the blood. She came to stand beside him and watch him watching himself in the mirror. His face was on backwards and the part in his hair on the wrong side. It made his face look twisted. She touched his shoulder. There was a Polaroid picture lying on the vanity and she picked it up and looked at it. Somebody who looked a little like him, only twenty years younger, with the sides of his head almost shaved, in a coat and a tie, holding a pretty girl in a white dress by the arm. Old happiness ingrained on their faces as they smiled at the camera, the future a bright promise on that day long ago.

"This is your wife," she said. She touched the picture almost reverently and put it back down. Then she moved it, so it wouldn't get wet, as if that time could be preserved by the image of its past existence.

"Was. Has it stopped?"

She looked at his neck, at his arms.

"Yeah," she said. "I think it has."

"Good. I ain't got no more Band-Aids, anyway. I was gonna go uptown after some but I never did go. I had me a few drinks and laid down. I should've went on."

"You want me to go get you some?"

"Naw, hell. I don't guess. If I could just get it to quit bleedin it'd be all right. What was it you wanted to ask me?"

"Nothin," she said quietly. "It don't matter."

"Hell, tell me."

"We just thought you might want to go out. She's wanting to meet Randy. We thought you might know where he is. He wasn't at home."

"You didn't have to come back here to ask me where he is. What else you want?"

She turned away from him and looked out at the black night beyond the back door. The little shed and the junk scattered around it were illuminated in the cold glow from the yard light.

"Frank's back. I don't want to stay at Mama's."

He stopped what he was doing and looked at her. Looked at her hair and her back and her tight jeans.

"I thought she run him off."

"She did. Two times. He called her beggin the other night and she told him he could come back if he'd leave me alone. He promised. I got my stuff and left."

"Why don't she just shoot the son of a bitch?"

"Aw, she says it ain't his fault and all this shit. Says I go around in front of him half naked and he can't help it. Every time I go in a room I look around and he's right behind me."

"He's wanting to fuck you."

"Hell. I don't know what for. You just as liable to walk in the door and catch em on the couch going at it as not. I'm sick of it. Sick of her, too."

He stepped back into the bedroom to pick up his drink but it wasn't in there. He got another drink of her beer.

"Well, they's another room here. You still work up at that cleaners?"

She turned around with her hands in her pockets.

"Yeah. I wouldn't need it long. Just till I save some money and get me an apartment. Or a trailer. I won't be no trouble. I won't tell her where I am."

He shook his head. "Shit. She'll know where you at."

"Who's gonna tell her?"

"Don't nobody have to tell her. She's called over here before looking for you. Wanting to know if I'd seen you."

"What do you tell her?"

"I don't tell her nothing because I don't figure it's none of her damn business. Hell, you're twenty-one, ain't you?"

"Three more months."

"Well. You old enough to where you can do what you want to."

"He's liable to come over here."

He laughed. "I hope to hell he does. I don't know why your mama supports the sorry son of a bitch. Long as I've known him he ain't never held a job. I put my old lady through a lot of shit but I always had a job. She'd have put me down pretty damn quick if I hadn't."

She'd been standing in the hall talking to him and now she came in and sat on the bed. She leaned up and got her beer and held it between her knees with both hands, watching him going through the closet.

"I don't want to get you in any trouble," she said.

"You ain't gonna get me in no trouble. You got a car, ain't you?"

"Yeah. That's mine out there."

"You got to carry her back home tonight?"

"Cathy? Naw. She's got her car uptown. I just have to take her to town."

He found another old shirt and put it on and closed the closet door.

"Why don't you let me ride up there with you, then, drop her off and take me to the drug store? I got to get some stuff to put over this. I'll ruin my sheets and everything else. All my shirts."

"You got it," she said. She got up from the bed and went to him. "I didn't know nobody else to ask."

"Hell, it's all right. You welcome to stay over here."

She kissed him, but he just patted her on the ass and gently pushed her away.

When they got out to the car, he made the other girl get in the back seat with the dog.

"Y'all start coming over here regular," he said, "you better get to know him."

They went back by Henry's for the deer meat, but she wouldn't go in. Cars and trucks were wedged against each other in the tiny yard with no possibility of exit for those hemmed in against the porch. They sat in the dark on the front seat for a few minutes while he tried to identify the vehicles of enemies who might have reason to challenge him in his weakened state.

"I won't be but a few minutes," he said. It was more like thirty. But later, in bed, he told her that he couldn't go in and not speak to anybody. He didn't tell her that he'd taken three hundred and twenty dollars out of the game during the time he was there. He didn't tell her about the eyes that shifted in the smoke when he walked in, the shadowed figures and drinkers spread out along the walls who paused in the moment a hush fell over the room. They saw him bleeding from the four holes and not a man asked the cause of his ills when he squatted with the money and the dice in the circle of light on the floor, the old boards and dust, the false teeth in his head gleaming like bones and his eyes bright with pain and liquor. He won the money and nobody asked him to stay and try to lose some of it back. But he thanked Henry for the tender-loin and even tried to pay him for it.

She was on her side now, breathing lightly and slowly with the glow from the yard lights coming through the crack in the curtain. Her long brown hair spilled in a rush over the pillow and under her back. He pulled his deadened arm out from under her neck carefully, and she mumbled something and drew up into a ball. He didn't wake her getting up.

The dog raised his head from where he lay on the carpet in a dim pool of light. Joe didn't turn the lamp on. He turned on the television and left the sound low and groped around in the half dark until he found the whiskey bottle and propped it between his legs on the couch. The dog lowered his head to his forepaws and lay still on the floor. The red glow of Joe's cigarette lived and died in the darkened living room. And the next morning she found him there, naked, sprawled beneath the faded bedspread like those revelers of old in cracked paintings whose names or makers she'd never known, would never know.

The boy was up and about with first light, creeping softly among the sleeping members of his family. He collected the scattered and crushed beer cans from where they lay in whatever places they'd been thrown and carried them outside and added them to the growing pile. The squirrels at the fringes of the yard clattered the pine bark with their claws at the sight of him and hid themselves on the off sides of the trees before clambering away over branches still wet from the rain. He was soaked to the knees after one trip through the yard. Beggar-lice clung to the cloth of his jeans in mats. He stepped back inside long enough to take just one of the frosted cakes from inside the safe. He looked at it for a moment. His little sister was in the corner next to Fay with a fishing seine thrown over her, her thin dirty legs drawn up almost to her chest, her hair in lumps of dust and spiderwebs and the tiny turds of mice. He took another package of the cakes out and went to her and eyed the old man in deep hibernation on the bed of leaves he'd made. The father had spent a half day gathering the leaves and had enlisted the little girl to help haul them up from the hollow in garbage bags recycled from the county Dumpsters. Don Shelby would shoot to kill if he could find them now. Fay was flat on her back with her head on one side, her hand drawn up over her eyes as she rocked and moaned through the bad dreams she made in her mind.

He shook his little sister until she woke. She seemed startled to see him there. With a finger to his lips for caution he showed her what he had in his hand and then slipped the little cellophane package beneath her minnow net and stood up and made motions with his hands. She stared dully at him, uncomprehending. But when he went out the door, she was sitting up and tearing softly at the plastic with her fingers, a silent child.

A path led down through pine woods. It was an old path in which needles had settled over the years, just the faintest impression of a trail. Soon he was out of sight of the house and treading quickly past an old cairn of rocks that he'd already dug among and abandoned. Such an abundance of squirrels fled before him that he wished for a gun to help stave off starvation. Some of them didn't know what he was and clung to the sides of the trees, barking like tiny dogs. To these he held out a finger and said *pow* silently. They inverted themselves and stood head-first and watched him go, their black eyes bright and hypnotic after him. He went down to the creek and stepped into the rock beds, where a thin trickle of water coursed musically over the shattered stones and fell from bench to bench ever lower into the hollow. A weak sun was trying to break through the tattered clouds. He probed into the clay banks with a long stick, testing for snakes, watchful of where he put down his feet. He'd seen the copperheads before, dull slow things brown as the leaves they pressed their cold bellies against, no more noticeable than the bark of one tree in a forest of trees. His eye caught a flicker of movement ahead and he walked closer to see a box turtle with patterns of yellow sunbursts on its back like the imprint of a kaleidoscope. He tapped the stick on its shell and watched the legs and head shoot inward and the door on the front of the lower shell come up like a drawbridge and close with a long slow hiss. He went on.

At the bottom of the hollow he turned west, keeping his feet out of the wet ground that seeped moisture in a wide track, going along beside it to a narrow wash that even in summer's months was never dry. He could see the springhouse now and he walked on up to it, a ramshackle structure long rotted and all but obliterated by wind, sun, rain and time. The delicate latticework lay soft with mold on the ground, the posts that once held the roof leaning inward across the pool. The boy knelt on one of the three wide flat stones covered with lichen and green with moss. From the center of the spring came a soft undulation that rippled the surface gently and kept grains of sand in motion, ceaselessly turning and resettling on the clean bottom. He bent and touched his lips to the water, much the way some foraging animal might. It was sweet with a faint taste of iron and so cold it made his teeth ache. There were two six-packs of beer in the bottom of the spring, the blue of Busch slightly distorted beneath. He drank again and caught his breath and then wiped his mouth and sat up and crossed his legs on the stone. The cake was a little stale, the icing partly melted from where he'd held it in his hand. He ate his breakfast slowly, looking around at the birds flitting and singing in the awakening woods. The spring sang to him a low and throaty warble. He wiped his hands on his pants when he'd finished and knelt once more and drank, then stood up and turned and stepped away from the spring.

There was a little white marble marker set in a clearing fifty yards away, a place kept free of vines and creepers for reasons he didn't know. Fan-shaped plants with thick green blades like knives were planted in a circle around the grave. He stood there and looked at it for a while. The marker was no bigger than a cereal box. He wondered why they'd chosen to bury him here, alone with the animals and the snakes and the deep green shade. Maybe only John Edward Coleman knew, ten years old for an eternity, dead and asleep with the worms these seventy-nine years. Perhaps he'd played here. Or died here. An old man now, Gary thought. If he'd lived that long.

He'd brought his little sister down and showed it to her and told her it was a grave and that there was somebody buried here, but she'd only looked at it. He could remember a time when she'd talked, but it had been a long time now since she'd said anything. If she cried there were only tears. In happiness only a smile played from her mouth. And few of those here lately.

He walked on, wandering aimlessly. He jumped a deer once, but there was only the brief flash of a long white tail bounding away through the trees and then it was gone. The timber here was second growth and sparse, not like what was close to the house. Fire had swept over it a long time ago, yet some of the trunks were still blackened. He came out on a bluff that overlooked a section of cane and thickets, the low tops showing in the distance more timber and a lazy coil of black smoke from a house somewhere just beginning its burn to the ground. Along the edge he walked, stopping to run his hands over the old knife scars of names and dates healed almost unreadable in the bark of a giant beech riddled with squirrel dens and half toppling out over the void below. A hollow tree, it was once burned on the inside by squirrel hunters, the flames from the bed of leaves running up it like fire within a flue. He looked up into the top branches. A fat coon stared down at him from a fork, then put its hands over its eyes and turned away, an obscure lump of fur residing most peacefully this fine spring morning.

He walked a fallen log on the ground and then walked it again, holding his hands out from his side and then stepping down. He turned.

They emerged slowly in the distance through the slanted trunks and matted tangles of briers, slashing doggedly at the trees and the nets of vegetation hung like the giant webs of spiders across their paths. Faint cries could be heard. They were a group of seven or eight black men, with their shirts tied around their waists, some with flashing silver tubes in their hands and some with bright orange, all of them spread out arms' width apart and traveling slowly to the trees, then around and around them, stabbing and slashing. He sat down on the log and watched them come. When they were almost abreast of him, he could see that there was one who moved among them holding plastic jugs in his hands, attending to them when they called out. They were shouting back and forth to one another things he couldn't make out, only a word now and then. Then, as he watched, the one nearest him threw up his hands and screamed. They all ran at first, scattering in all directions, but then they came back cautiously, tiptoeing over the wet leaves until they congregated at one spot on the ground and drew close in a circle and then with short cries and hysterical abandon began hacking and beating the spot with their sticks and poison guns, darting in and out like dogs on a bayed bear. They were all talking and shouting at the same time, a hoarse chorus of curses that echoed and disturbed greatly the solitude of the woods, and they seemed frantic in their fear of whatever lay so helpless in the face of this ferocious attack. Demented John Henrys beating something into the ground. When they finished with it they seemed still reluctant to approach too closely. One of the men thrust at the thing with a long stick and picked it up, and the boy could see the white belly of the snake rolled over on the stick and the twin lengths of its body hanging down either side. They shouted. The man flung it down and they beat it some more, the sticks whacking on the ground in relentless unison and sounding strangely hollow on the earth. They dragged it around on the ground some more and pushed its head into the dirt until they seemed to be satisfied that it was dead.

The boy sat watching them on the log and wondered at what they were doing in the woods. There seemed to be no logical purpose to their work. They were still grouped in a cluster, lighting cigarettes and jabbering loudly. Some of them had even squatted down when a white man came up behind them and said something. They turned and he said something else and came over to them. They pointed to the snake. He looked at it and stepped closer and took hold of its tail and pulled it out and studied it. He said something and they laughed. Now they began to stand up one by one and throw the cigarettes down and disperse back into their loose ranks. The man stood with his hands on his hips watching them and fished a cigarette from his pocket and lit it. With his hand on a tree he leaned and watched them go past. The boy could see a little white cloud of smoke hanging around his head, the grips of a pistol sticking out of his back pocket.

The man turned when he heard the boy coming down the bluff and he waited until he'd reached the bottom and made his way over to him.

"Hey," Gary said.

The man nodded, still leaning against the tree, studying him. There was a look of tolerant amusement about him. He wore a black cap with CAT written across it in yellow letters. He had a big diamond ring on one finger.

"Where'd you come from?" he said. "You ain't lost, are you?"

"No sir." He pointed. "I live right over yonder."

The man squatted and picked up a twig.

"Over yonder where? There ain't nothin but woods back in there that I know of."

Gary put his hands in his pockets and looked at the ground for a moment.

"We just live back in the woods over there. In this old log house. Where's that snake they killed?"

"Right there. Ain't he a nice one?"

Gary stepped closer and looked at it, a smashed loop of muscle as thick as his wrist slowly ebbing toward death in the torn leaves.

"Them hands said it was a highland moccasin but I asked em what was a highland moccasin doing down here in the lowlands. I'da hated to stepped on him."

"I would, too."

"You sure you not lost?"

"I'm just walkin around," Gary said. "I seen them fellers when they killed that snake. I saw a big old coon in a tree back up yonder a while ago."

"You did?"

"Saw a deer while ago, too."

The man nodded and didn't say anything else.

"What are y'all doin, cuttin wood?"

The man looked up. He shook his head.

"We deadnin timber. I ain't figured out where your house is yet. There ain't no houses back in here that I know of."

Gary pointed to the bluff. "It's back straight in through there, over about three or four hills."

"Yeah? Is it close to the highway over there?"

The boy thought and nodded his head slowly.

"Sort of. They's this road, this dirt road you go up and it's another road you cut off of and it goes up beside this big bottom where they got some beans planted. It's this old house sets up on top of this hill with a bunch of pine trees around it."

"Oh," the man said. "Who you rentin it from?"

The question seemed innocent but the boy didn't know what to say. He scratched his head.

"Well. We ain't really rentin it I don't guess. We just sort of stayin in it till we find us a place to live."

"We?"

"Yessir. My mama and my daddy and my two sisters. And me," he added. "Y'all kill these trees?"

"Yeah. We inject em. You see them guns they had?"

"Yessir."

"See where they've cut these? Look right here."

The boy walked over beside him. The tree he leaned against had cuts all around the base, and something like thin molasses dripped from the cuts.

"Poison," the man said. "You got that gun you inject it with. Then in about a week it'll start to die."

"What for?"

"Weyerhauser land. They kill the timber off so they can come in and plant pine trees on it. Next winter we'll come over here and put out little pines on it. All this'll die and be on the ground in about six or eight years."

"Why?"

The man looked at him as if he didn't have any sense at all.

"Well, this ain't good enough timber to log it. It's just scrub stuff, so all they want to do is get rid of what's on it so they can put pines on it." He unleaned himself from the tree. "I got to get on and see about these hands. They'll set down if I don't stay right on their ass."

He'd already turned away to go before it all came together for the boy.

"I'll see you," the man said.

"Them guys work for you?" Gary said.

The man stopped and looked back. "Yeah. You don't want to work, do you?"

The boy took three anxious steps forward. "Yessir. I need a job. My daddy needs one, too."

"Your daddy? How old's your daddy?"

"I don't know," he said, and he didn't. "But I want to work even if he don't. I need a job bad."

The man pulled his pants up slightly and coughed into his hand. "How old are you?"

"Fifteen. I'm just little for my age. When you want me to start? I can start right now if you want me to."

"Well," he said, considering. He looked at his watch. "You could get a whole day in if you started now. You want to?"

"Yessir. Just tell me what to do."

"You don't need to go back and tell your daddy?"

"Nosir. They all asleep, anyway."

"All right, then. Come on over here."

They walked across the floor of the woods maybe sixty feet and stopped beside a line of trees already injected. The man pointed.

"See this here? Where these trees done been poisoned? What's your name, anyway?"

"Gary Jones."

"My name's Joe Ransom. You got a Social Security card?"

"Nosir. I ain't never had one."

"You ever worked anywhere before?"

"Yessir."

"Where?"

"Lots of places. I picked a lot of produce. We been in Texas pickin tomaters but we left, Daddy said cause of the wetbacks. But I've worked all over. Georgia and Florida. I pulled watermelons in Georgia last year."

"I don't guess you're scared of work, then. I'll tell you what I do, now. I pay a day's pay for a day's work. We start in about six and quit at one or two. If we work to dinner and get rained out I pay for a whole day. That sound fair enough?"

"Fair enough," said the boy.

"All right, then. Just get on this line of trees and you can see where they've come this mornin. It's probably close to a half mile or so back to my truck. Stay on this outside line where they've injected and you can't miss it. You'll come out on a road over yonder and they's a big yellow dozer up on this bank. Go to the right, two or three hundred yards and you'll see my pickup. Old GMC. And the guns and stuff's in the back. They got a top that just screws on. Get you one and fill it up with poison and then come on back down through here just like you went out and you'll catch up with us somewhere. You got all that?"

The boy had already started off. "Yessir."

"You ain't gonna get lost, are you?"

"Nosir. I hope not." He started running.

"And bring one of those jugs of poison back with you."

"All right," he called back.

"We'll need it before we get through with this round," Joe shouted after him. He heard the boy answer back, some word, and the sound of his feet rapidly diminishing through the woods. Then he was gone. It was the first time he'd ever hired a hand who didn't ask what he paid.

oe was asleep on the couch one Saturday afternoon when his daughter woke him up, knocking on the door. He got up and let her in and cleaned clothes off a chair and told her to sit down. He moved the whiskey bottle to the side of the couch after he saw her looking at it.

"I just thought I'd come by and see you," she said. "See how you are."

"Aw, I'm all right. I talked to your mama other day up at the post office. I tried to get her to go eat lunch with me and she wouldn't do it. I don't know what she's got against me."

"She ain't got anything against you."

He didn't agree with that but he nodded anyway. He was still sleepy and knew he probably looked bad. He lit a cigarette and sat back.

"You still smoke?" he said.

"Not much. The doctor said whatever you smoke or drink the baby gets too, so I just about quit."

He drew one leg up on the couch and rubbed his face.

"Yeah, I guess that's right. You listen to him. Take care of yourself. How much longer you got to go?"

She smiled for the first time, this child who had grown up so quickly in other houses with him, the one whose only defense against the things in him had been kindness and which kindness he felt he'd never repaid, never could.

"Five or six more weeks. I got the day marked on my calendar. If it's a boy we gonna name it after you."

"You don't have to do that."

"I want to."

"Well, that's good." He didn't know what to say to her now, never knew now. "That's good," he said again.

"Mama said you told her you'd been doin real good lately. Said you told her you hadn't even been out anywhere in two weeks."

He nodded without looking at her, but she was looking at the bottle.

"I'm gonna fix me a drink," he said. He got up and made one and brought it back to the couch. They sat uneasily in the room, in awkward silence that lasted while he tried to think of things to say.

"She gave me some of that money you gave her. She gave me seventy-five dollars. I bought some baby clothes and stuff. Some diapers."

"You better have plenty of them."

"I got two dozen."

"You better get four dozen."

"Mama said you wouldn't never change our diapers."

"Well. That's right."

"Why not?"

"I don't know. Didn't want to, I guess."

He bent forward on the couch and held the glass with both

hands. It was hard for him to meet her eyes. She remembered him as being too busy for her and her brother. When they cried he never heard. Charlotte was the one who took care of them and raised them, Charlotte was the one they cried for when they were sick. Not him. It was never him.

"You know she still loves you, don't you?"

The questions were in her eyes that she wouldn't ask, had never asked. Why did you do the way you did? Why did you run us all away?

"She don't love me," he said. "I don't blame her. She's give me enough chances. Maybe she'll find her somebody that can take care of her."

"She won't. She's afraid to."

"Why?"

"You know why."

"I don't."

"She's afraid you'd kill him."

He tried to laugh it off, but his face felt as if it might crack. He shook his head and finally looked at the floor.

"That ain't what's stoppin her. She knows better than that."

"But you might. You know you might. I know how you can be when you get mad." She paused. "Or drunk. I'm sorry, Daddy. But it's true."

"Listen. Your mama can do what she wants to. I ain't married to her no more. If she wants to remarry I won't say a word. Is she wantin to?"

"She ain't even had a date. Anybody that knows you won't date her."

"Is that what she said?"

"I know that myself."

"Well." He turned the glass in his hands, feeling the weight of her gaze on him. "Y'all don't know everything."

"I know you," she said.

"You sound just like your mama. Y'all ain't happy if you ain't fussin at me."

"I ain't fussin at you," she said, and he was startled to see that she was close to tears. Her eyes were wet and her mouth had set up that little trembling just like Charlotte's always had when she'd been forced to gather the strength to stand up to him in the past.

"Goddamn, don't start in cryin."

"I ain't cryin."

"You fixin to."

She didn't wipe at her eyes. She kept her hands clenched in her lap, her fingers twisted together.

"I didn't come out here to fuss at you. I came to see you cause I miss you. I just wanted to see if you were taking care of yourself."

"I'm okay," he said, and he took another sip from his glass. "Y'all don't need to worry about me."

"You know if you'd stop drinking she'd take you back."

He shook his head.

"We done been through all that. I quit drinking one time and carried her up to Memphis, to this nice restaurant up there. I ordered one beer and she like to had a goddamn hissy. I hadn't had nothin to drink in two months. Hadn't touched a drop. And then she wanted to make a big scene over one beer. I told her to just get her ass up and go get in the car. I was tryin hard but that wasn't good enough for her. Ain't nobody gonna run my life for me. You don't know what I've had to put up with."

"I know what she's had to put up with."

"Yeah?"

"I growed up in it. She's tried."

He settled back on the couch and slumped down and looked out the window, rattling the ice·gently in the glass. How could he explain it to her? "I know she's tried. You can't live with somebody for twenty years and not know em like I know her. She's a big churchgoer and I ain't. She don't like to be around anybody drinkin, don't even like to smell it. I drink and I like to drink. That's it. If you have to argue with somebody day in and day out you're gonna get sick of livin with em. I don't care how much you love em. You can't fight all the time and not have it do somethin to you. There ain't nobody who can live like that. Me and your mama can't."

He stopped and shook his head. They could talk it over and over and it wouldn't change anything. She wasn't coming back. Nothing was ever going to change. He didn't know what Theresa wanted to come over here and start talking about it for. All it did was make him feel worse.

"Are you happy by yourself?"

"I'm used to it," he said. "That don't mean I like it. I can come and go when I get ready, and they don't nobody say nothin to me. Y'all wouldn't be here now even if we'd stayed together. When have you seen Randy?"

She smiled slightly and then winced as the baby kicked inside her. She grabbed her stomach and eased herself back, drew in her breath sharply.

"He kickin you?"

"Whew. Yeah." She smiled weakly. "He don't usually kick in the daytime. Mostly it's at night when I lay down. I'm all right. Can I get a drink of water or something?"

"Yeah, sure, what you want?" He set his drink on the floor and got up quickly and went to the icebox.

"Just anything," she said.

"You want some Coke? I got some orange juice or I can make you a cup of coffee."

"Just some juice if you got it."

He filled a glass with orange juice and brought it to her. He sat back down across from her and watched her drink it.

"You sure you ain't gonna have twins?"

"It's just a big baby, the doctor said."

"Say you ain't seen Randy?"

"Yessir. He come over to the house the other night and eat supper with us. Mama cooked us some steaks out on the grill and he worked on her sink some. He had to put one of them traps or whatever under there. And fixed the lock on her door. He didn't have a whole lot to say to me. I guess he ain't never got used to the idea yet. I guess he's ashamed of me."

"Well," he said. It was all he could think of to say. He knew she was probably right. He was almost glad his mother and daddy weren't alive to see this happening. Randy hadn't killed the boy and that was something to be thankful for, that he wasn't in the pen over it.

"I might still get married some time," she said. "This ain't the first time it ever happened to anybody, and it won't be the last."

"First time it ever happened to one of mine," he said.

"It's my baby. It ain't yours."

"It's your decision."

"That's right."

"If you want to keep it it's up to you. But it's gonna be rough on the kid and one of these days he's gonna ask you why. If it's a boy he's gonna have to learn how to fight. You know what other kids'll call him."

"I've done thought of all that."

"Have you?"

"I have. Me and Mama's talked about it. I can get a job later on. I want to go back to school later on. You can't get no kind of a decent job around here without an education. I used to couldn't see that. I see it now."

"Well, I'm gonna fix me another drink," he said. "You want some more orange juice?"

"I got to go," she said, and she got up and handed him the glass. He took it and then she put her arms around him and held him. He hugged her only a little, fearing to hurt the unborn child. She drew back and looked at him, the top of her head only level with his chin.

"I love you, Daddy," she said. "I'll see you."

She turned to go and he told her to wait a minute. He went back to the bedroom and got some money and brought it out to her.

"Here," he said. He held out a hundred and a fifty and some twenties. She looked at it and shook her head.

"I didn't come over here for money."

"I know you didn't. Take it. Hell. For doctor bills if nothing else. I know you got doctor bills."

"I can't depend on you for the rest of my life. Ain't none of this your fault."

"To hell with whose fault it is. Long as I'm able I'm gonna take care of you." He put the money in her hand and closed her fingers around it. "It ain't nothing but money."

But it was not money she was looking at now. He turned his head. Connie stood in the hall in a short blue bathrobe.

"Excuse me," she said, and went quickly back to the bedroom.

"Damn," he said.

"Yeah. Damn's right. She's the same age as me. You know that? She was in the same grade as me. You ain't never gonna change. Here. Keep your damn money. I don't want it."

She threw it in his face, and left. He didn't try to call her back.

Wade had been dubious of the job to begin with, and now he was trapped in a living hell of steaming green timber. The men around him were moving like beaters through the lush jungle, breaking through the undergrowth, flailing wildly at the trunks and vines. They'd call out for water or poison, and a man would come running, bearing his refills in plastic milk jugs. Like winos they staggered through the tremendous heat. There were no rests or breaks. But there were yellowjackets to be contended with, and poison ivy, and sullen copperheads, which lay motionless and invisible against the brown leaves, becoming an actual part of them, lethargic and sluggish until the moment they chose to coil and strike.

Joe watched his two new hands from the top of a ridge. The old man stopped every two minutes, looked around, and leaned against a tree. When the boy went ahead too far, he called him back. Joe noted that it took one man working nearly full time just to keep this reluctant tree-killer watered. He lit a cigarette and slapped at a gnat on his neck.

Down in the great green hollow the old man tripped and almost fell. He was approaching a creek. The boy had crossed on a log and was already attacking the young sycamores on the far side with a ferocity driven by the promise of money.

Wade mopped at his unfamiliar sweat and studied the flow of the stream. The banks were five feet high, clotted with vines and treacherous with mud. He walked upstream for twenty yards and stopped. It looked no better there. He went on up, fifty feet more, and paused. He stared back over his shoulder, searching, but Joe was crouched low beneath a young persimmon, silently watching him through the leaves.

The old man stepped behind a bush and sat down. The bossman closed his eyes briefly and shook his head.

At noon the hands walked out of the woods and congregated at the pickup. They piled their poison guns inside the camper hull, and a black dwarf began issuing the lunch sacks from a cardboard box on the seat. The boy was there and took his small parcel, his meal of Vienna sausage and crackers and a hot Coke and a Moon Pie, and sat on the ground and started eating. He could hear the thin tortured cries of his father coming up through the brush, could see not a shape but the mere suggestion of a body struggling, some crippled floundering going on down there among the vast interwoven tapestry of vegetation. Some of the men began to look about.

"Reckon at old man can get up outa there?" said one.

"Aw, he's all right," said Gary. "He just ain't used to workin is all."

Some had sardines and others potted meat. The radio was playing in the cab, and Joe had wandered off somewhere. From Prince Albert cans kept in back pockets against the sweat of their buttocks, they rolled cigarettes of homegrown dope and passed them around. They smiled, blew smoke in little streams, grew languid and happy. The boy munched his food slowly and sniffed at the air.

Finally the old man emerged from a slash, stumbling along in a strange gait, gone crazy, evidently, slapping at his head as if he'd slap it off. The more coherent ones among them could see the tiny dance of angry insects around his hat. Yellow-and-black, miniature dive bombers stalling their engines in midflight, poised, wings humming, stingers raised aloft before boring in madly, tail first.

"Don't bring em up here!" the dwarf yelled, but it was too late. They gathered up their drinks and cigarettes quickly, clutching sacks and fighting at the air, yowling like cats as they started getting popped. And within five seconds they were all jerking dementedly and slapping, running away in a drove.

Joe dropped these two off last of all. He pulled up at the entrance to their road and shut off the truck. He took a quick drink of the hot whiskey on the seat and shivered, then got out and walked to the back and peered into the camper. The boy was helping his father crawl across the spare tires, the poison guns and jugs, this elder moaning on all fours like a political prisoner newly released from a dungeon. He stood eyeing them and took off his cap. He knew the boy would work—he'd proven that—but the old man would hold him back. He swept one hand through his thick hair and resettled his cap and put his hands on the side of the truck.

"Can you make it out of there?" he said. He lit a cigarette.

"Aw. Yeah. I'll make it. I guess," Wade whispered. "Just help me over to the tailgate, son," he said in a broken voice. The boy had him by the arm, guiding him along. Joe watched him dispassionately and knew almost certainly that whatever the boy made, the old man would take from him. Probably every penny. He quickly figured in his head what he owed them, and had the money ready by the time the old man swung his legs over the tailgate. He counted it again and laid it down.

"What?" said Wade. He picked up his money. "You pay ever day?"

"Naw," said Joe. "I don't need y'all back no more. That's yours there, son," he said, nodding at the remaining bills.

"Well," Wade said, but that was all he said. Gary picked up his money and looked at it. Then he looked at Joe.

"I'd sure like to work some more," he said.

"Maybe later. I'll let you know." He started to say more, started to tell him to be out on the road at six in the morning ready to work, that he could always use somebody who worked as hard as he did. But he looked at the old man again. He'd gained strength suddenly, was already pushing himself off the tailgate, turning, starting to hurry the boy away from the road, not looking back. But the boy looked back. Joe could read his face. Panic. I need the money. Don't leave yet.

He got back into the cab and sat there. He took another drink of the whiskey and chased it with a sip of Coke off the dash. He wanted to see how long it would take, if he'd even wait until they were out of sight. He leaned across the seat, smoking the cigarette and thumping the ashes into the floor. They were going slowly up the dirt road. The old man held his hip, prodding it along. He stopped and looked back. Joe cranked the truck and pushed it up into reverse. He started backing, looking out at them standing a hundred yards away. The old man and the boy faced each other in the dust of the road, like boxers. Then the boy fell. He kicked the ground, on his back, holding his pockets. The old man bent over, pawing at him, but Joe didn't wait to see any more.

Their supper was cooked in a pot against the coals, and the blackening flames ran up the sides of the vessel as if they'd climb into the food. Nameless beans with a piece of rancid rind bubbling in the spring water, stale loaf bread in a bag. The boy's eye was closed and he kept soaking it with a wet rag. The old man had gone with the money. The four of them sat speechless in the yard with the dark trees all around. The youngest girl had her legs crossed beneath her dress, and she rocked, hugging her elbows in her hands. The old woman seemed entranced by the flames. Her face was like the faces of soldiers shell-shocked in the trenches whose minds had heard the enormity of the blast and could not accept it as real. Stunned into silence, remembering . . .

The car and the man and the woman. The music and the lights and how they weren't like them. How the cut grass smelled and the sounds of the children splashing in the fountain and the aroma of barbecue in the air, the lights strung from pole to pole and the microphones and the stage and the people milling everywhere and the quilts spread on the ground and the lawn chairs and coolers and picnic baskets they were eating from and how the bats soared briefly over the softball field and the heat and the children. She remembered him hitting her, although there was no memory of the pain, just the blackness she fell into and waking up later to find that Calvin was gone for good.

Careening softly and with his hands out before him, Wade went like a blind man down through the alley and out onto the street. Cars and trucks were parked nose to tail on both sides and others were cruising for parking places. He stood with his back against a wall and listened to the gigantic pounding of a great drum in the night that came from a brightly lit door in the alleyway where young people were walking in twos and threes, so many of them at the entrance they had formed a large group. A man at the door was checking them and herding them single file up a walkway like cattle. But it spoke of nothing if not the promise of drink. Wade pushed himself off the wall and went across with his arms dreamily coming up, astonished at the lightness of his feet. Past a beauty salon with padded chairs displayed in muted lights and big mirrors reflecting his movements as he glided past, a figure of unbalanced gait and slouchy posture. He eased up at the rear of the crowd, and they moved aside and made room for him so quickly that he felt welcome. Whatever lump of shabby currency his roving hand found first in the pockets of his overalls it drew out and clutched. Closer and closer to the magic door he drifted, the keeper of it already eyeing him and shooing the students in like chicks. Over their heads the bouncer watched this vision come forward with his tattered scraps of paper money. Music and smoke poured out the door into the alley, and the old man felt warm and safe and happy. As he drew nearer, such a deafening clash of sound emanated that the patrons and the keeper of the door shouted in one another's ears. He was alone suddenly, none behind him and none before him but the linebacker or whatever he was, a monster man, a giant blocking the way with his thick arms folded over his massive chest. His face was impassive and he did not speak. He blinked his eyes once slowly and heavily like some huge lizard and shook his head and stood his ground. Turn back, old man, begone. There is no room in the inn.

He turned away as he knew he must, down the boarded catwalk and past the white walls where someone patted his back. He did not turn to see the face. A black arrow pointed his way. He walked with great sadness in his heart past darkened cars and trash cans and a warehouse door studded with cracked windows. Into each life a little rain must fall but perhaps it monsooned in his. He trailed with his hand a yellow stripe at waist level and his shoulder scrubbed lightly at the brick. His feet tried to twist under him, and he told them silently to keep moving one ahead of the other until he stood with his hands in his pockets on another sidewalk. Cars went by, close, their exhaust fumes like rotten eggs. Across the street was a bank; and in a shop, darkened shoes in rows. He let another black arrow direct him west and walked until the street was bisected once more. Cars and buildings lined both sides of a roughly paved lane. There was a hole in a brick wall halfway down the left side that threw a square of yellow light onto the pavement, and he made his way toward it on his tired and wasted legs. He stepped past the corner of the doorway and stood there blinking at the stairs. What manner of establishment? He went up the stairs and peered in through a security door, cupped his hands around his face and watched what went on. Tables and chairs. Stools set up along a wooden bar and glasses shining in ranks overhead and the polished handles of kegs. All was not lost. Salvation lurked just beyond the glass. He opened the door and took himself inside.

Things got quiet when he presented himself at the bar. Pool cues rested, patrons turned and stared. The bartender ceased his whiskey-sour vibrations. The old man heard voices from below and craned his neck sideways to see concrete steps and the legs of people standing. Another world beneath this one. He slid off the barstool and made his way downstairs to find a beer bar and bearded drinkers with gold earrings and cutoffs and Harley-Davidson insignias on their skins and clothes. The floor was spotted with red paint, scuffed away by the shoes of many. He ordered Miller and was served immediately. He paid and lifted the bottle to his lips. Then he went back upstairs.

He tapped a cigarette out of the pack and lit it with a match, waving it slowly in his hand, dropping it on the floor. He crossed the room, sucking at the beer, and stopped to watch a game of eight ball. A thin boy dropped the ball in a corner pocket and another boy gave him a dollar. He moved on, deeper into the room.

He passed under some brick arches and out a door into an open room with no roof. He stood there and studied the stars in the heavens with the beer tilted up to his mouth. Everywhere around him loomed the walls of the old hotel. He finished the beer and set the bottle on one of the benches and opened the door at the far side of the room. He found himself on a landing above a cavernous room so packed with people and music and lights that it made his head sing for a moment. A girl sat at a card table in front of him with a cigar box full of money and a rubber stamp in her hand. He eased up to her and pulled out his green.

"How much?" he said.

She stood up and waved to somebody. Somebody waved back. She turned back around and watched him with eyes uneasy, not believing his ripped clothes, his gray whiskers, his black fingernails.

"Wait a minute," she said. She pinched her nose and deserted her post and went down the stairs. The old man pocketed his money and stamped the back of his hand with the rubber stamp and went down the stairs behind her. He was quickly lost in the milling crowd below.

Late that night the rain fell thinly in the streets around the square, slashes of water streaming diagonally in the air above the wet sidewalks. Passing cars sprayed it up from their wheels, and the blooming taillights spread a weak red glow across the pavement as the hum of their engines quietly receded into a night no lonelier than any other. The stained marble soldier raised in tribute to a long dead and vanquished army went on with his charge, the tip of his bayonet broken off by tree pruners, his epaulets covered with pigeon droppings. Easing up to the square in uncertain caution came a junkmobile, replete with innertube strips hung from the bumpers and decals on the fenders and wired dogs' heads wagging on the back shelf, the windows rolled tightly on the skull-bursting music screaming to be loosed from within. Untagged, uninspected, unmuffled, its gutted iron bowels hung low and scraped upon the street, unpinioned at last by rusty coat hangers, a dying shower of sparks flowing in brilliant orange bits. No tail-lights glimmered from this derelict vehicle, no red flash of brakes as it pulled to a stop. It inched forward in jerks, low on transmission fluid. The old man watched these things. Later that night he was thrown in jail.

A public drunk was reported, an inebriated senior citizen whooping out great obscenities on the county square, performing some unmetered step on the timeworn bricks. Two policemen in a dispatched cruiser picked him out, a sly sot now apparently dozing on a green bench. They threw the light on him. He tried to run. The cops left the cruiser idling in the middle of the street and took off after him. Their feet slapped loudly around the sidewalks as the old man hobbled down the steps to the street. Some drunken students from the university were going to their cars from The Rose, and they stopped to watch the fun.

But he was old and the police were young and they hemmed him up against the front of a jewelry store. He elected to make his stand against a backdrop of silver platters and bridal china, his eyes wild and red in the flashlight beams, his thin chest heaving from his exertions. The cops went closer and then suddenly stopped.

"Shit," said one.

"Goddamn," said the other.

They seemed loath to put their hands on him. A crowd of students had gathered by then, it being past midnight and the bars now closed, and they stood watching the feinting and dodging. One of the cops approached and the old man immediately tried to put a headlock on him. The cop flung him off like a bundle of rags and he dropped to the pavement and started moaning.

"Stop that," the cop said. "Get up here. Here."

The old man huddled into a wretched ball on the concrete.

"Go on and kick me, you sumbitches," he said.

They stood watching him, unsure of how to proceed.

"Put the cuffs on him."

"You put the cuffs on him."

"I ain't touching him. I ain't putting my hands on the stinking son of a bitch."

"What you gonna do? Walk him to the jail?"

"I'd rather, as to have him ride in my car."

"Listen, now. Get up from there. Get up off the ground. Ain't nobody going to kick you."

"I know how you do. Get me over to the jail and you'll whup the shit out of me. I been in jail before."

"Aw, no shit. Well, you fixing to be in jail again. Now you get your ass up from there and get over there in that car."

But he would not rise. He'd either passed out or was using a marsupial's ruse. They braced him up under his arms. His feet lolled, boneless. They staggered beneath the assault of his body odor. Chickens dead three days in the sun had never smelled so rank. Ruined elephants on the plains of Africa paled in comparison. The cops gagged and tried to lift him. He lay limp as a hot noodle, quietly exuding a rich reek, a giddy putrefaction of something gone far past bad, a perfect example of nonviolent protest. They went across the square in the dead of night, dragging their prisoner, hapless victims themselves of circumstance, booed and hissed loudly by the students, struggling along with his unwashed wasted carcass like exhausted mules.

City court. Wade sat on a bench with other defendants whose crimes against the town he did not know. He turned his hat in his hands idly. The windows were open in the high walls of the second-story room and the sounds of traffic on the square drifted in. A black uniformed bailiff was nodding himself to sleep in a chair beside the judge's podium, and Wade thought about just getting up and walking out. Everybody else seemed resigned to their fates. He got up and put on his hat and went to the door. Two lawyers in the room studying their documents looked up at him and looked back down. He opened the door and peeked. An empty hall, closed rooms. He tiptoed out, his feet soundless on the rubber tiles, and closed the door softly. From somewhere came the dull clack of typewriters. A girl turned the corner with a Coke in her hand. He started to ask her how to get out of the building, but he didn't want to arouse suspicion. When she went into an office, he looked around the corner and saw a blank wall. Halfway down the hall he opened a door and looked inside. A vacuum cleaner and dust mops. He thought about hiding in there for a while, but he knew that soon after capture was the best time for escape. He walked around the other corner and came to a bank of elevators. He punched a button and a soft little bell rang when the light came on. Sounds came to his ears of mechanical hissings deep somewhere in the entrails of the courthouse, sliding cables and turning gears. He waited. The bell chimed gently again and the doors slid open. He stepped forward. The two cops who had arrested him stepped forward to meet him.

"Where the fuck you think you going?" one of them said.

"I's lookin for the bathroom."

He waited a long time for his case to be called. They wouldn't let him smoke and nobody would sit close to him. The bailiff had given himself over totally to rest, mouth gaping and head back and eyes closed. Wade leaned back and listened as the judge droned on. Sally Bee Tallie, found guilty of assaulting Leroy Gaiter with a cowboy boot. She said the whole thing was her brother's fault. Roosevelt Higginbotham, a public drunk in his own yard, which he argued unsuccessfully was not a crime. The judge slammed his gavel and fined them or sentenced them to jail or set them mowing grass and picking up litter for the good of the public. People speeding, forty-five dollars a whack. The city making money hand over fist. The public defenders doodling on papers and staring out the windows like children longing for recess. The old man sat with his elbows on his knees, watching the proceedings uneasily with slowly shifting eyes. At last he was called and he stood up. The judge was a man not thirty years old, in a double-knit suit. He studied the papers before him carefully. The cops had long since resigned their chins to the cups of their hands. The judge looked up.

"They don't have any address for you, Mr. Jones. Where do you live?"

"I live out close to London Hill," he said. "I don't know what the address is. Ye honor."

Ye honor evidently didn't like that answer. He tapped his pen menacingly on the lectern. He looked at the bailiff but seemed reluctant to call the whole court's attention to the fact that he was asleep by waking him up. Indeed it was as if a glance at that peaceful face made him uneasy. He looked out over the room and raised his eyes until he was talking to a spot high on the rear wall.

"You've got to have an address, Mr. Jones, or we'll declare you a vagrant. You know what a vagrant is?"

"Oh, yes sir. I ain't no vagrant."

"You ever been declared a vagrant before?"

"Well. I been declared one. Shore have. They declared I was one in Oklahoma City one time, but they never could prove it."

The courtroom had almost emptied, and the cops sat regarding him with their arms crossed and their faces dull with boredom. The judge nodded somberly, chewing on his lower lip.

"Do you ever get any mail, Mr. Jones?"

"No sir."

"Well, just say you did. Where would the mail come to if somebody wrote you a letter?"

He thought and thought and at length said, "I don't believe nobody knows where I'm at."

One of the cops shook his head and the other one closed his eyes. The judge put the pen in his mouth and chewed on it and opened something in front of him. He read for a few minutes.

Then he wrote something down. He cleared his throat and looked down on Wade.

"Are you on a rural route, Mr. Jones? Are there any mailboxes around your house? You do live in a house, don't you?"

"Oh, yes sir, I live in a house. But they ain't no mailboxes around there nowhere. I ain't never seen one. Sir."

"All right, then. You might want to remember this. Your address would be General Delivery, London Hill, Mississippi, three eight six oh five. You're charged with public drunk and resisting arrest. How you plead?"

"I don't know what to do," he said immediately. "I'm afraid if I plead guilty it'll be a big fine, and I ain't got no money to pay it. What if I plead not guilty?"

"You mean, what'll happen?"

"Yessir. What'll happen?"

"Well then, we'll have to have a trial. You'll have to get you a lawyer and fight it."

"Yessir."

"But you'll have to go back to jail first. Or we'd have to set your bond. Can you make bond?"

"I don't know. How much is bond?"

"It'll be about a thousand dollars. Do you know a bondsman?"

"Naw sir," he said sadly, keeping his head down and shaking it. "I don't know no bondsman."

The bailiff jerked awake suddenly and gripped the armrests, his tipped chair slamming down hard on the boards. He glared wildly around.

"And, too, you'll have to pay an attorney and court costs. These two officers swore out the complaint against you. Why don't you just plead guilty and be done with it?"

"What'll it cost me if I plead guilty?"

"I can't tell you that until I sentence you."

Everybody was waiting to see what he'd say. Or waiting to get the hell out of there, one.

"What chance I got of winnin if I fight it?"

"Not much, I'd say."

"It's their word against mine."

"This court does not take the testimony of police officers lightly."

He knew they had him either way he went. But he was eating pretty good in the jail. Big plates of scrambled eggs and toast with coffee for breakfast and fried meat with two vegetables for supper.

"I reckon I'll plead guilty, then," he sighed. "Bad as I hate to."

"Mr. Jones, this court finds you guilty and fines you four hundred and fifty dollars, payable immediately." WHAP! went the gavel.

The old man staggered back, almost as if a visible blow had hit him.

"What!" he said.

"Of course, you can always work it off for the city if you can't pay the fine."

"Work it off? How long?"

"Oh, we'll round it off to about forty-five days."

"Do I have to stay in jail the whole time?"

"You certainly do."

"I don't guess I got no choice, then. What kinda work I'm gonna have to do?"

"Whatever needs doing, Mr. Jones. Bailiff, you want to take this man back to the jail? And maybe get a good night's sleep before court tomorrow?"

They set him to pushing a lawnmower the first day. There were rolling green hills of grass in the park, and against this immense backdrop he was a tiny worker toiling with exaggerated slowness in the early morning heat, a small wretched figure stopping every few minutes to wipe the sweat from his brow. Other captured felons with long knives whacked listlessly at weeds. The whole day and forty-four others just like it stretched endlessly before him. The park was deserted, baking, barren. Sober drunks with nails mounted in mop handles speared bits of trash and deposited them in garbage sacks tied around their waists. The mower blade was sharp and the motor ran smoothly. Wade talked to himself and cursed his luck with a sullen vindictiveness. Each pass he made was about three hundred yards long. They'd have cut it with a tractor and a bush hog if they hadn't had him, but they had him. He figured they had all kinds of things planned for him, painting curbs and hauling garbage, painting tennis courts and picnic tables. He had resolved to make his escape at the earliest opportunity, but he didn't know where he was. There was a line of woods rimming the east side of the park where he could conceivably hole up until darkness came, but at the rate he was going it would take him two weeks to get over there.

At midmorning the lawnmower sputtered and died. He stopped

and mopped at his sweat and stood looking around him. The city trucks were parked in the shade beside the pavilion and he made his way down to them. Two black boys were sitting in the shade when he got there, smoking cigarettes. They were park employees, kids hired for the summer maybe.

Wade rummaged around in the bed of a truck, looking for an antifreeze jug with gas. There were razorous joe-blades and green-stained weedwhackers piled up in there. He rooted among them, shoving things aside, sweat stinging his eyes. Finally he looked over at the boys.

"Y'all know where the gas is?" he said.

"They supposed to be some in there," one of them said.

He looked and looked. He found an antifreeze jug but it had antifreeze in it. He poured some out on the ground to make sure, and sure enough it was green.

"That ain't gas. That's antifreeze."

The boys looked at each other. One of them scratched his ear. "We supposed to have some," he said.

"Well, you *ain't* got none," Wade told him. He looked at him with what appeared to be barely controllable rage. His face was red and droplets of sweat were swinging on his jowls. "I can't cut the grass without no gas. By God, if I'm gonna work down here, y'all got to furnish me with some gas. I ain't gonna buy it myself."

"What you think?" one of them said.

"I don't know," the other one said. "I guess, run get him some."

"I'll get it," Wade said. He got in the truck and shut the door. They looked at each other.

"He supposed to be drivin that truck?"

He cranked it and pulled the shift down into low, popped the clutch and spun one small spurt of gravel from a rear wheel. They were without phone or radio and even though they chased him for a short distance, shouting and waving for him to come back, he was soon a small blue speck flying down the street. They stopped and stood looking after him as he disappeared from sight. They turned to each other.

"You gonna be in trouble."

"Me in trouble? It's you in trouble."

"It ain't me. It's you."

"They gonna put you back paintin that swimmin pool."

"I done painted that pool one time."

"You may paint it two times."

A few days later the old man stood in front of the liquor store for a long time with his hands in his pockets. He eyed the rows of brown bottles within, Dickel, Daniel's, Turkey, and wetted his dry lips slowly, as if he were astonished at the taste of his own tongue. It was ten-thirty and the regular winos were briskly conducting their early-morning business, shapeless men in rumpled clothes who emerged from the front door looking neither right nor left. He stood there until one went in that he thought he could handle and then he walked down to a laundromat and waited, squatting on the cracked concrete against the bricks, idly watching the cars move about in the parking lot. He whistled a low and tuneless hymn. Next door in Shainberg's, some women were adjusting stacks of jeans and moving over the polished floors and talking in voices that had no sound. He picked up a scrap of wood and turned it in his fingers.

An old black man came out and turned down the alley between the stores and shuffled past with a nylon windbreaker over his arm. Wade didn't appear to watch him shamble around the corner. He waited a few more deliberate minutes. He got up and dropped the piece of wood and stepped around the corner. There was nothing but discarded tires and mop handles and a broken compressor with one wheel missing, all piled against the back side of the building. For a moment he lost the shuffling figure. Then he looked toward the bypass and saw him in the act of halting his climb up the bank, putting one hand down, easing himself to rest on the sparse grass of a red clay hill. Wade watched. The black man put his coat down and drew his knees up and opened the bottle he had and tilted his head back. Wade started across the parking lot. With his head down he lifted his eyes and marked the man's position, noted the stream of cars flowing past behind him, high on the hill. The parking lot ended abruptly in a choke of kudzu and honeysuckle.

He stopped at the ditch and looked up at the man forty feet above him, lifted one hand in greeting.

"Hey," he said.

The black man said nothing, didn't look. He capped his liquor and wrapped it in his coat.

"I's wonderin if you could tell me how to get to Water Valley," Wade said. "Wife's in the hospital down there and I just now got here."

The old black man raised one long bony finger and pointed due south. His face was the face of stone, sullen, the eyes red and malevolent, his countenance ruined with the scars of small drunken wars. He bore small scraps, perhaps of cotton, in the dark wool of his head.

"How far is it?" Wade said. He stepped across the ditch and stood there looking up. He had his hands in his back pockets but his eyes searched the ground. He stepped a little higher and the black man rose in a crouch. One hand rested on the ground, the other clutched his precious bundle tightly.

"That the highway goes to it?" he called up.

The scarred head nodded yes. Just once. Don't come no closer.

Wade stepped forward another five feet, grasping a sapling to aid himself. He stopped and looked behind him. A boy was changing a tire on a tiny car behind Otasco, and a freight truck was backing up to Big Star. Blue milk cartons were stacked higher than a man's head on the dock.

"I just wondered was I goin the right way," he said to the ground.

The head above him nodded again.

"You don't care for me comin up there, do you?"

The man shook his head, soundless wonder etched on his face. In his troubled gaze he seemed to hold some terrible secret.

The old man went up the bank like a mountain goat and squatted next to the drinker. The black man didn't look at him.

"What are you drinkin?" said Wade.

A demented smile crept onto the face of the wino, three long yellow fangs bared in the purple gums.

"Fightincock."

"You ain't drinkin some wine, are you?"

"I may," he said.

"Yeah? Why, hell. That's all right. Lot of folks think a feller ought not drink at all." He wasn't looking at him. He was smiling to himself, talking to himself, looking out over the parking lot. "Little drink never hurt nobody."

The black man was watching him carefully now, perhaps seeing him in a new light.

"That right," he mumbled.

"Shoot," Wade said. "I get me a little drink when I can but the old lady raises so much sand I don't drink much around the house. I just usually get me a drink when I'm uptown like I am now."

"You wife in the hospital?"

He paused for a moment, thinking. "Aw yeah. Well, yeah she is —today. I got to get off down here at Water Valley and go see about her. That's where I was headed. What it was, I's supposed to got paid this mornin but the feller that was supposed to paid me ain't never showed up. I's gonna get me a little somethin to drink and head off down here to Water Valley and see how she was doin."

The man drew his bottle up to his lips, arms still wrapped in his coat, and untwisted the cap. He sipped it as if it were something forbidden. He wiped his lips and his face.

"What all wrong with her?" he said.

"Got cancer," Wade said immediately. "Got cancer of the leg. Just eat up with it all over, can't even walk. Gonna have to put her in the rest home, I guess."

The black man was sucking bubbles from the mouth of the bottle. He put it down and said: "Aw."

"Yep. A feller don't know from one day to the next which one'll be his last."

The scarred head nodded mute agreement to this undeniable truth. But he didn't offer the bottle in commiseration. The old man watched each swallow, each sip, like a hungry child. Clouds were bunching up high in the east, a dark bank of them that loomed up suddenly to banish the sun. In their hillside glade the shadows bled together. Wade saw that the rain was not far off. He hunched his shoulders against it even as he scanned the ground around him. But he was sitting on something, a hard bump beneath his shoe. He moved one foot and nudged it with his toe and it rose up from where it was half buried, brown and heavy and coated with a brittle corrosion that flaked away as he worried it with his toe.

"I believe it's fixin to rain," he said.

He let his right hand drop and pulled on it and broke the dirt around it free, a ringbolt twelve inches long, buried where some construction worker, long ago laboring on the shopping mall below, had perhaps flung it one day.

"Yes," he said, "I believe it's fixin to rain some."

He whipped the bolt straight across his body without looking and it landed hard on the forehead of the black man, who was in the act of passing the bottle, and knocked him whimpering into the grass with his eyes full of blood. He curled up and began a spasmodic kicking, until the old man hit him again, and then he stiffened and quivered. A sodden thump, a hammer on rotten wood.

He rifled the pockets quickly. Thirteen dollars in cash, three U.S. Government food coupon booklets worth sixty dollars each.

And the bottle of Fighting Cock. He got that, too.

T he sun had gone in too early and the sky looked like rain. The air was cooling and the wind shifted and moved among the stiff tops of the pines along the road. The ditches were rich with cans and Gary marked them to memory for later retrieval, for harder times. But these seemed hard enough. His eye was still swollen and black-looking but it didn't hurt. He could see out of it a little now, anyway.

He could hear the trucks and cars coming a long way behind him, but he moved to the shoulder of the road and did not turn and raise his thumb as they drove past. The mailboxes were slowly becoming more frequent, the land more populated, but the houses were too far from the road for him to want to ask directions. He kept walking, his stomach empty and hard and tight, his head light. It was all he could do to keep going. The road climbed and twisted through the land. At the tops of hills he could look out over green forests and hay fields far off in the distance, where barns and silver metal towers stood hazy under the gray and leaden sky. Beyond the last greenery he could see was another line, blue as smoke, the last trees of the horizon. Earlier he had come through a bottom where hawks hunted over the sagegrass or merely perched on limbs thin as pencils, watching over all that moved before them, but there were no hawks now. There were neat fenced pastures and deep oak hollows and muscadine vines growing beside the road. Posted signs, barred gates. Little gravel trails stretching away to nothing through lanes of pine trees. He kept seeing mailboxes and he watched for them to stop. He didn't know for sure if he was on the right road. He was just trying to do something, do anything. He didn't know how far he'd come but he guessed five miles.

In another thirty minutes there were more houses, closer together. The sun tried to peek back out but the clouds moved over it and hid it again. In two more hours it would be dark and his journey all for nothing.

It had been easy money to him and he couldn't understand why Joe Ransom had let them go. Maybe the man wouldn't even be home now. Maybe he wouldn't find his house.

The rain came, thin drops that spurted dust from the roadside gravel, small explosions of brown dirt. The sun was trying to shine. He could see the rain marching against the forest, bending the treetops with the wind it brought and waving the boughs wildly. He started running, looking, and when he saw the big rusted culvert, he went down the bank over the loose gravel and beer cans and slipped and caught himself with one hand and stepped down into gray muck that sucked his shoetop in. He pulled his foot loose and bent and stepped into the culvert, ducking his head and entering a cavern of corrugated blackness. In the round mouth of the thing he squatted and watched the rain beat the grass flat and slowly grow into a curtain of water that obscured the trees twenty yards away. He bent with his feet spread wide. Before long he felt the first trickle come between them and watched it pipe out in a spout over the lip of the culvert. He tried to put his feet up higher on each side of the barrel, but soon there was four inches of water racing down and rising. It flooded his shoes, then his ankles.

"Well, crap," he said. He braced himself up like a cat facing a dog until his back met the roof of the tunnel he was in. The roar was a din and the color of the water was like pure mud. One foot slipped, then one hand, and he flew out of the culvert and landed churning in the middle of a creek rising to an angry level, foaming with bits of straw and trash and sticks. He pawed his way through the brown water to the bank and clambered up over the edge of it, his knees coated with mud, his shirtfront and his hands slick with it. The water was cold and the wind was a solid thing he could push his body against and feel it push back. There was nothing for shelter. Leaves were wafting across the road as they were torn from the trees and sucked out of the woods. He tried to go up another bank slippery with mud, but it defeated him again and again. His ears were full of water. It didn't seem possible to him, but the rain doubled in intensity. The world was gone, nothing left but gray disaster. He squatted on the side of the bank and dug his heels in, covering his head with his arms and waiting for it to be over. He was washed clean by the rain. Every drop of mud ran from his clothes and shoes. He had never seen such a rain. He had never even imagined that such a rain could come.

ay would keep her own promises. The lights she dreamed of, the clothes she would wear, the distant cities shimmering in the highways of her mind.

"He ain't comin back," she said.

That old woman she had watched grow older and older until she was bent and wasted neither turned her face nor gave any sign that she'd heard. There was something bubbling before her in a lard can, set atop a niggardly fire banked with dirt on a rotten sheet of rusted tin in the floor. The smoke had settled comfortably in the ceiling, to drift at its leisure out the windows and shift slowly among the hewed timbers. They could hear the wasps dropping like lead shot on the floor in the other room. Not one penetrated that wall of fumes. By morning they would all be gone, scattered to the four winds, their paper home a fabled trophy for a small boy to prize.

"If he was comin back he'd of done been back."

The little girl paid no attention. She'd made a doll of sticks and rags and she was rocking it to sleep. On its burnt face she laid some sweet kisses that almost made the older sister stay. Fay watched her mother, perceiving not even the rise and fall of her chest to mark her breathing. Just the thin bubbling in the lard can, the wisps of steam playing below her face. She could almost hate her for staying with him for this long, never having a house to call her own. Nothing but squatting before a fire like this one for as long as she could remember. She couldn't remember now how long Tom had been dead. Maybe it was ten years. Maybe it was twelve. And Calvin. Wherever he was, if he wasn't dead, he was better off than them.

"I seen him in a dream," her mother said.

"Hush."

"He was in a car. Had the longest purtiest hair, like a woman's. Long and curly, down on his back. Like Absalom. Absalom was on a mule runnin away from his enemies and caught his hair on a limb. I member the picture from the Bible was in it. He was tryin to cut his hair loose with a sword. Things'll get better."

"Things won't never get better here."

"They can't get no worse."

"That's where you wrong, Mama."

She stood up. She slipped her feet into her shoes and she picked up her purse and she looked around in the room. She had the clothes she was wearing, a skirt stuffed into the purse, and that was all she had. She looked at her little sister once. She was curled up in the corner, talking silently to the stick baby.

"I'm gone," she said.

"If you goin to the store I wish you'd bring me back some Kotex," the old woman said.

She didn't look at her mother again. She stepped across the

floor and down the rickety set of steps and gingerly, dodging the briers, picked her way out of the yard and through the honey-suckle vines and only looked back once, at the ruined house and the smoke coming out of the windows and the tall black pines growing blacker as dusk fell.

J oe almost didn't hear the dog for the rain on the roof. The sound of the growling was an undercurrent, an accompaniment, something that might have been there for a long time. The noise stopped, then it started again. It got a little louder.

"Is that that dog?" he said.

Connie was in the chair with just panties and a robe on, a beer in her hand. They'd been drinking since afternoon but he hadn't touched her. There were days she couldn't make him.

"I don't know," she said. "Is somebody out there?"

"I don't hear anybody. Ain't heard no car drive up."

"It probably ain't nobody. Ain't nobody with any sense out in this."

He nodded and lit a cigarette, coughing a little. "Why don't you fix me another drink, baby?" he said.

She got up and took his glass to the table and got out some more ice and Coke and whiskey. She didn't put much whiskey in it. She stirred it with her finger. When she handed it to him, he took a small sip and didn't look away from the television, just held out the glass and said: "I can't even taste that."

She took it back to the table and poured more whiskey in it. She gave him the glass again and got her beer and sat down in the chair.

"We gonna go anywhere tonight?" she said.

"I don't know." He looked at her. "Where you want to go?"

"I don't know. I just wondered if we was."

"I hadn't planned on it. Unless you want to."

"We don't have to."

He looked away. "I'm just sorta enjoyin settin here with the TV," he said. She had cleaned the house from one end to the other, washed all his clothes and ironed his shirts, cleaned all the bad food out of the refrigerator, feeding the scraps to the dog and trying to make friends with him. He guessed it wouldn't hurt to take her somewhere, but he hated to get up and take a bath and get dressed and drive to town in all this rain.

"I guess we could go eat," he said. "Get us a steak somewhere. Or would you rather have some seafood?"

"It's just with you. I don't have to go nowhere."

What the fuck'd you bring it up for then? he wondered.

"I don't guess we got anything here," he said.

"Hot dogs."

"I meant to give you some money and let you go to the store. I guess we need to do that before long."

She nodded. The dog kept growling under the house.

"Stick your head out the door and see what that damn dog's so unhappy about," he said. She got up and went to the door and opened it. It was dark out there. She looked.

"They's somebody out here."

"Hit the light."

She turned it on. A bright yellow glare lit up the mud and the streaming grass.

"Who is it?"

"I don't know. He's just standin out there by the road. What you want me to tell him?"

"Tell him to come on in."

She looked back at him. "He ain't gonna come in long as that dog's out there."

"Say you can't tell who it is?"

"Naw. I don't know who it is."

"Well, fuck. It's somebody either wantin a drink or money one," he said. "That's the only reason anybody comes to see me, anyway."

He got up off the couch with his drink and went to the door. He looked out. There was a thin dark shape standing out by the road, just standing there. He squinted.

"I can't tell who it is," he said. She pulled her robe closed and held it with one hand. The rain slanted brightly in front of the porch light, obscuring the form standing so still in the glistening road.

"Shut up," he said, but the dog wouldn't hear. "I wish I could tell who it is."

"Well, don't make him just stand out there in the rain all night."

"I ain't making him stand out there. Didn't even know he's out there."

"He's scared of that dog's what it is," she said.

"Well, go down there and hold him. He won't bite you."

"That's what you said last time."

"He knows you now, though."

"Shit."

"I don't want to get out. I ain't got any shoes on."

"I ain't either. I wouldn't touch that dog if I did."

"Aw, go on."

"Not me."

"I wish to hell I knew who it was," he said.

And then the little wet shape called out: "Would y'all hold that dog?"

"Aw, hell," Joe said. "Here. Hold this."

He went down the steps barefooted and snapped his fingers until the dog came out to stand beside him, then squatted in the rain and took him by the collar. He patted him. The dog strangled with his rage.

"Settle down, now. Ain't nobody messin with me," he said. He tightened his grip on the hamestring.

"I got him," he said. "Come on in."

"You sure you got him?"

"Who is it, Joe?"

"This boy I know. Come on, now, I'm gettin wet."

The boy stepped off the road and came slowly across the muddy yard, never taking his eyes off the dog. His feet were encased in gobs of red mud.

"Go on up the steps there," Joe told him. "Take your boots off."

The boy bent over and started fumbling with the sodden laces on his boots.

"Go on up the steps," Joe said. The boy straightened and looked at him, looked up at Connie.

"You can set down right here and take em off," she said. She moved back from the door, and he went up the steps and sat on the doorsill.

"Y'all hurry up," Joe said. "I'm gettin wet."

The boy got his boots off and set them together on the top step and stood and turned and walked to the center of the room, where he stood shedding water onto the carpet. Joe turned loose of the dog and shoved him under the porch with his foot and slammed the door going in.

"Damn, Gary," he said. "How long you been out there?"

"I don't know. A good while."

"Let me get you a towel," Connie said.

"Bring me one, too. Boy, you soakin ass wet. You liable to be sick from this. Why didn't you holler?"

The boy looked up, small, muddy, forlorn. Quietly dripping all over the floor. "I hollered one time," he said. "That dog almost come after me. I's afraid if I run he'd come after me anyway." He motioned helplessly with his hands. "I's sorta trapped," he said. "Couldn't get no closer and couldn't get no further away."

"What's you gonna do? Stand there all night?"

He thought about it. He shook his head. "I guess I would've. Fore I'da had him get ahold of me."

Connie came back with the towels and gave him one. He dried his hands and then started rubbing his head with it.

"He ought to get out of them wet clothes," she said. "He'll have pneumonia."

"Aw, I'm all right," Gary said. "I just wanted to talk to you about workin some more."

The bossman draped the towel over his shoulders and picked up his cigarettes. He smiled a little crooked smile, not unkindly. "Work? Boy, don't you see what it's doing out there? It's pouring down rain."

"Yessir," Gary said. He rubbed the towel over his head. He put a finger in it and drilled his earholes a little.

"Where's my drink at? Have you got some pants he can wear? What size waist you got, anyway?"

He looked down at himself. "I don't know what size," he said. "My mama gets my clothes for me. I just wear whatever she gets."

What he was wearing was a pair of khaki pants that were pinched up around his waist with a belt that was six inches too long. A Kiss T-shirt and a pipe welder's cap.

"I think I got some jeans he can wear," she said. "Let me go in here and see."

"Well, set down," Joe told him. "I didn't know you were out there. You oughta hollered."

"I figgered if I hollered again he'd nail me. I bet nobody comes messin around here when you ain't here."

"Why I got him. I ain't here much. Way things are now, some sumbitch'll back a truck up to your door and just load up what he wants while you gone to work. He won't bother somebody just walkin down the road, though. A dog's smarter than you think. Anybody comes in this yard they better have a gun. I got to be here when they read the meter. Long as you stayed in the road he didn't bother you, did he?"

"Nosir. He just growled was all."

"You could have walked on off and he wouldn't have done anything. The road ain't his. He knows what's his."

"Here," Connie said, and handed him a pair of jeans. "Try these on. I believe they'll fit you."

He took the jeans and looked them over and looked around.

"Bathroom down the hall," she said, pointing. "You can change in there."

"Yesm," he said, even though she wasn't four years older than he was. He found his way down the hall and went into the bathroom and shut the door. Then he groped around in the dark looking for the light switch. Feeling all over the wall. He turned it on and then he stood for a minute just looking at all the products scattered on shelves and around the sink and lined up beside the bathtub, a wide assortment of ointments and creams and shampoos and deodorants and colognes and aftershaves. He opened some of them and sniffed, and looked at their labels. Meaningless symbols printed there whose messages he could only imagine. In the mirror stood a wet boy-child whose hair was twisted all up over his head like a rooster's comb. He found a brush on the sink and pawed at his hair with it, slicking it down long over his ears. There was long downy hair all over his chin and neck that he'd never shaved. Finally he pulled the threadbare shirt over his head and unbuckled the belt and pulled the wet trousers down over his knees and stepped out of them and stood naked in the room, his balls shriveled and drawn from the cold and the wet. He dried himself all over and put on her blue jeans. They were almost a perfect fit except that her legs were longer than his, so he turned them up at the bottoms four inches and went back up the hall. They were sitting down in the living room when he walked back in. He stood there holding his wet clothes in his hand.

Joe got up. Worse than he'd thought. Wandering urchin wafted up on the shores of human kindness. Asking nothing but the chance to earn. Offering his hands not to take, but to make.

"You feel better now?" he said.

"Yessir. I sure do. I been wantin me some blue jeans for a long time. These is Levi's."

"You welcome to them," Connie said quickly.

"You walk all the way over here?"

"Yessir. I got caught in some bad rain about three miles from here. It come a storm over there."

"How'd you know where I live?"

"I didn't. I was just lookin for you. I'll work. I need a job bad. I'm tryin to save my money and get me a car. Or a truck. If I had me somethin to go in I could get me a regular job. That's what I need. But I can't get a car till I get a job. That's why I wanted to talk to you. My daddy don't care if he works or not. But I do."

Joe paused to phrase his answer.

"Well, son, I don't know when we'll get back to work. It just depends on the weather. We can't even get into the woods till the roads dry up a little. That'll be two or three days if the rain ever stops. But if it rains some more I don't know when it'll be. I wish I could tell you somethin but I don't know myself. I'd a whole lot rather be making some money than sitting around the house here."

"Yessir," Gary said.

"Would you work in the rain?"

"Yessir. It don't matter to me."

Joe smiled and reached for his drink.

"Well, I hate you walked all the way over here for nothing," he said. "Let me slip my shoes on and I'll run you back home. You ain't moved from where you were, have you?"

"Nosir. We ain't moved."

"Just let me go back here a minute. Come on, Connie."

When they got back to the bedroom, she shut the door and turned around to him.

"I feel sorry for that boy."

He sat on the bed and started pulling on his socks.

"I can't give him work when I ain't got none myself. He can work when we start back if he wants to. Long as he don't bring his daddy. That son of a bitch ain't worth killin."

"I'm gonna give him one of my shirts. I got some old tennis shoes in here he can have, too."

He looked around at her and picked up a shoe.

"Why don't you just go ahead and get dressed and we'll go to town and get us something to eat. If we going out we might as well go on and eat supper. We got plenty of time."

She sat down on the bed beside him and folded her hands between her knees. "You reckon they've got anything to eat?"

"I don't know. I don't know whether they have or not."

"Why don't you ask him?"

"Ask him? Hell, I don't want to ask him that. I don't want to embarrass the boy."

"Well, what if they ain't? What if he's waiting on y'all to start back to work before they can get anything to eat?"

"Shit," he said. "I don't know. Maybe they ain't. They livin up there in the woods. I ain't been up there but I know where they're at. I used to birdhunt up there and it ain't nothin but an old log house. Ain't nobody lived in it for fifty years, I bet."

"Fifty years?"

"Hell, it ain't nothin up there," he said, and got up to find a shirt in the closet. "Only people you ever see up there is either huntin or fuckin, one." He turned around and gave her a grin. "Or huntin a place to fuck."

"Reckon who hit him in the eye?" she said.

The bossman didn't bother to answer that.

The rain was streaming down the sides of the glass, the wiper blades hardly able to keep it at bay, when they pulled to a stop in front of the store. There was a watery visage of gas pumps and posts and a screen door, a yellow bulb on a cord illuminating the mosaic of bottle caps packed tightly into the red sand.

"I reckon he's still open," Joe said. "How about puttin about ten dollars worth of gas in the truck?"

The boy was sitting next to the window, and he got out wordlessly and went back to the pump and turned the lever, unhooked the nozzle and twisted off the cap. Joe went inside.

Cigar smoke hung from the ceiling in layers, wreathing the old man, who was leaning back against sacks of flour with his endless newspapers and magazines and Civil War books. The roar of the rain on the roof shut out every other sound. He picked up his cigar and looked at his friend.

"What you say, Joe?"

"Reckon it's ever gonna quit?"

"Four inches on my gauge. These farmers is gonna be in a mess."

He didn't know if the boy would come in or not. If he did he did.

"Would you ring up some stuff for me, John?"

"Sure."

He closed his paper and rose stiffly and went around behind the counter and laid the cigar in an ashtray. Joe picked things that didn't have to be refrigerated, or things that didn't need to be cooked. Vienna sausage and canned chicken and soups and chili and potted meat and Spam.

"Would you slice me up about two pounds of ham and a pound of cheese?"

With the thunder cracking all around, the noise was near deafening. The old man went silently to the refrigerator, his hands slow and orderly. The electric saw ran unheard and the meat fell silently onto the tray with each pass. He got crackers and loaf bread, mayonnaise and mustard. He piled the cans up in his arms and carried them to the counter. The old man laid the wrapped packages beside them and rang everything up.

"Have you got one big sack you can put all that in, John?"

"Ought to have. This rain's bad on y'all."

"Yessir, it is. Looks like every time I get a little ahead it starts in again."

John Coleman laid his pencil down and looked up, touched the side of his glasses with a forefinger.

"Twenty-seven even, Joe."

"Ten dollars gas." He gave him the money.

"Out of forty. Three dollars. You don't want all that in two sacks?"

"This is fine," he said, sliding it off into his arms. "I'll see you, John."

"Don't hurry off."

He stopped at the door and looked back. "I'm headed to town. You want anything?"

John stood looking down, leaning one hand on the counter, scratching at the side of his neck.

"You going by the liquor store?"

"Yeah. What you want?"

"Get me. Get me two fifths of some good whiskey."

"What you want? You want some Jack Daniel's?"

"Naw. Don't get that. Get me two fifths of Jim Beam if they got it."

"They got it. You want some beer?"

"Naw, I got some beer. Curt and them brought me some beer today. I wouldn't mind having a drink of whiskey, though."

"All right. You gonna be up later on?"

"Yeah, I'll be up."

"All right then."

He went out and the screen door flapped hollowly behind him. He went around to the other side and opened the door and slid the sack in on Connie's legs. The boy was seated beside her once again, keeping close to the door.

"Boy, you gonna get wet again," Joe said.

"Yessir. Reckon I will."

It was no better when they stopped again. They sat for a moment, the wipers beating gloomily at the downpour. Joe was thinking that the sack would be all to pieces before he went a hundred yards. He pulled out the handbrake.

"Wait just a minute," he said.

He went blindly out into the rain and raised the door of the camper hull, cursing, getting mud off the tailgate on his clean pants, fumbling in the dark for what might not even be in there any more. But it was. His hand found it and pulled it out.

"Here," he said, when he opened Gary's door. The boy got out.

"What?" he said.

"Put this over it. Maybe it won't fall apart before you get home."

Connie put the sack down on the seat and he slid the plastic garbage sack upside down over the groceries while the rain lashed him. When he had it wrapped he gave it to the boy.

"I hate I can't take you no closer. You couldn't get up that road in a Jeep now."

"This mine?" the boy said. He acted as though he couldn't believe it.

"Hell, it's just some stuff. I'll come see you when it dries up. We got plenty to do when the weather gets right."

He didn't wait for an answer but shut the door on Connie and went around to the other side. He got in and shut the door, pushed in the handbrake and ground the transmission into first. He blew the horn and they pulled off.

In the black and howling night the boy stood there with his heavy sack in his hands and hugged it tightly, one dim red eye moving away from him and the sweep of white light boring a tunnel of rapidly diminishing size down the rain-slicked highway, the water flashing in front of the lights until it passed from sight, until the sound of it ebbed, until even the tires sang away to nothingness and he was alone.

He turned his face up to the streaming heavens and they answered. He was immersed. He let it pelt his face. Blacker nights he'd not yet seen. Ground bled to sky, woods to road. But he knew the way. He turned and started up through the mud.

The creeks were raging with dark water, angry and swollen. He stopped on the bridges and rested. The mud was thick and it made for hard walking in his new tennis shoes. The food was in his hands and no one would know if he stopped now and opened something and ate. But there was a black wall of nothing that somewhere held his family, and his home, and it was that he headed into with ever quickening steps.

The owner of the package store on top of the hill had the doors open at ten o'clock sharp. He was sandwiched between a pizza parlor and a hair salon, and it was a good location because business sometimes bled over from each flanking establishment. He kept his clocks exactly on time, so he knew it was not yet a minute past ten when the first customer of the day stepped inside and nodded. A patron of dubious financial stability who might have spent the previous evening in a ditch, judging from the amount of dried mud slathered on his boots and overalls and flaked on the side of his face. An old man with rolled-up sleeves and a battered hat and a nervous tongue that he dabbed across his lips. The owner straightened from his newspaper and looked at the first customer.

"Can I help you with something?" he said.

"I's just lookin," Wade said. He moved over in front of a shelf and stood there with his hands at his sides and studied the bottles. Looking at the prices, the owner decided. To see what he could afford. Probably had some quarters and dimes in his pocket, hoping it was enough. Or waiting for a chance when his back was turned to grab something off the shelf and run outside with it.

The owner took three steps and cut off his only escape route and stood between the door and the counter, idly studying an inventory list. He was low on the Turkey half-pints and the Popov fifths. Two cases each. He made little notations on his sheet. He glanced around at his customer. An unpleasant aroma was beginning to fill his immaculate little store. He narrowed his eyes at the man. The man didn't move, didn't look around.

They usually headed straight for the wine cooler, for the Thunderbird and the Boone's Farm and pure grain alcohol. He didn't like them loitering, had signs forbidding it, in fact.

"If you're looking for something in particular I can show you where it is," he told him.

"I don't know what I want."

"The wine's in the cooler."

"I don't want no wine."

"Well, what do you want?"

The old man turned just his head in an odd way. "I know what I want but I don't know what you call it."

The owner sighed. Dealing with these people over and over. With the depths of their ignorance. The white ones like this were worse than the black ones like this. Where they came from he didn't know. How they existed was a complete mystery to him. How they lived with themselves. He tossed his list onto the counter without ever thinking he might have helped make them the way they were.

"Can you describe it?"

The old man turned around. He looked at the bottles on the opposite wall. "Well, it's clear," he said.

"Is it vodka?"

"Naw."

"Is it gin?"

"Naw, it ain't gin. It's kindly thick-like."

The owner wiped a hand across his face. He could have sold the whole thing at a good profit to his son-in-law months before. He went back to the cooler and opened the glass door and reached in, brought out a cold half-pint of peppermint schnapps and held it out.

"Is this it?"

"I don't know."

He carried it to him, all the way to the front of the store. He handed it to him.

"Is that it?"

The old man was looking at it carefully, holding it close to his face and moving his lips.

"I don't know if this is it or not. It looks kindly like it. What is it?"

"Schnapps."

"What's it taste like?"

"I don't know. I don't drink."

The old man looked at him curiously. When he looked at the bottle his brain seemed to stop working. Finally he raised his head.

"I don't know if this is it or not. What if I buy it and this ain't it?"

"You mean, what if you drink some of it and then decide you don't want it?"

The old man nodded vigorously.

"Yeah. What if I do that?"

The store owner rubbed his temples.

"Well, in that case you simply bring back the unused portion and we cheerfully refund your money and put the rest of it back on the shelf."

"Aw yeah? I ain't never seen a place that would do that before."

The owner sighed and went around behind the counter. He unlocked the cash register with his key and rang it up.

"Two dollars," he said.

The old man hadn't moved. He was looking back toward the coolers. "Wait a minute," he said. "Have you not got this in a bigger bottle?"

"I thought that was what you wanted. I've already rung it up."

"I may want a bigger bottle."

The owner put both hands on the register and looked at his customer. I am a fool, he thought. I am a fool and I am going to make sixty-five cents profit by fooling around with this other fool. He walked out front and took the half-pint away from the old man. There were some fifths on the opposite shelf, hot ones, and he walked over to them and pointed.

"We have fifths and half-pints," he said. "No pints."

"Can't get it in a pint?"

"No."

"How come?"

The owner lied. "They don't make it in a pint."

"Why's that?"

He took a deep breath. Just a few more minutes. Just a few more minutes and he'd be gone.

"There's a reason for it," he said. "It costs more to make a pint bottle than it does to make a fifth or a half-pint bottle. It's not the liquor. It's the glass."

"Well, I be damn. I didn't know that."

"It's a little known fact of the liquor industry, actually," he said.

"Well, I be damn."

"Do you want this fifth of schnapps?"

"I don't know," Wade said. "How much is that?"

"Six twenty-five."

The old man didn't say anything. To the owner he looked as if he had lost what little brains he had. He held up a finger and pointed.

"A half-pint's two dollars, and a fifth's six twenty-five?"

"Right."

"Well, I's just kinda figurin," he said. He rubbed his chin whiskers a little. "Let me ask you somethin."

"Anything."

"How many half-pints would you say was in a fifth?"

"What?"

"How many . . ."

"I heard you. I don't know. How many would you say?"

"I'd say four or five. Or maybe a little over four."

"Maybe. But I doubt it. Now if you want this take it. If you don't I'm going to put it back on the shelf."

"I's just tryin to figure the best deal," he said. "If it's five half-pints in a bottle and at two dollars, that's about ten dollars worth at that rate in a fifth, right?''

"I don't know what you're talking about," the owner said. "I have no idea what you're talking about."

"I wish they made it in a pint. I bet a pint wouldn't be over about four dollars, would it?''

"I told you they don't make it in a pint."

"I wish they did."

"I wish they did, too. Now," he said. He was offering the bottle and its companion on the shelf like a sacrifice, a grail, a chalice. To take one of them or leave or whatever.

"Shit, just gimme the fifth," the old man said.

"Fine," the owner said. He went over to the shelf and got one and handed it to him. He still had the half-pint in his other hand. He headed back toward the cooler with it, to put it back inside, all the way to the back of the room.

"I think you'll be happy with your . . ."

But the door slammed the instant he opened the cooler, and he paused. He didn't even look around. There was no need. It was done.

He set the little bottle back inside the cooler, gently among its brothers, so as not to disturb them, knock them over. He shut the door a little sadly and stood looking over his goods momentarily. They were lined up in neat rows, perfectly straight. He checked his cooler about thirty times a day to see that everything was in order. He couldn't stand disorder, couldn't abide sloppiness.

After a while he went up to the front of the store and sat down in the high-backed chair behind the counter. He took out his pipe and reached for his tobacco and slowly put it in, tamping it lightly, sighing to himself with enormous lassitude. He lit it with a match, turned the match slowly in the flame, puffing lightly, until the whole bowl was glowing red and consumed in fire. He shook out the match and drew deeply, and turned in his chair to gaze out through the large plate of glass where the name of his own little business was written backwards in paint. He didn't know where the man had gone. There was nothing but kudzu across the road, an apparently impenetrable jungle of green vegetation that crept softly in the night, claiming houses and light poles, rusted cars and sleeping drunks, the old and the infirm, small dogs and children. He wondered if maybe the old man lived in there and had trails like a rat, like the slides of a beaver or the burrows of a rabbit. Perhaps it was worse than he thought. Perhaps there was a whole city of them under there, deep, sheltered from the rain and shaded from the sun, with tents and canopies pitched beneath, cooking fires, camps where the children played and where they hung their wash. Where else could they hide? Anything was possible. And they only came out once a month, when the welfare checks and the food stamps were issued, and they stocked up on everything, and disappeared back into their lair. Maybe one day he'd look. Maybe one day he'd lock the store and walk across the road and peer over the edge of the creepers and look down, to see if he could spot a wisp of smoke, to see if he could hear their radios playing, their TV sets. Maybe they had Honda generators and refrigerators. But he knew, really, that he wouldn't look. He wouldn't look because he didn't really want to know. He didn't want to be right.

The days went by and the rain would not stop. Or it would stop for a day or a day and a half and Joe would gather his crew and park on the highway and send them up the muddy slopes only to blow the horn for them an hour or two later when the drops began to pelt down on his truck, where he was sitting drinking whiskey. He hadn't gone after the boy because he hadn't wanted to walk up the muddy road. But the boy had walked it. He'd walked it every morning the sky wasn't cloudy and waited by the highway, pacing, studying the sky and listening as the cars and trucks came within hearing. The old GMC never showed. He gave up hope late each morning. He knew they wouldn't start at that time. There was nothing to do but go back through the mud to the log house and idle his day away. The food went rapidly. His mother would say nothing of Fay. After a while he stopped asking.

Joe stayed in the living room when Connie was at work, playing the same songs over and over on the tape player, watching game shows and soap operas. His needs were few and his money was stacked in sheaves. Some days he and John Coleman sat behind the stove and hid their whiskey from the women and children who came into the store. John told stories of dogfights over the African deserts, of wading rivers behind the German lines, of nightmare fights with knives and gunstocks. They ate pigskins and crackers and poured Louisiana Hot Sauce on their sardines. Sometimes in the afternoons the store would be closed without warning. They'd have the curtains drawn over the door and hear people knocking and see them trying to see in, dim figures with one hand cupped over their eyes as they leaned against the glass, wanting gas for their pickups or Kotex or a loaf of bread or a pack of cigarettes or a dozen eggs for breakfast.

John Coleman had returned from the war in 1945 a quiet man, a wounded man with shrapnel close to his spine and shrapnel beside the bones of his legs, and in his head that same torn steel. A man with few words for people, who had seen all of the world he wanted to see. Not sullen, just a somber aloofness that no one could see was sadness for what men did to other men. He had inherited the store from his father and had kept it open all these years and each day of the year. He was a prodigious reader, a drinker with capabilities near legendary, a man with plenty of money. He ordered rare volumes, collections, series of books and chronicles of war. He studied and memorized little-known facts. He stayed inside the store days and in his little house across the road nights and never went anywhere. Joe would not go to town most times without stopping and asking him if he needed anything.

The days of May drew by and the fields stayed wet and the woods dripped water. Joe fished in his tedium, cutting canes in the river bottom and rigging set hooks with cord and lead and jabbing them deep into the bank. Morning and evening he checked them, carrying a five-gallon bucket of live crawdads along the path, stopping to take off the fish and checking every hook to see that it was baited. Then back at the house by eight or nine, skinning the fish with pliers while they hung shivering on a post, stripping the living skin from their pale bodies and flinging the offal to the waiting dog, whose jaws snapped shut in midair over the flying morsels. One morning he eased up to the bank after baiting all his hooks, after standing around for a while to see if the fish were biting. He squatted at the lip of the bank and took a cigarette out of his pocket and lit it, smoking and watching the smoke drift across the slow brown water. Limbs in the current dipped and swayed, rose and fell. He looked down and thumped the ash with his little finger. And not a foot below him, there in a little cutback in the bank, lay a snake with scales the size of his thumbnail. He didn't say anything. He might have just sat down on the bank without looking and hung his legs over. It wasn't coiled, just lying there, and he couldn't see its head. So he just looked. He could even smell it now that he had seen it, a dry sour smell like dead vines in a garden or carrion that is almost wasted away, until the essence of its scent is almost gone. He only wished that he had his pistol and could see its head to shoot it because nobody would believe it without the evidence of its dead body. There was probably no safe way he could kill it. He watched until he grew tired of it, until he convinced himself that it couldn't really be as big as he thought it was. Then he got a stick and poked it. The head flew out in a blur, hard enough to jar the stick in his hands, and he drew back a little, not certain it wouldn't come up the bank. He leaned over and poked it again, but the snake bunched and moved and began to flow into the river, loop after loop of steel muscle sliding over the mud, an impossible girth of snake that ended in a stubby tail. He stood back and watched for it to surface in the water, but it never did, python, boa, anaconda of Mississippi. And he was careful never to run the hooks at that place again, to watch the ground when he walked near there.

Mornings he would park his truck off the road, hidden from view in a copse of trees close to the river and near the place where he got on the path. He was laden with fish one morning coming back to the truck, a stringer cutting into the flesh of one hand and the crawdads in the bucket sloshing sluggishly in stagnant black slough water in the other. He was tired of dressing fish and being out of work and his hands were tired of carrying these things for half a mile. He stopped within view of the bridge to rest his legs before the climb up the bank to his truck. He squatted in the wet weeds and smoked a cigarette, mopping at the sweat on his forehead with his arm and wrist. A rifle cracked suddenly, close, then again and again. He looked toward the bridge and saw a man standing there, facing away. But he knew him anyway. With one hand he caressed the healed holes in his neck, and then he hunkered down, keeping bushes and trees between them, went closer. The .25 was in the truck and was no good for even shooting snakes, you couldn't hit anything over six feet away with it.

The rifle spat from time to time as turtles floated up to see if it was safe and found it was not. He went closer and closer, silently up the overgrown bank next to the bridge until finally he could pull his head up over the bottom rail with most of his face hidden behind a post and examine this fool who had leaned his rifle on one side of the bridge while he drank a beer on the opposite. He went up over the side and walked carefully down the concrete curbing until he was within twenty feet of the gun. He grinned then. He walked to the gun and picked it up with no noise. Then he leaned against the side and held the rifle in his arms until the man felt him there behind him and whirled. The eyes were wide in the blasted face.

"Surprise, motherfucker," Joe told him.

Willie Russell dropped his beer when he saw the gun leveled at him.

"Don't shoot me," he said.

"Why not? Son of a bitch, you shot me."

"I's drunk, Joe. I didn't mean to do it."

"You know I could kill your ass right here and nobody would know it?"

He lowered the gun to waist level and took out the magazine and jacked the round out of the chamber. He dropped the gun and it clattered on the concrete.

"I ain't goin to walk around the rest of my life lookin over my shoulder for you," he said.

"I ain't gonna mess with you no more, Joe. I promise."

"I ought to beat your goddamn face in worsen it is. That's what I ought to do. I just hate to go back to the pen over a piece of shit like you."

"I'm sorry, Joe."

"You better be. You better listen to what I'm tellin you. You got it straight?"

"I got it straight."

"All right, then," he said.

Russell walked over immediately with his hand stuck out. "Let's be friends," he said. He caught a left with his nose and a right with his throat, went down strangling, his eyes enormous, blood running down his shirt. He knelt, choking, on his knees.

"That's for shootin me," he heard. "I ain't shakin hands with you, you son of a bitch."

Russell was trying to say something. He was trying to make some words come out of his mouth. He was crying silently and Joe left him there for people to see as they eased across the bridge in their cars and slowed and almost stopped and then went on. He walked back down into the woods and got into his truck, thinking no more of fish or the river and only of whether or not this would settle it and if he had done the right thing and knowing that he probably had not since he had left him alive.

The rain ended that day and the woods stood steaming as they slowly dried. He sharpened the poison guns with a file and rounded up plastic milk jugs and went to Bruce for more poison and, on the seventeenth day of May, went back into the woods with nine black men and one white boy.

When the old man came back to the log house he was drunk and disorderly. He staggered in through the door one Tuesday morning about nine o'clock and stood there staring dully about, his face cut by briers and lumpy with mosquito bites, the clammy legs of his overalls plastered to his shins. His wife looked up to see him and he said, "Goddamn you," and went for her. She rose like a cat with her fingers curved into cat's claws and they met in the center of the room in a rush of dust. He slapped at her face and she pushed him out the door. The steps were rotten. He stumbled. There was a splintering of wood and he crashed to the ground. He had to stay there a moment, lolling his head drunkenly, looking for a stick maybe, the young summer sun burning a hole in his head. He lurched up onto his knees and tried to throw one leg up onto the floor of the house as he clutched at the sides of the door frame, grunting, halfway in and halfway out. His eyes were maddened, his tongue sticking out between the gaps of his teeth.

"Come on," she said, motioning to him. "Come on in."

"I ever get up," he said. He pawed his way into the room on his hands and knees and grabbed a windowsill to pull himself erect. He opened his arms and waddled spraddle-legged across the room and enveloped her in what he must have thought was a crushing embrace. They waltzed around the room, little scrolls of dust leaping from beneath their feet. The little girl sat crooning to her doll and not watching them, changing paper diapers and smoothing paper hair. The woman pushed at his face and tried to take his arms from around her. This married couple of thirty-six years tumbled out the back steps and lay there groaning with their hurts in the hot grass, until she rolled over and tried to get away from him. He grabbed her leg. She fell on him. Kissing him all over his face and pulling at his clothes, jerking up his shirt.

"Make me a baby," she said. "We got to make Calvin again," she said. He tried to crawl away and she caught him by the leg, trying to take off her pants. He tried to get up, but she leaped on his back and rode him down. He was begging her to stop and all but crying for her to turn him loose. The little girl watched from the window, her thumb caught in her mouth, as her mother and father moaned and groaned and crawled in the yard half naked. Strange sights but not as strange as some she'd seen, others that kept her silent. Endless nights in bitter cold, shaking with no covers and drawing no warmth from the knees pressed against her chest and the wind screaming through the cracks, or summer days and them like desolation angels through a desert wavering with heat and the blacktop burning their feet with every step they took. But he was down now, she was holding him.

"I got him," her mother called. "Let's kill him."

The only thing in the room big enough to do it was a brick. The child grabbed it up and tore through the room and leaped out the door and across the yard. He saw her coming and tried to get away. He was up, jerking his leg, sliding his wife along the ground, trying to get into the protective woods. When the little girl got close she threw the brick. It missed. She ran back toward the house for another one. She was going to rob the fireplace, one at a time. She squatted beside the blackened bricks and tugged one loose, then another one. She gathered them up in her arms, but when she went back he had pulled himself loose and was leaning against a tree with a big stick in his hand, while her mother lay in the yard with her legs spread, calling out to him to come on and do it to her, him shaking his head, trying to find a smoke in one of his pockets.

It was past three when the boy returned. He came up the road with his shirt wrapped around him, his hands empty. They were sitting in the back yard and he looked at his father. The others went into the house.

"When'd you get back?" the boy said.

The old man had two or three hot beers spread in the grass beside him. He was drinking them slowly, cupping each one in his hands. He had no answer for this upstart of his loins. The boy stood there. His hands were cut and bruised, his eyes burning from the poison that had splashed up into them.

"Where's your money?" Wade said.

Gary shrugged. He squatted a ways off. "He ain't give us none yet." His mother leaned out the door and said that supper would be ready in a few minutes.

"Gimme some money," Wade said.

Gary looked at him, looked away.

"I ain't got none."

Something flickered over the old man's face. The boy had hard muscles in his arms. He was crouched lightly in the yard, the waiting over for a day that had seemed so far off in the future down the lonely roads of years past and was now here without warning.

"He ain't paid you?"

"He ain't paid me. He'll pay me Friday."

Wade sucked the last of the suds gently from the can and eased it to rest beside his leg in the grass.

"Gimme some money."

Gary didn't even look at him. "No," he said.

The old man reared up drunkenly.

"What'd you say?"

"I said no."

Wade came across the grass after him and caught him by the leg, and they rose, holding each other until the old man began to hit him in the head with his doubled fist. The boy clenched his father close and smelled the awful stench of him, pushed him back while receiving the blows on his face and neck.

"Now quit it," he said. His father's breath was coming harder. His arms were swinging, his knotted fists finding no target as his son pushed him away. He swung so hard at Gary that he turned all the way around and fell. He lay on his back, scrabbling at the ground like an overturned turtle. He made it up on one knee and pushed off with his hands.

"I ain't got no money," the boy said. "He ain't paid us yet."

"Pays ever day," said Wade, coming after him.

"Just cause he fired us that time."

He backed around in the yard. His father followed him, but his breath was beginning to go and his legs were shaking. His steps were wobbly. Drinking hot beer in the sunshine had given him an uncontrollable head. Finally he went to his knees, his tongue out. His eyes were rolled up almost white in his head. He pitched over face forward into the grass and then he didn't move any more. The boy looked at him. He looked back at the house. His mother and his one remaining sister were standing in the doorway watching.

"Drag him around in the shade and come eat," his mother said.

Joe began to drive them harder as the last days of May slipped away. He stayed with them constantly now, taking a gun himself and joining their ranks as he tried to finish the tracts he had contracted for. He hired more hands, a load of them that bellied the pickup down so that it scraped and dragged over every rough spot in the road and ran down the highway canted up, and still they were not enough. He could see now that June would catch him unfinished, a matter of a lot of money. He pushed them more and more, harrying them around their edges, shouting, prodding the slow, the lazy, the hung-over, his own head throbbing and pounding under the summer sun. Clouds of gnats enveloped them and the yellowjackets rose boiling from their nests in the ground, and they moved through the green and tangled veldt like zombies in a monster movie or the damned in some prison gang, until under their breath they cursed him and work and the heat and the life their ways had led them to. They began to quit one by one. Three quit one Saturday and he made them understand they'd walk back to the truck and wait until the working day was over before he'd take them back to town. They stood in a small group, muttering, their eyes baleful and lowered, watching him narrowly as he moved away with the rest of the crew.

"Hey!" one of them said.

He turned back. "What?" he said. He had sweat in his eyes and he was already angry over their quitting. He'd been stung five times that morning and all he wanted to hear was one wrong word.

Gary was listening but he wasn't looking back. He had his head down, making overtime. Taking all he could get and glad to get it.

"You need to take us back to town," a man named Sammy said.

"You want to go back to town you can walk," Joe told him. "I ain't got time to run you back to town." He turned to walk off again.

"I ain't walkin back to town."

"Then you gonna have to wait on your goddamn ride."

"Hey!"

Joe threw his poison gun down. He turned and walked back. "You got anything to say, say it. I got work to do."

Sammy must have thought the other two were going to back him up, but now they stepped away. He looked around at them.

"Y'all gonna let him do this to us?" he said.

"I ain't done nothin to you," Joe said. "I hired you to work and if you don't want to work when I need you, I ain't got time to mess with you. I ain't worked you no harder than anybody else. Look yonder." He pointed. "They all still workin." But they weren't. They had stopped and turned back to watch what happened.

"Ain't hired on to work no nine hours a day. Didn't say nothin bout workin weekends."

"You didn't have to get in the truck this mornin, Sammy. And I can't do nothin about the weather. I got till the first of June to finish up and if you don't want to help you can go set in the truck. But I don't want to hear no more of your mouth. You've laid on your goddamned ass all your life and drawed welfare and people like me's paid for it. That's why you don't want to work. Now shut your fuckin mouth."

He turned one last time to go away and be done with it and heard the quick movement behind him, stepped back and spun as the knife passed under his arm, coming up, the steel flashing bright and quick to make a burning red stripe on his tricep. He hit Sammy in the nose and Sammy's nose exploded. The knife fell. He went to his knees and Joe grabbed his collar and pulled him forward. Nothing was said, no sound but their gasping breath in the early morning stillness and the scrape of their feet in the leaves. Sammy swung wild, once, then closed his eyes when he saw the next one coming. It snapped his head back and then it was over. Joe stood over him, a thin trickle of blood winding down his arm like a red vine and, drop by drop, falling off his middle finger to spot the leaves crimson, little spatters on the floor of the woods, like the trail of a wounded deer.

He said: "If they's anybody else don't want to work, or got somethin to say, you better speak up now."

Nobody spoke. They stood immobile in the hush with the thin calling of tree frogs the only comment.

He said: "I don't give a fuck if ever one of you wants to quit right now. I'll load the whole bunch up and pay you off. Last chance."

Gary turned away and slashed at a small bush. He went up to a tree, stabbing, pumping the poison into it. He mopped his forehead with his arm. The rest of them turned away one by one and fell back to work. Joe walked over to his poison gun and picked it up. The two who had quit with Sammy looked at each other uncertainly, now that their mouthpiece had been silenced.

"What you want us to do with Sammy?" one called out.

Joe cut and slashed and checked the time by his watch. "I guess you better drag him back to the truck if you want to ride to town this evening," he said.

An hour later he noted that all three had fallen back into the ranks silently and were working beside everybody else. Nothing else was said but he paid those three off that afternoon.

It came up one day at lunch that Joe was going to get rid of his old truck and buy a new one when they got finished with their tracts. The boy chewed his bologna sandwich dry and worked up enough spit to ask him how much he wanted for the old one. Joe turned his head and looked at him.

"Why? You want to buy it?"

"I'd like to have it," Gary said.

"It needs some work done on it."

"I can fix it."

"You ever worked on a automobile before?"

"I can learn."

"Oh. Well, you might have to work on that one a good bit. I

spend about as much time workin on it as I do drivin it. Course it ain't nothin major wrong with it. Just little shit. Old motor uses a little oil. Needs some brakes on it. Needs that shifter fixed for sure."

"How much?"

He thought about it. They wouldn't give him anything for it on a trade-in. Two or three hundred dollars at the most. The body was beat all to hell, the tires were slick. The front bumper was hanging loose on one end.

"I hate to price it," he said. "I ain't ready to get rid of it right now."

"I won't need it long as I'm ridin with you," Gary said.

Joe lit a cigarette and stretched out on the ground. He looked at his watch and called out to his workers: "Y'all hurry up, now, it's almost time." They were only taking fifteen minutes for lunch now, but everybody kept quiet about it. He was paying them time and a half after two p.m. and double time on Saturdays and Sundays.

"I couldn't guarantee it, now. That truck's old. Got a lot of miles on it. You might do better to just try to find you one in town somewhere. Or let me look around for you one."

"It wouldn't look too bad if it was washed up. I'd take that camper bed off it. Fix that bumper. All it needs is a bolt in it probably."

He looked at the boy. Then he looked at the truck. It was old, it was dirty, it was junky. But he guessed he wasn't looking at it from the boy's side. The boy had probably never had anything to call his own. He started to just say he'd give it to him.

"I'll take two hundred dollars for it when I get my new one," he said.

Gary stuck his hand out. "That's a deal."

Joe took the hand, squeezed it, then got up. He put his hands on his hips and called out that it was time to start back to work.

The boy worried about how he was going to pay for it all afternoon. He had to have some way to hide part of the money while he was saving it, and he had to have the money by the time Joe got ready to trade, which wouldn't be far off. The end of the month. It presented other problems. Gas and oil to buy, and his job would be over. But he reconciled himself with the thought that he could find something else to do. There were jobs everywhere, he figured. You just had to get out and find them. And he needed a vehicle for that. He hit upon it as they were taking a break from the heat that afternoon.

"What if you was to hold some of my money out and keep up with it?"

Joe was taking a drink of whiskey and when the boy came out of nowhere with that, he didn't know what he was talking about. He squinched his eyes almost shut and searched for the Coke on the dash and grabbed it and took a swallow.

"What are you talkin about, son?"

"To pay for my truck. How bout if you hold out about fifty dollars a week and let me pay for it like that?"

"Well. We probably won't work but about two more weeks. Hell, they all ready to quit. They been ready. Only reason they've stayed this long's cause I had to hit Sammy that day."

The boy fell silent. He had fifty dollars hidden under a rock down in the woods behind the house. The whole family was living off him now. His father robbed his pockets at night until there was nothing left.

"Where were you born?" Joe said.

"I don't know."

"Where's the rest of your family at?"

"This is all of us, I reckon."

"Where were you raised?"

The boy looked down. He still remembered Tom falling off the truck and the truck behind them going over his head, how everybody gathered around in the hot Florida sun, looking at him sprawled there dead. Was he four or five? And Calvin. Little brother. Gone now too.

"Different places," he said.

Joe looked at him. He knew nothing of him except that he would work. But his work was almost over. It was a long time from June to December.

"We finish this tract," he said, "they'll settle up with me. They'll shut us off after this one. They won't be no more work I can give you until this winter."

"What do you do?"

"You mean when I ain't doing this?"

"Yessir. When you ain't doing this."

Fuck. Drink. Gamble.

"I get by," he said.

"You know of anything I could do until this winter? I got to keep a job."

"Y'all can't stay in that damned old house this winter, can you?"

Gary turned up the last of his hot Coke and drained it. He set the can on the ground and pulled out his cigarettes. He had taken to smoking regularly since he was making money regularly.

"How cold does it get around here in the winter?"

"Shit. It gets cold as a witch's titty. We had ice stayed on the ground four days last year. You couldn't even get out on the road. I stayed up at the store with John about half the time. It didn't do to try and drive on it. They was cars all up and down the road in ditches."

"What did people do about goin to work?"

"They didn't go. The ones that live out here didn't. It stayed below ten degrees for three straight days. People had water pipes froze and busted and couldn't get into town for parts to fix em with. We couldn't work. Ground was froze solid."

The boy sat there, studying the situation. "I got a little money saved up," he said, finally. "If we could work two more weeks I believe I can get enough up to pay you."

"Well. We'll worry about that later. We'll work it out. Let's get on up and hit it."

The other hands rose in a group like a herd of cows or trained dogs in a circus act when they saw the bossman stand up. They picked up their implements and thumped their cigarettes away. The whole party moved off into the deep shade with their poison guns over their shoulders, the merciless sun beating down and the gnats hovering in parabolic ballets on the still and steaming air. The heat stood in a vapor over the land, shimmering waves of it rising up from the valleys to cook the horizon into a quaking mass that stood far off in the distance with mountains of green painted below the blue and cloudless sky. Joe stood in the bladed road with his hands on his hips and watched them go. He surveyed his domain and the dominion he held over them not lightly, his eyes half-lidded and sleepy under the dying forest. He didn't feel good about being the one to kill it. He guessed it never occurred to any of them what they were doing. But it had occurred to him.

The shelves in the old wooden safe that stood in a corner of the log house were now stocked with food. Gary couldn't remember when they'd ever eaten so well. There were proper pans to cook in and Joe had given him a little green Coleman stove that burned each evening with a cheery blue flame. Their windows were tacked over with Visqueen, which admitted, in brightest sunshine, a pale murky light, like half-light, that kept the interior in a gloom through which their restless figures moved without shadow. He'd chinked the cracks between the logs with old cotton found in a pen in a field. In the dead of night under their mildewed quilts recycled from the hands of the haves, these have-nots lay with their ears pricked in the darkness as the drone of the mosquitoes moved toward them like supersonic aircraft, their radar just as deadly, just as accurate. He bought poison and sprayed for ticks, whacked with a broken joe-blade the assemblage of overgrowth surrounding the house into some semblance of a yard. He kept an eye out for a castoff screen door, but these seemed hard to come by.

His routine was to charge his things and get Joe to drop him off by John Coleman's on Fridays to pay his bill. This Friday Joe put gas in his truck while the boy was inside and then followed him in to pay his own bills. The storekeeper was counting some money back into the boy's hands. The boy said thank you and went out and got in the truck.

"How about addin up my bill, John?" The old man reached for a pad of notes and a pencil. He started punching buttons on his adding machine, sucking on a cold cigar.

"Y'all bout to get wrapped up?" he said.

"We like about another week, I believe. We ought to done been through but we just had so much to do. All that rain early."

John rang it up. "Looks like twenty-two fifty."

"Thirteen gas, John."

Joe gave him the money and took his change back and stuck it in his pocket.

"Thank you, John."

"Thank you. Listen," he said, his eyes cut toward the door. "That boy there that works for you."

"Him? Yeah. I wish I had about ten of him. We'da done been through."

"Is he not that Jones's boy?"

"Who?"

"Wade. I know that was him come in here the other day and wanted to charge some stuff to that boy. Said they both worked for you. I wouldn't let him have nothin till I talked to you. But the more he stayed in here the more familiar he looked. If I ain't mistaken he lived here a long time ago."

Joe looked toward the door and pulled out his cigarettes.

"That boy's last name is Jones. His daddy's sorta fat and don't ever shave. I don't reckon he ever takes a bath, either. Smells like he ain't had one in about twenty years."

"That's him," John said. "I knew that was him. Have you not ever heard em talk about all that shit that happened down there on the Luster place a long time ago?"

They had leaned closer to each other over the counter and were talking in low voices like assassins plotting, like revolutionaries talking revolt.

"Seems like I heard Daddy and Uncle Lavert talk about it one time. It was somebody hung down there, wasn't it?"

"Hell yes. It was three years before I went to Europe. That boy's daddy was in on it, they said. He left out. Oh, it was a hell of a mess. It was Clinton Baker they hung. He was down there three days before they found him. Hangin in a tree and buzzards eatin on him."

"Aw hell." He had to think about that for a moment. "How come em to kill him?"

"Don't nobody know. J. B. Douglas was in on it, him and Miss Anne Maples's oldest boy. Buddy. And that boy's daddy, they said. But he run off. I thought that was him."

"Well damn," Joe said. He looked out at the boy. The boy was in the truck looking down at something, saying silent words. "What did they do to em?"

"Well, they all run around together, Clinton and Buddy and all of em. They had a old house they gambled in down there. After they found Clinton and went and got him down and all, they went over to J. B.'s house to talk to him, see if he knowed anything about it. Sheriff went over there. That was old Q. C. Reeves. He pulled up in the yard and started across and J. B. come out the door with a shotgun. And fore they could even decide what he was up to, he set down on the porch and stuck it in his mouth and blowed his brains all over his mama's porch. With her standin in there in the kitchen fixin to put dinner on the table. I never seen so many flowers at a funeral as his had. It was the worst thing to happen around here in a long time. Buddy Maples went to the pen but he died or got killed down there, I still don't think the truth was ever told about that."

"What, did he admit to doing it?"

"He admitted he was in on it. Or admitted enough to where they talked him into pleadin guilty to murder. Hell, they didn't even have a trial. But he never would tell how come they done it. That was the thing of it. They was every story in the world told about it."

"Like what?"

"Aw, hell, you can hear anything. It was told they poured gas on him and struck a match to him. I don't know if it's true or not."

"Goddamn," Joe said. "Well, could they not still get him? His daddy, I mean?"

"Shit, I don't know. It's been so long ago. I knew damn well that was him come in here other day."

Joe looked out toward the truck again. "I wouldn't let him have anything if I was you. That boy would be the one that would have to pay for it. He owe you any money?"

"Him? Not a penny. He's bought a good bit but he's always paid."

"Well." He looked up at John Coleman. "What in the hell would they want to burn him for?"

The old man lit the cigar and took a long slow puff of it and laid it in the ashtray. He leaned on his elbow and turned his head away.

"They's probably drunk," he said.

They coasted to a stop beside the growing cotton, where the honeysuckle blossoms hung threaded through the hogwire in bouquets of yellow and white, the hummingbirds and bees constant among them and riding gently the soft summer air. The boy held some money out.

"Here's half of it," he said.

"Half of what?"

He pushed the money at him. "A hundred dollars. You said you'd take two. You ain't changed your mind, have you?"

"Just keep it. You can pay me when I get my new one. I got to have this one to drive till then."

"I wish you'd go on and take it while I got it. Or keep it for me."

"Just hang onto it."

"I'm afraid I might lose it or somethin'll happen to it."

But Joe wouldn't take his money, and finally the boy put it back in his pocket. He got out and pulled his shirt off the seat and shut the door. He leaned in the window.

"I'll see you Monday," Joe told him. "Be out here at six, okay?"

"We ain't gonna work tomorrow?"

Joe looked up the road, then looked back. The boy seemed worried.

"Naw. I got to have a little break this weekend. You know what I mean?"

He was sure he didn't but the boy nodded that he did. He stepped back sadly. Joe shifted into gear and let out the clutch, tossing his best worker a wave of the hand. When he looked back through the camper glass he could see him walking across the road. Dark was half a day away. And it didn't matter what his daddy had done, what he did was all that mattered.

He reached under the seat for the whiskey and got it up between his legs and twisted the cap off. He laid it on the seat and took a drink. It was hot, he had no chaser, it burned going down. Summer was coming and soon it would be Friday night. And yes, they had probably been drunk when they burned him. A man did things he wouldn't normally do when those little devils were running loose in his head.

He called Connie from a pay phone outside a drug store that was just down the sidewalk from B&B Liquors. He was chewing gum and he had set his fifth on the concrete so he could dial. The telephone rang in his house three times and then she picked it up and said hello.

"What you up to?" he said. "Naw, hell, not right now. I just got some stuff I need to do." He listened to it a little while, not long. He never listened to it long.

"Well, I's probably drunk when I said it. You ought to know by now not to pay attention to me. I'm liable to say anything."

He coughed into the phone. A police cruiser crept at an idle around the parked cars and rounded the end of the lot and stopped.

"Listen, I got to go. They's a goddamn cop settin right here watchin me. I guess the sumbitch thinks I'm drunk. Me? Naw. Not yet. Hell, I don't know. Go shoot some pool or somethin. Go out to Vivian's. I might be out there later. I don't know what time. Naw, I ain't gonna promise. Well, suit yourself then." He hung up. "Goddamn women."

He picked up his bottle and walked straight as an arrow in front of the police car and got in his truck. He halfway expected the car to follow him. It did, for a while. It went out of the shopping center after him. But halfway up the hill it turned off and he went on about his business.

There was nothing but a porch light showing at Duncan's house. Joe parked the truck behind a green Grand Prix and got out and took a drink from the bottle. He put the pistol under the seat.

He could hear it raging behind the door when he knocked, its barking harsh, the growling a little hysterical. Then the sound of somebody cursing, a yelp of pain from the Doberman. The door opened two inches. He saw an eye, a chain, a black muzzle three feet above the floor, where ivory fangs drooled a ropy spittle.

"That son of a bitch bites me I'm gonna kill him," Joe said. "Go put him up."

The door closed. Other doors were slammed inside. Brown beetle-bugs bombarded him and the porch and the light. The door cracked open again and then it opened all the way. He stood there, waiting.

"You got that bastard put up?"

"He's in the kitchen," she said. "Come on in. He ain't going to bother you."

He wanted it made plain, though.

"I'm tellin you, now. That sumbitch bites me I'm gonna blow his fuckin brains out."

"He ain't gonna bite you."

"All right, then," he said, and stepped inside. There were women wall to wall, old and young and fat and skinny. They lay on couches and sat on the floor eating popcorn and watching movies from a video store. He guessed it was a slow night. He had to step over some of them. The worn dowager who had let him in went to the small bar she tended and waited there, her bosom like mangoes, her lips like blood.

"Can I fix you up with somethin, baby?" she said. She scratched absently at something in her hair.

Joe leaned on the bar and set his whiskey down.

"Come here and give me some sugar, Merle. I want you to lay them lips on me."

"Where you want me to lay em, honey?"

"I ain't decided yet."

She smiled and bent over to him. He kissed her for about a minute and then pulled away.

"Damn," he said. He picked up her hand and held it. "Why don't you just marry me, Merle? We wouldn't even have to fuck. Just kiss and cook supper."

"You asking?"

"Hell yes."

She laughed and went to the icebox and got a canned Coke out. She took a glass from the cabinet and scooped ice cubes from a tub in the sink. He looked at her sad rippled legs and the bra that cut into her back, and shook his head.

"I ought to asked you about twenty years ago," he said. "For real."

She mixed his drink using his own whiskey and set it before him. He held her hand again.

"What you got the blues over tonight?" she said. She reached for a barstool, still holding his hand, and drew it up close and sat.

"Hell, I don't know. I'm all right."

"I've heard you say that before. I believe you said that the night you shot that cop."

He lowered his head. "Well."

"Can you still fuck?"

"Not much. Just ever once in a while."

"You the only one I ever seen that would admit it."

"What you see is what I am. Last time I tried it I couldn't do nothin. Just bump up against it. I done got too old, I guess."

He picked up his drink and sipped it, and took some money from his pocket, the leaves of green not missed by the eyes that watched from the dark living room.

"Here," he said, and gave her a five. "Keep it."

As she put it in a drawer under the counter, the Doberman walked out of the hall and stood looking at him. Coal black, a chain of silver, sleek and lithely muscled, and the lips lifting ever so slowly from the white teeth that lined his mouth. The dog hated him, had always hated him, ever since he was a puppy. He wished for the pistol under the seat with a slight chilling of his blood and felt that something that hated so strongly for so little ought not be allowed to hate anymore. The dog stood ravenous and slobbering on the bright yellow linoleum, the flanks tense and the brown eyes not blinking. Joe looked into the animal's eyes and the eyes looked back with a deep and yearning hatred.

"Harvey," one of the girls called. "Harvey, settle down."

Joe watched him, watched him hear her voice and relax, all the muscles so keyed going slack at once, the hide sliding shiny and loose over the back and legs. The dog walked to a water dish and lapped three times and raised his head and looked at him again. He growled.

"Put the son of a bitch up," he said again.

Merle got down off her stool then and whistled the thing back, and Joe sat there sipping and hearing the toenails clicking down the hall, until she shut the animal away in a darkened bedroom and turned and came back to sit with him.

"What do y'all keep that goddamn thing around here for?" he said.

"Duncan says it's a good idea. Says it stands to reason that a deputy sheriff or anybody else we don't want in won't come in with something like that standing in the door, gives everybody else a chance to run out the back door and hide. I don't believe he likes you," she said.

"Hell naw, he don't like me. He'd like to eat my ass up is what he'd like."

It hit him then that there wasn't any reason for the thing to be here and there wasn't any reason for him to keep coming over here as long as it was because eventually it was going to nail him. Somebody was going to take it too lightly, one of the girls who could pet it was going to turn it out on him one night.

He looked down into his drink and heard the Doberman scratching at the thin door with its nails, whining and wanting out. He could imagine the dog in there in the dark, growling low, sitting on his haunches, leaning forward to gnaw and worry the wood. He lurched up suddenly.

"Where you going?" Merle said.

It smelled the Doberman when he opened the truck door and let it out in a flow of white liquid muscle. He told it to hush when it started whining and then he caught it by the collar. They dragged each other toward the door, him trying to drink from the bottle with one hand and hold his dog in the other. When they got up on the porch it barked and pawed at the door. Joe knocked, three thunderous blasts upon the flimsy wood. A pale girl opened the door and took one look and slammed it back, but he pushed it open before she could turn the lock. He went on in with the dog in tow. Only three of the girls were still up and they began to edge to the corners of the room. The dog had begun a low insistent growling and was straining forward an inch at a time, its toenails digging in the shag carpet.

"Where's he at?" Joe said, and then it got away from him. He grabbed for it and missed. It hurtled down the hallway to the room and bounced once against the door, and the Doberman spilled out in a rush of clicking teeth and flying saliva and slobbering outrage. In that tight little space they reared and sought each other's throats, the sounds they were making fearsome and out of control. The half-Pit came dragging him backwards into the kitchen, the blood already soaking into the white muzzle, where the Doberman was held, locked by the throat.

"Kill his goddamn ass," Joe said. The girls were screaming and going out the door. He pulled up a chair and sat down to watch it. There wasn't much to watch. The Doberman was shitting on the floor of the kitchen, while the half-Pit went deeper and deeper into his throat, mashing the blood out like water from a sponge, throttling and shaking him, droplets of blood flying over the clean walls and the table, the floor slick with it. The Doberman went down in the blood, his eyes glassing over slowly, the shine of life fading. The half-Pit turned him loose, licked curiously at him once, whined and looked back at its master, its face gore-stained and its tail wagging

"Good boy," Joe said, petting his dog.

They made it eight miles down the road before the deputy's car caught up with him. He wouldn't pull over. The dog had its head hung out the window, its long ears flapping in the breeze. He'd always liked to ride. Joe pulled over in the middle of the road with blue light flashing inside the cab. Through the side mirror he saw the car drop back, heard the big engine start to scream. It shot forward and tried to come around the left side, but he pulled over to the left, watched the car slide sideways and halt briefly with dust rocketing and swirling before the headlights. He could hear gravel flying behind him. He got another drink of the whiskey and closed one eye so that he could see how to stay in the middle of the road. Orange fire barked from the window of the deputy's car, shots aimed for the tires. He reached over and found a half-warm beer on the seat and opened it, started using it for a chaser while they reloaded.

They finished it where 9 runs into Calhoun County. A state trooper had his car parked sideways in the road and he was down across the hood with a shotgun to his cheek. Joe wouldn't have stopped for him, either, but he misjudged by two feet the amount of room it would take to go around the left side. His wheel dropped off a culvert and he turned down into the ditch, jerking the wheel to no avail. The brakes wouldn't stop the tires from sliding in the dewy grass. At five miles an hour he slammed into an oak tree three feet wide and broke the windshield open with his head. The dog went out the window and ran.

When he came to, the headlights showed dark green jungle depths and bugs danced in the halos of light they made. Far down and away through the black night came the wail of sirens faintly, like sirens singing, like souls lost in the sky. Through the trees, faint blue flashes of light.

When Joe woke the first time, it was to summer heat that held not a breath of air. Someone had taken a lighter and held it against the ceiling while kneeling on the upper bunks and writing strange fuck-slogans in smoke up there. There was a white man in T-shirt and skivvies and shower shoes sitting at a table with a black man in a rumpled suit and a red tie, playing cards. They regarded him as he came awake and then they ignored him. He slept again.

He woke to the sound of banging. If anything it was hotter. What he'd have given for a cold drink of orange juice. He couldn't believe where he was.

He felt of his pockets. Shirt, pants, back pockets. There was nothing on him, no money, no cigarettes. He rose up finally and sat on the edge of the cot, his shoes still on his feet. With his fingers searching carefully he found blood caked above his eye and a knot above his ear. No memory came forward to attest to the reasons for their existence. They were only there and had somehow come with the rest of it. The walls were green and there was a little fountain above the commode. If he wanted a drink, he'd have to drink from that. What he'd been lying on was a stained striped mat about an inch thick. Other men lay sleeping on other bunks throughout the cell. He looked at the card players.

"Has one of y'all got a cigarette I can have?"

The white man looked around. "I've got a Kool if you want a Kool."

He got up and went over and took one offered from the pack and stuck it in his mouth.

"I ain't got a light either. You gonna have to kick me in the ass to get me started, I reckon."

"Here's some matches. You want to sit in on a hand?"

"Thanks. No, thanks."

When he had his smoke going, he went back and sat on the bunk. From the heat in the cell he judged it to be afternoon. He remembered standing in the road at night and seeing the truck against a tree, the lights shining. He thought he remembered somebody pulling his hair while he was hitting somebody else. He touched his scalp with his fingertips. It was tender, sore. There were small bare places where some of his hair had been pulled out. He couldn't remember faces, complete events, just nightmare scenes that were vague and surreal, like glimpses of a movie he might have seen.

He finished the cigarette and dropped it on the cement and ground it under his heel. The door to the cell was solid steel, with a small rectangular hole large enough to admit trays of food. He got up and went over to it and bent down so that he could look out into the hall. There was nothing to see but another wall and nine or ten cases of beer stacked against it.

"Hey. Jailer." He rested his head on the cool metal ledge and thought he might throw up from the idiocy of it all. From not learning his lesson, from the subservience he'd have to effect. There was no telling what he'd done. Murder maybe. Mayhem, at least.

Steps sounded in the hall. A man bent over and looked in.

"What you want?" he said.

"I want to get out of here."

"No shit. I magine everybody in there'd like that."

"I get a phone call, don't I?"

"Yeah, you get a phone call. Who you want to call?"

He thought for a moment. Not Charlotte.

"I don't know yet. Can you let me out and let me get some cigarettes? Did I have any money when I come in here?"

"We got your money in the desk. You want me to take enough out to get you some cigarettes?"

"I guess so. What have they got me for?"

"I'll have to go ask. I wasn't here last night."

"You mind?"

"Naw. Just hold on."

The steps went away slowly. He heard a door open and close. Somebody was yelling in another cell. Down the hall a tray slot opened. "Hey. Hey! Somebody. You hear me? I'm sick. I want to go to the doctor. Open this door."

The door to the hall opened. A voice called down: "What you yelling about now?"

"I want to go to the doctor. I'm sposed to be takin medicine."

"I done told you you ain't going down there. All you wanting is some more dope."

"Naw, I ain't wantin no dope. I'm sick. I need to go see the doctor. I was sposed to done been down there."

"Go back to sleep, Roscoe. You got three more weeks."

"I can't stay in here three more weeks. I got to go see about my kids, you son of a bitch."

"You stop that goddamn cussing. You been yelling ever since you got here. I'm tired of hearing it."

"I don't give a fuck what you tired of. Now, goddamnit, open this door and let me out, you cocksucker."

"You better shut up."

"I ain't gonna shut up."

"I'll get that strap."

"Well, *get* the fuckin strap!"

He shouted some more things but the door closed on him and his words fell on no ears that wanted them. After a while he sobbed. The tray slot pulled back shut and there was silence. Joe rubbed the scabbed place over his eye and wondered if it had been stitched, or needed stitching. In a few minutes the hall door opened again and the steps came back to his door.

"You still on probation?"

"Naw. I been off probation three years."

"Well. They can't find a field officer. Said he was out feedin his cows."

"Hell, they don't need to talk to a field officer. I ain't on probation."

"They seem to think you are."

He groaned and held his head. He was trying to think of a name but now when he needed it most it wouldn't come to him. Bob or Bill Johnson or Jackson.

"What they got me charged with?"

"Shit. A heap. DWI and assault on an officer. Resistin arrest. Whole buncha stuff. You gonna need you a lawyer."

"Can you get me a bailbondsman?"

"I can try."

"They's a card in my billfold if you'll look in there. Did you get me some cigarettes?"

"You never did say what kind."

"Any kind. Salems if you got em. Anything. Can you get me a Coke?"

"I'll see."

The steps went away again. It was nearly an hour before they returned, but he wouldn't bum another cigarette. The jailer called him to the door and let him out. He stood with his head up in the hall while the jailer locked the cell behind him. The tray slot opened down the hall and a mouth came into view.

"Why's he gettin out? Huh? How come he's gettin out?"

"Knock it off, Roscoe," the jailer said. To Joe he said, "Walk in front of me. Now hold it. I got more keys than Carter's got little pills."

At last he stood in the dayroom with lounging cops and trustees with their feet up in chairs watching television. They eyed him warily.

"Where's my truck?" he said.

The jailer was dumping his personal belongings from a manila envelope onto the cluttered desk. Keys, a ring, change, his wallet and comb and pocketknife. He was presented with a typed list of items which he himself had signed for.

"Check to see that everything's here and then sign. Count your money."

He picked up the billfold and opened it. He didn't know how much he was supposed to have but there was nearly two thousand dollars in it. It tallied with the inventory sheet.

"It's all here," he said. He slipped it into his back pocket and picked up his other stuff and signed. He looked up. All the city police were watching him. All their eyes were hostile. One had a Band-Aid on his chin.

"You can't learn your lesson, can you?" this one said.

"You talkin to me?"

"There ain't nobody else standing here, is it?"

Joe ignored him, though he hated to, and turned to the jailer.

"You know where my truck is?"

The jailer had settled in a chair and was unwrapping a sandwich from waxed paper. It looked like egg salad with hot peppers and tomatoes, and the jailer was reaching for a bottle of Louisiana Red Hot sauce.

"I believe they took it to King Brothers," he said.

That would be about fifty-five dollars if he could even drive it home.

"Can I go now?"

"Not till you make bond. He'll be here before long."

There was nothing to do but wait on the bondsman. Nobody

ever got in a hurry about something like this. There was a water fountain on the other side of the room and he started walking toward it.

"Hey," the cop said.

He stopped.

"Yeah?"

"Ain't nobody said you could walk over there."

"Ain't nobody said I couldn't, either."

He went on and bent over the fountain, drank the cold water for a long time. When he finished, he wiped his mouth and turned around. Somebody was coming in, a man with a briefcase.

"There's my man," he said.

They had him on $2500 bond and he was surprised it wasn't higher. They hadn't set his court date and it took only a few minutes to get released. He paid the bondsman the money and they said he could go. He had his hand on the door to freedom when the cop with the cut chin spoke again.

"We'll see your ass in court, Ransom. You going back this time. This time they'll keep you."

Ten years before, it would have been different. Now he would not let himself say anything. He wanted away too badly. They'd had him once and he had promised himself they would never have him again. Now they had him. He opened the door and walked outside.

The cars moved along the streets in the hot sunshiny Sunday afternoon. Couples with children sat on the low brick wall in front of the jail, talking in quiet voices, plans made, promises promised, hands clasped and hearts maybe shuddering with fear. For some it was almost a home, but he wanted it for his home no more. He went down the concrete steps and across the narrow street, the bells in the courthouse tower starting to chime. They tolled two times and he marked each sound in his head and stopped for a car that was cutting through the parking lot of the bank. He was glad of not calling her and of her knowing nothing of this. As the car went past he raised his eyes to see the driver who had already seen him. He wasn't sure. She had on sunglasses. It might have been anybody. He watched the car until it went out of sight, but she never looked back.

Dawn on Monday found the boy waiting beside the road with his gloves in his hand, squatting in the pale dust, his ears tuned for the sound of a motor. Cars and trucks appeared as specks down the road and grew larger and gained form as they hurtled toward him and sped past but not one slowed or stopped. Not one was an old GMC with a wrecked camper hull.

He sat there until the mist burned off, until the sun rose and lit the fields and dried the dew from the cotton. It hadn't rained. He sat until the sun held the land in its grip for another day and he knew he wasn't coming. Then he got up and faced down the road where the black strip of asphalt curved away toward the crossroads, toward distance and futility and nothingness. Nothing stirred anywhere. No breath of wind nor any sound. A light sweat broke out on his back. It was five miles, but he had a little money, and good credit. There was nothing to go home to anyway. He started walking, that old familiar thing that made riding such a joy.

*

At midmorning he trudged up the last little hill and walked between two pickups just as two men came out the door. He stepped aside for them to pass and he nodded. The boards of the floor just beyond the door were patched with printer's tin and tacked insecurely and they crinkled when they were stepped on. He went inside and stood looking around. It looked empty. He waited. There was a single lightbulb in the ceiling, a yellow glare of illumination in a cavern of bad cereal and atrophied potato chips, long forgotten and stashed behind the bug spray. The coal stove sat at the rear of the room, lacquered with tobacco juice. Flystrips hung from the scorched ceiling with their victims mummified, handfuls of black rice flung and stuck, untouchables. There were crazy patches of tin all over the floor. He reached back and pushed the door open a little and let it fall to. The old man parted the curtains behind the counter and stepped out.

"Hey, Mr. Coleman," Gary said. He went over to the blue Pepsi box and slid the lid back. He felt among the cool bottles, examining the caps. In the dark water he found the letters R and C. The old man came from behind the counter slowly and eased himself down on the bench, the cigar cold and dead between his fingers. Gary closed the lid and went to the rack of cakes and got a double-decker banana Moon Pie.

"You ain't seen Joe, have you?"

He turned at the old man's question.

"He never did come by. You seen him?"

John Coleman leaned back and rubbed his forehead with his fingers. A crescent scar hung there, hung in flesh like an eighth of a moon. In his skull likewise lay the shrapnel he thought had killed him one day long ago. The boy could not know that it itched, it always itched, it never stopped its itch.

"He wrecked his truck the other night. I believe they've got him in jail."

"Jail?"

"I magine."

He looked down at what he had in his hands. His hunger seemed so small then, so stupid. He wrecked *his* truck the other night. He slowly opened the RC on the drink box and sat on the bench on that side, held the bottle between his legs while he opened the cake.

"I waited on him a long time," he said.

The old man sat like a statue. He seemed to read some bad news on the screen door. A car passed outside, a flash of red that went out of hearing. The air pump kicked on and it chugged and chugged. John Coleman stretched one leg out and reached into his pocket for his lighter.

"How bad did he tear it up?" Gary said.

"Tear what up?"

"That truck."

"Oh. I don't know."

The lighter snapped and the smoke flooded out of his mouth. He bent forward and stroked his knee absently with the silver rectangle. Finally he dropped it in his shirt pocket.

"I wished I knew," the boy said. "I was supposed to buy it. I hope he ain't tore it all to pieces."

The storekeeper offered no response. He seemed to hate to have anybody in there with him. The boy ate his Moon Pie and drank his RC and formed possible lines of conversation in his mind.

"Reckon when he'll get out?" he said.

The old man shook his head. He crossed his legs and put one hand on the bench. The wood there was smoothly worn, polished, shiny.

"Depends," he said, finally. "Last time they got him they kept him two weeks."

"You don't know what happened?"

"Had a wreck was all I heard. I think the highway patrol got him."

That was all he'd say about it. He got up and went back behind the curtain where secret things were that nobody ever saw. A cot, shelves of books, shoe boxes of old money both rare and near extinct. Hot Budweiser in cans that he'd drink when he took the notion. A framed photograph of an old man and an old woman, their faces like leather in a tintype portrait, poised uncertainly and fearful on the porch of their log house. Theirs was the one that lay near the spring house, entombed there after the first house burned down, far away now from where they slept their eternity away on the hill. He sat there for a while, until he heard the boy call out.

He'd laid a dollar on the counter when he stepped back out.

"I need to pay you for that," he said. "I had a big RC and a Moon Pie."

He put the burning cigar in the ashtray and punched the buttons on the register. He rang it open and said: "Sixty-five."

Going out the door the boy looked back at him. John Coleman seemed like something made of china, a being or mannequin with living flesh but wires for bones. His glasses caught the tiny sunlight and flashed it across the room.

"You come back," he said.

n the countryside by nights without the moon, there sometimes roamed an indigent, a recycled reject with eyes sifting the dark and sorting the scattered scents, walking beside deep hollows and ditches of stinking water. The hours he kept were usually reserved for the drunk and the sleeping. With his sloe-lidded eyes that in the daytime tried to hide from the sun, he spied treasures all over the land. No thing unlocked was safe from his grasp, he who could squat in the road and talk to the dogs and still their dying growls, all save one.

With his myriad transactions he would convert these Troy-Bilt tillers and battery chargers and bugwhackers to a small amount of money and show up at the store wet to the knees and clamoring for Pepsi and peanuts, tomato juice and Alka-Seltzer. He went in on John Coleman one day with a fistful of food stamps. The old storekeeper was lying back against a pile of flour with a book in one hand and a cigar in the other. He had gone to sleep, and now came a crafty assassin and thief whose feet toed soundlessly over the worn and creaky boards. The hand with the cigar had come to rest against his stomach and he held the book to his chest, his snores long, sonorous, drafty. He'd once drunk three big Pepsis poured into a pot on a dare of not stopping and all but died from it, long before rumors of war, before the talk around his father's store altered from general topics and became focused on one thing: war. He had been reading about the fallen on the field of Shiloh and about the retreat into the Hornet's Nest and about the bullets in the orchard cutting the peach blossoms like falling snow. He could only shake his head over it, a war like that, that long ago. But he had been drinking that morning, as he did some or sometimes many mornings, and the heat and the beer and the book had done him in.

Wade crept about the room and eyed the register warily, ready at any moment to assume the position of a customer just entered and just as surprised as the one he feared might wake. He reached out and tapped his knuckles on the glass pane of the candy case. He rapped three times. The slow sighing and tuneless whistling sawed through the air. He took two steps closer to the counter, then stood finally with his hand on it, regarding the merchant caught in his dreams. John Coleman's neck was wrinkled like a turtle's and a slow pulse beat steadily at the corner of his jaw. His glasses had fallen sideways on his nose and he appeared old, weak, vulnerable. But there against his leg lay an automatic pistol blued with rust, close to hand, the snout shiny with age and use. Wade put both hands in his pockets and nudged John's foot with his toe. The eyes opened like a child's with no sleep in them, and the first thing he did was straighten his glasses.

"Ho," he said, and he got up, the hand trailing the pistol now by his leg and behind the counter where it was placed in some strategic spot not known to anyone but himself.

"I hate to wake you up," Wade said.

"I wasn't asleep. Just had my eyes closed. What can I do for you?"

"Aw, I just need to look, I reckon."

He was eyeing the shelves, gripping with his hand in his pocket the wad of food coupons he had taken off the dead black man. He looked over the shelves and noted what was there, the bags and boxes and brightly colored cans. Nothing was marked, for the old storekeeper kept the prices in his head. If he didn't know the price he would immediately name one. He gave credit to the reliable and the unreliable alike, slow to ask for payment, didn't really need it. On the pagan holiday a masked drunk stooped, smiling, behind the counter, wearing a plastic face, the lights out, hearing the tiny cautious steps outside the door, the cars idling, the parents watching as the little ones came inside. He always lit a coal-oil lantern and set it in the floor. To the young it gave an awesome quality to the room, small glints of shine on the shelves, fearsome shapes behind the stove. It was one of their favorite places to go. He'd hear them stop, hear them whisper to each other, gathering their courage. He'd let them say it three times before he leaped out with the flashlight, a white-haired frog with wings of hair on the sides of his head ratted up with a comb, cackling like an insane rooster. He loaded up their bags and they came back every year until they were too old to come in costume any more. And he would not even touch one of these that he had so badly desired to sire. He could only watch them grow from year to year, become men and women over and over, send their own inside for trick or treat.

"What you need?" he said to Wade. He was sure now that the

one rumored was in fact the same. There was no smile on his face, nothing but a hard glare.

"Aw, I'm just lookin," he said. He stepped to the shelf and hefted a can of Viennas. "How much?"

"Fifty-five."

"Goddamn, you high, ain't you?"

"You don't like the price go buy it somewhere else."

Wade got three cans. He got three packs of cigarettes. John saw that he was shopping and stepped behind the curtain and opened the refrigerator. There was a bottle of Jim Beam half full in there, and he tilted it out and took the cap off and turned a good drink down his throat. He stuck an eye to the crack in the curtain and watched Wade slide a flat tin of sardines down in his overall pocket. I got my goddamn eye on you, he said to himself. Then he got another drink. He wanted something to chase it with then, so he brought the whiskey out and set it on the counter and came around and went to the drink box. From an eye corner Wade watched him get a small green glass Coke, open it on the box and drink about half it. Then he watched him walk over to him and reach into his overalls and take out the sardines and put them back on the shelf.

"You holler at me when you get through," John said, and he went back behind the curtain. Wade stood stunned. He didn't even try to use the food stamps. Half drunk like he was he just walked out the door.

When John Coleman stuck an eye to the curtain there was nobody standing inside. He came on out. There was no money on the counter. He locked the register, then unlocked it and rang it open. The money was packed in there, stuffed tightly, the tens, the fives, the ones. He slammed it shut and locked it again and got his pistol and put it in his pocket and went outside. The screen door slapped shut behind him. He strode quickly between the whittled benches and past the square red tank coated with oil and insects, with the pump handle on top to dispense the kerosene, and stepped over the board the red sand was shoveled against and walked to the middle of the road and faced left. There was nothing beside the slow figure going down the road trying to open a can of Vienna sausages except two houses on the right and an abandoned one on the left and Mr. Frank's barn that might or might not have a cow in it. He pulled the pistol from his pocket. Then he looked at the store.

"Well shit," he said. He rushed back inside. The whiskey was sitting on the counter where he'd left it. He rushed back outside. Wade had become a small target but an immobile one, his fingers holding each juicy sausage and moving them into his mouth rapidly. John Coleman in his sixty-sixth year jacked the action back on the Llama and let it fall to, slipped the safety and aimed. Nora Pinion, horrified suddenly, almost pulled up for some gas. Wade leaped when the first bullet furrowed the asphalt and droned off heavily into the catalpa trees on his left. He spun, and the second bullet sprayed his leg with supersonic grains of sand.

"God*damn*," he said. He could see the storekeeper, slightly squatted to steady his drunken hand, drawn down on him at the top of the hill. He raised his hands and everything fell out from under his arms. He hadn't thought to get a sack. The voice drifted down to him, slow, clear: "You bring that stuff back up here."

Wade gathered his purloined goods with one hand, one hand in the air. He wanted no misunderstandings. By the time he got back up to the top of the hill, John had put the pistol away. He held the door open for Wade and Wade marched to the counter and put two cans of Vienna sausage and three packs of crackers on the counter, the crackers broken, crumbled inside the cellophane, not desirable but edible.

John Coleman walked behind the counter and unlocked the register. He stared across until Wade unloaded the cigarettes.

"Don't come back in here," he told him.

The word traveled fast, it seemed. One fine morning the boy woke on the quilt he used for a bed and lay turned on his back to hear the live things around him: the wasps buzzing busily overhead in the hot air in their obscure comings and goings; the jays outside his window screaming their curses to the squirrels that shook the branches and the dew from them as they scurried about; the far-off voices of other birds deep in the woods and the high thin piping of tree-frogs so loud and ventriloquistic they could never be found. The sun was shining on him through the window and it became too hot to sleep any more.

He got up and put on his clothes and went through the house. The little girl lay like one shot dead, and his father and his mother were nowhere to be seen. In the pie safe and on shelves nailed together from boards there were cans of soup, dry rice, Granola bars. He got a Granola bar with raisins and almonds and munched it while scratching himself and wondering where his parents could be.

Going down the road later in the hot morning sun, he passed a field of hay being baled. There was a flatbed truck inching along the rows of hay, and men were walking beside it throwing the bales up to another man who stacked them behind the cab against a high wooden wall. He stopped in the dusty roadside weeds to watch them labor. Already the heat made the toiling figures hazy and vague in the distance. He could hear faint cries, the revving of the truck motor from time to time. The baler was working along with a steady drumlike sound, the red machinery pushing each bale out in stages until it leaned toward the ground and fell off the chute and another appeared behind it to follow.

He lifted a finger and drew it across the beaded sweat on his brow and flung it to the ground. He saw what looked like a boy his age and studied him. The boy was having trouble with the bales. Twice he saw him drop them. Once he broke the strings on one and the man on the truck yelled down something to him. They moved in a palpable mist of heat under a disastrous sun amid clouds of chaff. Gary tossed his can sack into the ditch and stepped down after it. He found a sagging place in the wire and stepped over the top strand.

He had to follow the truck for a while because it didn't stop at first. On the ground were two old black men and the white boy. A white-haired man at least sixty was on the bed of the truck. A hard unfriendly face, a visage carved from burnt leather looked out from under a shredded-straw cowboy hat that held his face in shade. Gary kept trying to talk to him, but he kept looking around and going back to catch the bales. Finally Gary ran and caught the back end of the truck and swung himself up onto it. The old man leaned around and hollered into the window and the truck stopped.

They all turned and looked at him. They had on long-sleeved

shirts and gloves. Their faces were encrusted with bits of hay and they were wet with sweat. The boy he'd been watching was red in the face and looked ready to drop. It looked as though they were putting on the first load.

The old man was chewing tobacco and now he leaned his head over the side of the truck and spat and hit the webs of his thumbs together twice in the gloves. He didn't look happy.

"What you want?" he said.

"You need any help?"

The old man looked dubious. He leaned back against the wall of hay and looked out over the field. Most of it was still in long raked piles all over the ground.

"I reckon we can handle it. Throw that damn bale up here, Bobby. What you waitin on?"

The boy on the ground had been listening. He was chubby and soft-looking. He bent and grunted up with the bale and said, "Well, you stopped." He just barely got it up over the edge of the bed and with a herculean effort at that.

"I'll be goddamned," the old man said.

A sharp voice inside the truck said a name.

"Well, any damn body fourteen year old ought to be able to pick up a bale of hay. Give it here." He snatched the bale off the bed and threw it over his head into place and then glared down at the boy. The boy wasn't looking at him. He was walking ahead. The two ancient blacks were each standing beside a bale but the old man didn't yell at them. They were both older than he was. One of them had a solid white eye and wore glasses, the lens cracked over the bad eye as if in simultaneous injury.

"I just thought you might need some help," Gary said. "Didn't figure it'd hurt nothin to ask."

"You ever hauled any hay?"

"Yessir. I've hauled a good bit."

"Where at? Who for?"

"Well," he said. "I ain't never hauled none around here. I've hauled a bunch in Texas. I hauled all one summer down there."

The old man worked his cud and looked at Gary's thick little arms and legs.

"Can you throw one up on the truck?"

"Yessir."

"Let's see you throw one then."

He got off on the side of the truck and walked to the bale nearest him. He bent his legs and muscled the bale up against his chest and walked to the truck with it. It was seventy or eighty pounds, felt like. He tossed it up over the side onto the stack and all the old man had to do was hit it on the side and settle it straight. He looked down on him.

"How old are you?"

"Fifteen, I reckon. I'm just little for my age." He was looking up and shading one hand against the sun in his eyes.

"You gonna work in that?" He was pointing to the black T-shirt Gary was wearing.

"Yessir. I ain't got no other shirt with me. It don't matter."

"That hay'll stick you."

"It's all right. I've hauled in a short-sleeve shirt before."

"You ain't got no gloves."

He worked his fingers open and closed once. "My hands is tough," he said.

"Well." He called down to one of the black men: "Come on, Cleve." Then: "All right. Get over here on the left and maybe you can help this boy keep up. We done had to crank the baler out twice cause he couldn't pick em up."

"Yessir. Thank you." He walked behind the truck and the old man leaned around the hay. "Let's go," he said. The gears clashed as it went into first and the truck started rolling. Gary walked fast alongside it and hurried on to the next bale, going by the fat boy who barely got his on before the truck moved past. When it came by Gary he handed a bale up to the old man. When he went by the cab again, he saw a woman with a straw hat behind the wheel, a brown stain of snuff on her chin. She had both hands in a desperate clench on the wheel, with the truck crawling about two miles an hour. The old man cursed every time the fat boy tried to put one up.

"How much does hay haulers make in Texas?" he said.

Gary handed another one up to him and he turned and stacked it. "It just depends," he said. "Who you work for. I worked with a bunch of Mexicans one day and got two cents a bale. I never did go back and work for that fellow no more, though."

"Well," he said. "I pay a nickel a bale and dinner. That all right with you?"

"Yes sir," he said. He could already envision the feast. "How much we gonna haul today?" He was working and hurrying and throwing the bales up while they were talking.

"They's another field down yonder," the old man shouted. "Other side of that creek. See yonder?"

Gary looked. He could see a pale green square of flattened grass shimmering in the distance.

"We got another truck comin after dinner and three more hands," he said. "We gonna haul till dark if we can. You think you can stand it?"

"I can stand it," Gary said. The baling twine had already made deep red lines in his palms. He hurried ahead and picked up a bale and stood waiting with it.

"Uh uh," the old man called. He put it down.

"Now see there. You havin to pick it up twice. Don't pick it up till the truck gets to you. Wait on the truck."

"Yessir."

"Now, come on with it."

He tossed it up.

"I thought you said you'd hauled before."

"I have. It's just been a while."

"How much of a while?"

"Aw. A year or two."

"Well. It's all the same. In Texas or Missippi. All you got to do's put it on the truck."

He walked past the other boy and stopped beside him just as he was starting up with a bale. He was bent over from the waist, his back bowed.

"Use your legs," he said.

The boy looked at him. He was white around the mouth.

"What?"

"Use your legs. Don't pick it up with your back. Look here."

He bent over a bale with his forearms resting on his thighs.

"See here?" He raised the bale with his arms like a weightlifter doing a curl and straightened his legs at the same time. When he came erect the bale was at chest level. When the truck passed he threw it up.

"See there? It's easier like that. It don't give your back out like that."

He smiled at the boy but the boy didn't smile back. When the old man went to the other side to catch the hay, he walked up next to Gary and said, "That's my granddaddy. Daddy makes me come out here in the summertime and help him. All he ever does is fuss at me, though."

"You get paid?"

"Shit," the boy said. "I wouldn't come out here and do it for nothin. What you think I am, crazy?"

"I don't guess."

"I wouldn't even be out here if I didn't have to.

"Aw."

"I don't care if I don't never make any money or not."

Gary didn't say anything to that.

"Plus I have to mow the yard and hang out clothes, too."

"Yeah?" Gary said.

"And they don't even pay me for that."

Long before dinnertime the old man saw the red welts forming on Gary's hands and gave him an extra pair of gloves. When they had the truck loaded they stopped and tied the load down, the old man on top crawling around and rigging the rope, Gary kneeling under the truck and throwing the free end of the rope around for him to take up the other side and tie off. They rode on top to the trees that held the shade at the fence and left that truck and took an old '65 Chevy pickup back out to the center of the field. The baler was finishing up and they had what looked like about two hundred more to pick up.

"We'll have a hundred and thirty-five on two loads," the old man said. They had water in plastic milk jugs that had been frozen solid and wrapped in grocery sacks. It was cold and sweet and Gary knew it would ruin him if he drank too much of it. The fat boy, Bobby, turned the jug up time and time again. They took a break under the shade when they had both trucks loaded.

"You smoke?" the old man said. He pulled a pack of Winstons out of a dry shirt he'd put on.

"Every once in a while," Gary said.

"Well, here." He gave him a cigarette and then gave him a light. They sat crosslegged on the ground and the man looked at his watch.

"Ten-thirty," he said. "Where you live?"

Gary drew on the cigarette and looked out over the field. He rested his weight on one arm. He tensed it, felt the muscle bunch, untensed it.

"We live up on Edie Hill," he said.

"Edie Hill?" The eyes were flat and gray. The boy could see the lifetime of hard work in them, the hundreds of days like this one still remembered and not banished by time.

"Yessir," he said. He flicked at the fire on his cigarette with his little finger. It was quiet on the ground there, the heat rising around them and drawing the sweat effortlessly from them and already dampening and darkening the old man's fresh shirt.

"I used to know some folks lived up around there," he said. "Didn't know nobody lived up there now."

"We just livin in this old house up there," Gary said. "I don't reckon it belongs to anybody."

"Is it back up there around a big pine thicket? Got some old sheds and stuff around it? Old log house?"

He drew deeply on the cigarette and studied his feet. He didn't look up. The burning air had twisted the hair on his neck into wet locks that curled up and cooled his skin. "It's a log house," he said.

"You one of them Joneses that moved back here?"

"Yessir."

The old man nodded and looked off into the distance, the blue denim of his overalls tattered and faded. He waited a few moments before he spoke.

"How much you reckon's on them two trucks there?"

Gary looked. "I don't know," he said.

"A hundred on this one. Thirty on that one." The old man got up, pulling his billfold from his back pocket. "Six dollars and fifty cents."

The boy sat on the ground watching him, the cigarette smoking between his fingers. "What is it?" he said.

The old man didn't answer. He stuck a thin thumb between the leather jaws of his billfold and pulled out a five and a one. The two paper bills fluttered to the ground like wounded doves and were anchored almost immediately by two pitched quarters that landed flat and soundlessly and pinned them to the faded green stubble in front of his feet. He looked up. The old man was staring down on him now with his eyes hard and unfeeling. He bent over and picked up the gloves the boy had been using. The woman and the fat boy were standing by the other truck. They had not spoken.

"Let's go," he said, and they climbed into the cab. The haymaster put one foot on the rear hub and gripped the bed with his dark and freckled hands and pulled himself up over it like a seal clambering onto an ice shelf. But there was no coolness in that field. Long after they had gone Gary sat motionless beneath the shade tree, watching their wavering figures struggling relentlessly over the parched ground, their toiling shapes remorseless and wasted and indentured to the heat that rose from the earth and descended from the sky in a vapor hot as fire.

Sometimes in the singing underbrush the boy could hear sounds that came only at night, strange rustlings and movings that lay dormant in the daytime and rose after the sun fell into the deep green beyond the creek faded to black, the hushed voices and far-off crying dogs that rushed and swept through the dark timber, the faint yellow lights moving across the bottomland. Sometimes he'd go down there to hear them better.

He could follow the path without a light and climb a hill behind the house and come out on a dirt road washed with shadows, where he could see little puffs of dust rising and falling beneath his bare feet. He'd stop on the wooden bridge and listen, squatting there in the warm night. He could hear men talking, the quick baying, the short rush of dogs through the woods.

One night he sat motionless on the bridge with the rough wood under him and heard the quick splash of little feet in the shallows. He knew it was a coon. He could hear the dogs far back, trailing. There was no sound around him but the slow musical trickle of the stream and the slow wind that rustled the cane. The little feet came closer, stopped. He saw the coon, one small dark blob on the creek bank, a scurrying shape bent south with humped and pumping legs. The dogs came upon him in a rush; it wasn't until he heard their feet striking the water that the first one opened again. Five dogs, mottled moiling shapes indistinct in the dark, splashed down the ribbon of water and flowed beneath the bridge with their voices like hammers, sudden shocks of noise that disrupted the peace and serenity of the night, tore it apart with their anguished cries, swept past the bridge and down the bank, their voices louder than he could have imagined, echoing up and down and back behind him, all around him, until the whole of the woods rang with the sound of the race. The boy heard them catch it, heard the angry sounds of the dogs and the high thin chittering of the coon as they pulled it apart with their teeth. He saw the yellow lights struggling up through the woods as the men who owned the dogs came to see after them, and he got up, and waited a moment, some longing deep within him he couldn't name, and went away before they came too close.

omebody was beating on something down the road. The boy had been walking for a long time and he could hear the sound of it now. It was midmorning and he was on his way to the store again, their supplies low, empty bellies all around him. He still had money saved back, hidden under a rock a long way from the house, but already he'd seen the old man in the woods, bending, stooping, looking. He knew he'd have to move it soon, maybe find a hollow tree or even bury it. There was a good bit in his pocket but he would hide that before he returned home.

The sound of banging was irregular, hollow and muffled, and as he got closer he could hear small random curses. It appeared to be coming from near Joe's house. He rounded the last curve and the old GMC was there, the hood up, the left front fender off, the bossman kneeling over it on the ground and attacking it with a ball peen hammer and a tire iron. The boy stood watching him for a moment. Then he smiled. He walked on up the road and turned into the yard. Joe was laying the flat end of the tire iron in the wrinkles in the metal and drawing back and whopping it with the hammer. He would hit a few licks and then pause to examine his handiwork.

"Hey," Gary said.

Joe looked over his shoulder at him and smiled.

"Hey, boy," he said. "What you doing?"

Gary walked up beside him and squatted. The fender was lying with the painted side down and he could see the edge of an anvil sticking out from under it.

"I's headed to the store. What are you up to?"

Joe laid the hammer down and sat back on his heels. He fished a cigarette out of his pocket and lit it. Sweat had soaked his shirt.

"Ah hell, I'm trying to beat some of the dents out of this fender. You still want this truck?"

Gary got up and went around to the front of it. The mangled grille was lying on the ground. He looked inside the engine compartment. The radiator had been pulled out, but what looked like a new one was lying on a piece of cardboard beside the truck.

"Is this all that's wrong with it?"

"Yeah. I done had a new windshield put in it. I got another hood and put on it."

Gary looked. The glass was new and it had a new inspection sticker in the corner. The hood was a pale green.

"How did you get it to the shop?"

"I had to go over to the junk yard where they towed it. They put that hood on for me and put that windshield in. I drove it home but the radiator had a leak in it. I got James Maples to bring me a radiator from town yesterday. I'm fixing to put it in quick as I get through with this fender. Come here and help me hold it down, how about it?"

The boy sat down and gripped the edge of the sheet metal. Joe put his tire iron on it and beat a wrinkle flat.

"It may not look too good but it'll beat not having one on it at all," he said.

"We gonna work any more?" the boy said, in between licks.

Joe didn't pause with his hammering. "Nah. We through. I got to get cleaned up. And go to Bruce. Get my money. Try to find my dog. You want to go?"

"Yessir."

"All right. We got to put this back on. Put that radiator in. I ain't been able to find a grille."

The boy didn't know whether to ask him about being in jail or not. Maybe Joe knew what was on his mind. He stopped hammering and looked up.

"I guess you heard what happened to me."

"Well." The boy looked down at the fender, looked back up, squinting against the sun. "Sort of. I heard you had a wreck."

"That all you heard?"

"Nosir. I heard you got put in jail."

"It wasn't the first time," said Joe. "Probably won't be the last. Did you know I'd been in the penitentiary?"

Gary shook his head slowly. "Nosir," he said.

"Well, I have. I did twenty-nine months for assault on a police officer. The motherfuckers pulled me over behind a shopping center uptown and thought they were gonna whip my ass. I wasn't doing nothing. Waiting on an old gal to get off from work. Now I was drunk, I'll admit that. But I wasn't fucking with them." He looked up and smiled grimly. "But I had put one of em in the hospital about a month before."

The twisted piece of metal in front of him was beginning to resemble a fender again, just a little.

"What I need are some dollies. I used to be a body man a long time ago."

"What's that?"

"Dollies?"

"Body man."

Joe glanced up at him briefly and then back down.

Sometimes it seemed that the boy didn't know a lot of things a boy his age should know. They'd been driving by the Rock Ridge Colored Church one day back in the spring and the boy had asked him who lived in that big white house.

"That's a guy that fixes cars after they're wrecked. You know. Put on new doors. New fenders. Or like this. Straighten the old ones. It's cheaper. Sometimes it don't look as good. You got to know what you're doing. I used to paint a lot but I started having nosebleeds and I had to quit it."

The boy nodded.

"I'll give you a job this winter. We'll start in setting pines about December. We'll work on that till March or April. You can make you plenty of money then. Planting pays more than deadening."

"You mean we're gonna set out trees?"

"Yeah."

"Well, how you do it? You have to dig a hole and everything?"

"Naw, naw, it ain't like that. Here, let's move it up a little this way. Make sure that anvil's under it. All right. Hold it right there. See if we can get this big crease out of it. No, we set em with a dibble. Little old iron bar. It's got a dull blade on it. You just kick it in the ground and it digs a little hole. You just stick your tree in and then close it up, stomp on it. Go on to the next one. Takes about five seconds."

"Five seconds? How big's the trees?"

"Oh, they're just little bitty things. Baby pines. About a foot long. Naw, but what I was telling you about them motherfuckers . . . see a cop can fuck over you if he wants to. Don't get me wrong, there's some good ones. But you live in a place and get on the wrong side of the law like I did. Like I do. They'll look for you. They find out where you hang out, they'll park and wait for you. That's what they did to me that night."

"You mean the other night?"

"What other night?"

"The night you had the wreck. Got put in jail."

Joe looked up at him and pointed to the fender with the hammer.

"You mean this?"

"Yessir."

"Naw, naw." He shook his head. "I'm talking about what I got sent to the pen over. Move it a little more that way. Hold it. Hell, I been out a good while. Stayed in two and half years. They tried to shoot me. After I whipped all three of them they did. Or one did. He went for his gun and I grabbed it. He was fixing to kill me. Told me he was. But all he did was blow his kneecap off. Hold it right there, now."

The boy watched him while he hammered, watched the muscle bunching in his bicep and the pellet hole there and the crooked nose and the dark hair curled in ringlets on the back of his neck. Watched the tanned hands and the scarred knuckles, outsized, knotty with gristle.

"Only way I got out light as I did was my lawyer got him on the witness stand and made him mad." He looked up, looked back down. "I told him they'd been fucking with me. He went and looked it up. They were gonna put me in as a habitual offender. You can get thirty years for that. They'd pulled me over seventeen times in sixty-four days. They'd arrested me once. That was when one of em hit me in the back with his stick and I put him in the hospital. My lawyer went to the police station. He looked at the arrest records. A good lawyer's worth his money. I got old David Carson up at Oxford. He's high but he's good. It took me two years to pay him off after I got out of the pen. But it would have took me a lot longer if I'd still been in."

He laid down the hammer and the tire iron and lit another cigarette.

"Let's see what she looks like now," he said. He raised the fender and turned it over. It resembled something of its original shape. "Hell, that ought to be good enough. Long as the bolts'll go in."

"What you want me to do?"

"Help me hang it back on the fenderwell. I got all the bolts over here in a hubcap. Hold it a minute."

The boy stood holding the fender in place. Joe stooped and picked up the hubcap and set it on the breather.

"Now just hold it until I can get one started," he said. He had a socket and a ratchet in his hand. "You just hold it and I'll put em in. Yeah, old David's a good lawyer. He's been out here and deer-hunted with me. I've got access to some good timberland. I get it about a year before they cut it."

The boy didn't say anything, just stood holding the fender while he started the bolts and ratcheted them down. When he had three in, Joe told him he could turn it loose. He stepped back and looked inside the cab. Mud was caked on the floormats. The seat had a huge rip across the driver's side. There was a rubber-coated gunrack mounted above and behind the seat. The dash was piled high with papers. There was a long brown sack with a bottle in it lying against the hump in the floor. Joe looked around the corner of the hood.

"You want to do something for me?"

"Yessir."

"Reach in there and get me one of them beers out of that cooler in the back. Damn if I ain't done got hot."

He went to the back and raised the camper door. It fell twice before he got it to stay up. There was a big yellow Covey cooler with a red top in the back. He pried the lid open and looked inside. There were eight or ten bottles of beer covered with ice and water. He got one and looked at it.

"This here?" he said, holding it out.

"Yeah," Joe said, without looking up. The boy walked back and handed it to him. He put the ratchet down and twisted the top off the beer and tossed the cap out in the yard. He turned the beer up and took a good third of it down, then looked at his watch.

Nearly eleven o'clock. Damned if he wasn't starting earlier every day. He set it down on the fan shroud and balanced it precariously there and picked up another bolt.

"You like beer?" the boy said.

"Yeah. Do you?"

"I ain't never had one."

Joe looked around at him and grinned. "Ain't never had one? How old did you say you were?"

"I think I'm fifteen. That's why I ain't never got a Social Security card. I ain't got no birth certificate."

"I thought everybody had a birth certificate."

"I ain't. My mama said the place I was born you couldn't get one."

"Why hell, I wouldn't worry about it, then. You won't even have to file income tax. Long as you don't hold a public job. You won't even have to register for the draft. You ever been to school?"

"Nosir."

They stood looking at each other across the ten feet that separated them.

"You can't read."

"Nosir."

He picked up the beer again and drank some of it. "There's worse things, I guess. How do you sign your name?"

"I ain't never had to."

He bent under the hood of the truck again. He couldn't understand how the boy could have come this far without knowing what a church was.

"Can I buy one of those beers from you?"

He leaned around again and looked at him.

"What?"

"I'm kinda thirsty. I was headed up to the store to get me something to drink. Can I buy one of them from you?"

Fifteen. Maybe. And never had a place to call his own, don't know where he was born. He'd go up to the house one day and get him. See what kind of shape they were in up there.

"I tell you what, son. You can drink one of them beers if you want it. I don't reckon your daddy would care, would he?"

"I don't reckon."

"But you can't buy one from me. Friends don't buy things from one another."

"Yessir."

"And don't say sir so much to me."

"Yessir."

Joe bent under the hood again.

"You still want to give me two hundred dollars for this truck?"

An hour later he had it running with the radiator full of water. He had changed his clothes and had most of the black grease washed off his hands. The boy had finished his third beer and was sitting in the yard.

"Come on and get in," Joe told him. "I need to go by the store and get some gas."

The boy climbed in the other side. He wasn't saying much. He'd already noted how good those cold beers were. He understood now what the old man was after on all those nights and weekends and weeks sometimes, what he went for and what he wanted to feel. Nothing mattered now, he knew it the first time he met it. He was with the bossman, who was going to take care of him, and he probably wouldn't even have to worry about walking back home. He was going to get the truck, some way, some day, and then he'd learn how to drive it.

Later he remembered stopping by the store and getting ice and gas, the long ride to Bruce and the long wait in the hot sunshiny cab of the truck at the Weyerhauser plant, the big chain-link fence and the piles of logs as far as the eye could see, the water spraying over the stacked lengths of them. Joe stayed inside nearly forever, it seemed, and he got sleepy in the truck. They ate somewhere, thick hamburgers and fries in little white cardboard containers. A roadside stand had T-shirts and the bossman bought him one, AC/DC, although neither of them knew their music; the shirt was for a boy who needed one because he didn't have one on and might need one wherever they wound up. Two kindred souls, one who sat on the tailgate drinking another beer while the other one kicked the bushes and stomped the clumps of grass beside the freshly skinned tree, whooping and hollering and looking all around. Many houses, many yards, one where Joe struck up a conversation with a pretty young housewife, making her laugh easily, admiring her with his eyes, her knowing it. No, but she hadn't seen the dog. And now she had his number if she needed to call him. There was an old man in a rocking chair in another one. Joe pulled up right beside the porch, where the old man had a cane planted firmly between his shoes, hand-rolling his cigarettes, the little bag and paper pinched up tight against his chest, nodding or shaking his head; the bossman was genial and deferential to advanced age, good natured, easy, but each time, he pulled away from a house, saying *Goddamn, I won't never find him.* Down dirt roads they drove, past houses off dirt roads, little yards enclosed by high woods and brush, enclaves carved out of the wilderness where deer came at night and sniffed at the children's toys. Once he thought he slept. They were miles removed from where they had been, Joe having given up on asking folks and just riding the roads in a dry county and drinking whiskey, trying to find his dog, telling Gary over and over what a good dog he was. *He wouldn't have done anything to you, maybe just nipped you a little.* Sometimes they met cruisers with uniformed deputies or even the real bad boys, the highway patrol, military, hardass, looking for people like them. *Don't never wave to them. They know you guilty of something when you wave.* Days and nights in the ring at Fort Jackson when Joe held the middleweight title for sixteen months and defended it successfully nine times—Gary heard about that. Women and divorce and rolling the bones, jail and a grandbaby coming, he'd raised that dog from a puppy, had been the only friend he'd had in a while. Everybody thought he'd gone crazy but he hadn't gone crazy. *They tell ever kind of lie on me it is. The bastards would hang murder on me if they could get away with it. You listen to what I'm telling you. A poor man ain't got a chance against the law. How can some rich son of a bitch do something and get off? And a poor man go to the pen? It's money. The rich ones know the judge and play golf and shit with him. Hell, go out to the country club and have a few drinks. Weighs about a hundred pounds. He's got long ears but a docked tail. Well yessir I meant to get around to doing that but I sorta did a halfway job on him.*

Oh, he's a unique looking dog, I promise you that. But if you happen to see him. It don't matter what time you call. Day or night. Yes sir. Thank you, sir. A deep green creek stirring beneath a steel and concrete bridge, the bossman wearing shades and holding his dick in one hand and a whiskey bottle in the other, grinning and saluting him where he stood pissing in the road. Having to jump in and zip up his pants quickly because somebody was coming. *You ain't drunk, are you? I used to know an old gal who lived around here. Now, son, you talk about some good stuff. I wonder where that damn dog is. He's got to be around here somewhere. Some where.* Stopping at a store for cigarettes, his head lolling out the window, pigskins to sober up on that were of the hot variety and made him drink more. He didn't have to be home at any particular time, he was sure. *Just drive yonder way*, the boy kept saying. *Just drive yonder way.* He got it in his head that somebody had stolen the dog, or that the police might be holding him against his will. And there he was finally, standing not fifty yards from the tree Joe had hit, then loping, staying out of the road, where the cars whizzed by at sixty, even when they saw a man trying to get his dog by the side of the road. *You got more sense than I thought you had. Get back there. Lay down and behave. We going home right now.* The sun growing gentler and the evening light changing, going softer, touching the horizon beyond the road faintly blue, the clouds rolled up high in white masses steadily changing shapes. Once again roads that he knew or had been on if even briefly. Here the bridge where the man he had to hit with the rock. *You point the motherfucker out to me. I'll settle his goddamn hash.* The same fat cows, the same lush grass. A doe deer feeding among them now, little wild cousin with lespedeza hanging from her working mouth, the heartprint hooves. Both of them drunk now, a roady buzz that would linger for a while. Lights beginning to come on in London Hill, the storefront lit, a flashing glimpse of the old man standing under the naked bulb where it hung from a cord in the soot-stained ceiling. *I'll drop you off if you're ready to go.* They stopped and let the dog out. Joe held him and made Gary pet him and the dog accepted it and licked his hand. The broad tongue raspy, pink, wide. The creased forehead with its knots of tooth-marked scars. *Yeah, but all them dogs is dead. You better sober up a little before you go home. Oh? You ain't ready to go home? Well, I could find some place else for us to go, yeah.* Late evening coming, little flocks of nine and ten doves sailing over the light wires or perched on the same with their feathers ruffled and squatting in deep composure. Meeting people with parking lights on, the air suffused with the smell of things living, the trees green and standing with their grapevines twisted about them and their roots knurled deep in the good earth. A warm late spring or early summer evening with the branches beginning to merge together, for things in the distance to grow less plain, finally until night fell and all the lights had to be turned on and the day was another event.

The old man was shaking where he lay next to the house, nearly fetal with his clenched hands pillowing his head. The blacks inside had run him out again and now he didn't know what hour it was or day it had been or even where he lay. He would doze a little as sleep tried to close in on him, but always the fear he had of them kept his eyes opening and blinking him not to go to sleep, not here, where he feared they might cut his throat and lift the few bills he had and put him in the river for the turtles to feast on.

The underside of the house close to where he rested was strewn with broken beer bottles, odd lengths of pipe, here and there money fallen through cracks in the floor. A few feet away lay a dead cat, its bones showing through the rotten hide like yellow tusks. The old man heard feet walking on the wood above. A questioning voice raised a question. An answering voice answered it. An exclamation. Once in a while an angry word. And once in a while the electric strokes of a guitarist choking down a neck with fingers greased by skill, and there were no voices then.

He determined he would make it back inside and see what was

happening. If maybe there was anything to eat. He could see a dark cow in the dark pasture looking at him under the house and swinging her tail. He rolled himself over onto his belly and crawled out from under his hiding place. He had to beat the dirt off his clothes. It bounced out in large brown puffs. He thought there was a piece of a drink left somewhere.

He stumbled around in the back yard, which was littered with spare tires, grass grown up through the lug-bolt holes, with rotted wooden barrels sawn in half that had once held flowers. The back porch was of rough sawmill lumber and it leaned to the left. Screened in with rusty wire, patched with cotton thread. He lurched toward it feebly in the night. The cow raised her head and shook her horns, a gesture not lost on him. He'd already noted that the dogs didn't like him worth a damn.

There was his glass, left where he'd put it on the bottom step. He knelt and drank from it.

T he lights were on low and now there were no unfriendly growls to make a man nervous. They had a movie going on the TV and VCR but the sound was low, too. It was warm and cozy and the girls were showing plenty of leg. Joe had the one named Debi in the corner, talking to her. Gary was alone in another chair in the corner, eyes shifting, drinking a tenth beer. It was four a.m.

Joe leaned over and poured another little shot of whiskey into her glass. "How late y'all stay open?" he said, then leaned over and kissed her again. She was a little chubby but marvelously assembled, no dog you couldn't take home to Mama. Her hair was blond on one side and brown on the other, just the reverse between her legs.

"Never past daylight. When me and you going back?"

"Hell, I can't do you no good."

"Since when?"

"Hell, I'm about too old to fuck. I wouldn't never get my money's worth."

"I'll give you your money's worth, baby."

She leaned around him and looked across the room. "How's your friend doing?"

"I think he's sobered up now. Goddamn, we been a long way today. He helped me find my dog."

She looked at him with a half smile.

"I'm surprised you even over here. You seen Duncan?"

"Naw, I ain't seen him. Why, he lookin for me?"

"I don't figure he is," she said.

He looked at the boy and saw him pretending to watch the movie, but saw each time he lifted the bottle to his lips the quick darting movement of his eyes toward the girls giggling and whispering on the couch. Three of them in their underwear, two fat, one skinny. Joe leaned toward the one he had his arm around.

"How'd you like to do me a favor?"

She smiled and gave him a kiss. "Sure."

He pointed with his drink.

"Break that boy in there."

She looked at the boy and then looked back at Joe. There was an amused little grin on her lips.

"Him?"

"Hell, he ain't never had none."

"How you know?"

Joe shook the ice in his glass and drank off the half inch of liquid that was there and sat up. He ran his fingers through his hair.

"Shit. I need to get my ass up and go on home. What time is it?"

"Little after four."

"A little after four."

"Yeah."

He set his glass on a table and leaned back on the couch. "Y'all got time to make it before daylight. Hell, it won't take him but a minute."

"How you know how long it'll take him?"

"Cause. I remember when I was fifteen. Go on and take him back."

She looked at the boy and shook her head doubtfully.

"I don't know," she said. "He looks mighty young. You sure he's fifteen?"

He reached in his pocket for a wad of money and peeled off a fifty and handed it to her. "Here," he said. "I need to get him home before daylight."

She looked at the money for a second, looked at the boy, then put the money in a little purse that was hanging on her wrist.

"Well, hell," she said. "What's his name again?"

"Gary."

She seemed to resign herself to it. "Gary. All right."

She got up and smoothed her chemise and her stockings and put her cigarette out. Joe saw the boy watching her. His face kept lifting as she got closer until finally she was standing over him and he was looking up at her. She put one hand on her hip and said something to him. He nodded and said something back. She sat on the arm of his chair and crossed her legs. Joe smiled to see that the boy couldn't take his eyes off her. She talked to him for a while and the boy kept nodding. She reached out and took his hand and pulled him up out of the chair. She started leading him out of the room, and he looked back at the bossman, his face terror-stricken, mute yet pleading, maybe for some words of instruction, explanation, until she pulled him out of sight.

He went down the hall with her tugging on his hand and followed her into a room with a parachute tacked to the ceiling. There was a lamp in the room and a bed and a chair and a bowl of water on the floor. The covers on the bed were rumpled, the pillows lumped together. She pushed him down on the bed and he sat there looking at her with wild eyes.

"You ain't never done this before, have you?" she said.

"Done what?"

She bent over him and he looked into the deep cleavage she had.

"This." Her mouth came down on his and then quickly pulled away. "Damn."

"What's the matter?" he said.

"Your breath is awful. Do you not ever brush your teeth?"

"Naw."

"Well, you need to."

He just looked at her. She opened a door at the back of the room and light spilled out over him. He rose up a little. He could see a mirror and a sink, and towels hanging from rings on the wall. She stepped into the room and started running the water, looking through drawers.

"Come in here," she said.

He got up and set his beer down and staggered into the bathroom. She held up a blue implement that was foreign to him, made of plastic and with white bristles. From a tube she squeezed a white paste onto it.

"Here," she said, and held it out to him. "Do me a favor and brush your teeth. I got some mouthwash, too. I ain't gonna fuck you if I can't even kiss you."

"What am I supposed to do with it?"

"You supposed to brush your teeth with it."

"Well, how you do it?"

She glared at him. "Shit, do you not know nothin? Here."

She showed him. He stood beside the sink with her, marveling at the foam that built over her lips. She turned the tap on and bent her head under the faucet and finally spat clear water into the sink and turned it off.

"Now here. I ain't got no germs, I don't reckon. I thought everybody knew how to brush their teeth. Where you been all your life?"

"Just around," he said.

"I'll be in here when you get through. Hurry it up."

She left him in the bathroom and shut the door behind her. He stood looking at himself in the mirror, holding the toothbrush in front of his mouth, puzzling over it. He put it in his mouth and touched his teeth with it. He turned the water on as she had done.

"Hurry up," she called, a muffled voice from beyond the door.

It felt strange and hard in his mouth. But he started brushing and it made his teeth feel good. So good that he kept on and on until she snatched the door open and stood there naked behind him. He turned with foam on his mouth, the handle of the tooth-brush hanging slack.

"Well goddamn, are you coming on or what?" she said.

"I'm just brushin my teeth."

"Well, you done brushed em long enough. Come on and get it if you going to get it." She flounced her fine ass away and got on the bed, waiting for him.

He rinsed his mouth and turned off the water and put the toothbrush down. Looked at himself in the mirror and turned the water back on. He was still a little drunk and he wetted most of his face, rinsing his mouth out some more. When he had finished he shut off the water and looked at himself in the mirror again. In the mirror she lay behind him small on the bed, the dim lights showing her legs and stomach. Her red fingernails lay alongside her thigh. He cut off the light in the bathroom and went to her.

"Hey."

"Hey."

"I got em brushed."

"Well good. Now come on. Kiss me."

"Like that?"

"Naw. Open your mouth a little. Shit. Don't push so hard."

"I like that."

"Lay down with me. Just relax. You're nervous. Why don't you take your clothes off?"

"What for?"

She raised her head three inches off the pillow and stared at him. "What the hell you think I got mine off for?"

"Well, I didn't know."

She got up and threw the chemise over herself and found her cigarettes and lighter and lit one. Her face leaning to him in the lamplight was so young, so childlike and so smooth and so unwrinkled. She had a few freckles.

He reached over and got his beer and drank from it. He knew he was supposed to do something but he didn't know what it was. And what he was looking at between her legs was to him a strange and hairy puzzle.

She walked around the room for a while, smoking her cigarette, her arms folded.

"Take your clothes off," she said.

"We got to go in a little bit," he said.

"Shit." She went to the door and stuck her head out. "Joe!"

Gary lay on the bed and looked at her. She talked for a while with her head stuck out in the hall and then Joe leaned his head in.

"Boy, you all right?"

He waved his beer.

"I'm doin fine."

"Well, you better hurry up, now. We got to get you on home before long."

He heard her say something about giving him his fifty dollars back. There was some more arguing. After a while she shut the door and came back and sat down on the bed beside him.

"Listen," she said. "Do you want to do it or not?"

"Do what?" he said.

"Hell, boy, fuck. What do you think?"

He didn't know what to think. He had heard the word, from his daddy and Joe and the hands. Things were beginning to dawn on him.

"Shit," she said, and crawled down off the bed. "Take your pants off."

At first he thought she was going to hurt him and fought against her. He didn't want any teeth down there. But he understood soon and, like Joe said, he didn't last long.

When the light was turned on and Joe stuck his head back in, he was still lying back across the bed with his pants around his ankles. Debi was gone, had sought herself a darker nook.

"Boy, you all right?"

"Yessir, believe I am."

The boy walked up in the dust of the road and saw his mother standing in the yard, looking at him. The sun was high and she had a stick in her hand. He put his hands in his pockets and felt of the money there. He turned around and headed back the other way.

"You come here," she called after him.

"I'll be back in a minute."

"You come back here."

"In a minute."

"Now."

He didn't answer but walked around the curve of the trail out of sight of the house. Bees were buzzing in the patches of clover between some of the trees, and he looked back to see if anybody was following him. He looked to his pocket and brought the money out all wadded in his hand and started counting it as he walked. Money to him was something that was hard to make and hard to hold onto once it was made. But he enjoyed making it and he enjoyed saving it, and he began to look around for a good place to hide some more of it now that the work was over. The truck money was already hidden, but he never walked near it, would only walk there once more.

In front of the house the pines thinned away to scrub oak and bushes and sandy soil with scattered rocks. He looked back again and stepped off the trail, sighting on a big den tree where he'd seen coons leave in the evenings and return in the mornings, regular as bankers checking in and out of their offices. The woods were hot and dry and the leaves were noisy underfoot. He slowed down and stepped more carefully, as if he were stalking something. He had his first hangover and his head was not feeling good.

There was a creekbed that was nearly dry in the bottom of the hollow and he stepped across that and looked up at the coon den. A young one regarded him from his hole high in the tree, just his head poked out, then withdrew his face and was seen no more. The boy stood beside the tree, scanning the woods around him. He was tired from his night but he thought of the girl constantly, every second, never stopping. He had begun to feel a feeling for her that he could not describe even to himself.

When he had stood there for a minute or so, his eye picked out a small gray rock on a little hillside where pines had fallen long years ago and nature had weathered them down to their hard skeletal hearts. The rock lay among these lengths of prime kindling, and he walked over and knelt down beside it, looking back once to line up the den tree with his position. There was an old pay envelope in his pocket, and he pulled it out and put all the money in it except for one twenty-dollar bill. On both knees he scanned the woods around him, his eyes moving slowly, searching, noting particular trees and the clumps of honeysuckle and the matted nests of briers and the downed timber, listening for any sound there might be, but hearing nothing. When he had satisfied himself that he was alone, he carefully rolled the rock over and put the money beneath it and replaced it exactly as it had been for who knew how many years. There was a sudden feeling of eyes on him and he jerked his head up, both hands on the rock, but there was nothing, only the silent woods and the birds flitting through the tree limbs, the brief rattle of an Indian hen on a dead and acoustic trunk. His heart grieved with worry over the money, but the quiet woods lulled him with trust. He got up and moved away from the rock, careful not to disturb the leaves, and sighted back on it once more when he got to the den tree.

The rock sat in a bright patch of sunshine, streaked with pale veins and bearing small growths of velvety green moss. The sound of his steps receded through the woods and diminished, faded, was gone. The wind blew gently and the shadows wavered over the ground. The fallen pines lay around the rock, the woods warm, airy with light, flushed with sunshine.

After a time another noise appeared, a hushed step, a careful approach. The noise grew louder, a slow crunching of leaves underfoot, stealthy, heard only by one. A foot stopped beside the rock, an overall-clad knee came down to rest. A gnarled and shaking hand spread out over the rough warm face of the rock, trying to hold its secret there deep in the snakey woods.

The new pickup sat idling at the curb in front of the liquor store, and he came out of the door with three fifths of whiskey in his arms and got in it. He liked the way the new truck smelled. It had a V-8 with an automatic and the salesman had talked him into getting one with air conditioning. He was glad of it now. He rolled the window up and turned the air on. He had owned it for about an hour.

There was a new cooler in the floorboard with a case of Pabst iced down in it, and he shoved the top aside and got one out and put the top back on. The gas gauge was sitting close to empty but he figured he could make it to London Hill.

He met a sheriff's deputy not a mile out of town and looked in the rearview mirror to see if the deputy would hit his brakes. He did, briefly.

"Fuck you, sumbitch," he said, and turned his beer up. The truck had a good radio and he found a country music station and turned the volume up. George Jones was singing "He Stopped Loving Her Today." He sang along with George, at peace with the world. After another mile or two the black car appeared far down the road behind him, trailing him slowly.

"You motherfucker," he said. He watched it for a while and saw that it was slowly gaining. The blue lights were not flashing. He sped up a little, eyeing the gas gauge, muttering under his breath. He went into a curve, and once he got out of sight of the deputy's car and crested the hill, he drove onto another blacktop road that intersected Old Six, Camp Lake Stephens Road, pulling the wheel hard to the right and sliding the whiskey bottles across the seat. He mashed hard on the gas and drove to a small driveway about a hundred yards down the road and turned around. He sat there for thirty seconds and then roared back down the blacktop road. He pulled up to the highway and turned to the right again, then pulled out and took another drink of his beer.

He caught sight of the cruiser again within three more miles. The car in front of him slowed and he eased up behind it. He could see the deputy looking back at him through the rearview mirror. Joe waved to him but he wouldn't wave back.

He followed him down the road for another mile and the cruiser sped up and pulled off. It went out of sight up the highway around a curve. When he went past Manley Franklin's old store four miles later, it was pulled up on the other side of the building, facing the road, and it sped out after him, the blue lights flashing.

"I figured that shit," he said. He put on his blinker and pulled over on the shoulder and waited while the car eased up behind him. He dropped the empty beer bottle in the floor and lit a ciga-rette. The deputy took his time getting out. Joe rolled the window down and sat there.

The deputy walked up beside him, and he was a new man Joe didn't know, a stranger behind shiny sunglasses.

"Nice truck," the deputy said.

"Thanks."

"Noticed you ain't got a tag on it. You just get it?"

"About five minutes ago. I do something wrong?"

"Not that I know of."

"What'd you pull me over for then?"

The deputy rubbed his chin. He rested the knuckles of one hand on the butt of his gun. The leather holster creaked like a new saddle.

"How much have you drank?"

"I ain't drank nothing but one beer. I got three bottles of whiskey right here if you'd like to examine them."

"They told me you were a smartass."

"Who told you?"

"You think that was funny a while ago, trying to outrun me?"

"I wasn't trying to outrun you. I got off the highway and took a piss. Ain't no law against that, is it?"

He was a young man, with thin arms. The widest part of him was the belt and the gun around his waist. Joe pulled the gearshift down into drive and stepped on the brake.

"If you're through shootin the shit I'm ready to leave."

"I ain't through talking to you."

"I think you are."

He pulled off and left him standing there, reached in the cooler and got another beer. He watched through the rearview mirror as the deputy got back in his car and killed the blue lights. The car had not moved from beside the road by the time he lost it from view, and he didn't think about it or look back any more. Randy Travis was singing a song of love and heartbreak on the radio, and he was much more interested in that.

He pulled in at John's store and got out, took the gas cap off and locked the premium nozzle open so that it flowed slowly into the tank. He carried one of the fifths inside the store.

"Hey, John," he called.

He turned at a noise beside the door and the storekeeper was standing out there with his hand on the screen, looking at the pickup. He stepped inside, shaking his head.

"How about loaning me about ten thousand this afternoon?" he said.

Joe set the whiskey on the counter and pulled a wad of bills from his pocket, thumbing through them for a twenty. He pulled one out and put it beside the whiskey.

"I think I got a good deal on that one, John."

"It's pretty."

"Thanks."

"I like that color."

"I looked at a red one I started to get but I liked that one better. Come on and get in and we'll go for a ride."

He was just kidding, but the old man looked at his watch and said: "By God, I don't guess there's no reason I can't."

"Well hell, good, come on. Wait a minute."

He went out the door and released the lock on the nozzle and finished filling the tank, twenty dollars even. When he stepped back inside, the old man had put his money inside a bank bag and was holding his pistol and a couple of cigars taken from a box on the counter, and was standing there with another cigar in his mouth and the whiskey in his pocket.

"Twenty even, John."

The storekeeper nodded and said, "Let's hurry up and get out of here before somebody comes by."

"You taking that pistol with you?"

"Hell yes. I got about sixty thousand dollars in here."

"Damn. You got another gun I can borrow?"

"This one'll do."

Joe held the screen door open for him, then opened the door of the truck so he could pile his things on the seat. John Coleman walked back to the store on nimble feet, wearing socks and sandals. He locked the door and slammed it shut and started out to the truck but went back and unlocked it and reached in and cut off the power to the gas pumps and then locked it again. A car came down the road, slowing down hurriedly, swinging in.

"It never fails," he said, from where he stood beside the truck just about to climb in. He lifted the lid on the cooler and looked inside. "Lord have mercy, boy," he said. He looked up at Joe. "Let's go. Quick."

They got in and Joe pulled the shift down into drive.

"You don't want to wait on this guy?"

"Hell naw, don't wait on him."

But the driver of the car had already gotten out and was walking over to the truck. He had long black hair, a dirty T-shirt, and very greasy hands. He wiped his nose and leaned in the window of the truck. Joe noticed how close his hands were getting to the upholstery of his nice new nice-smelling truck.

"Mr. Coleman? How bout opening up for me?" he said. He shook his head and looked around inside the truck.

"I'm going somewhere," John said. "I'll be back after while."

"You ready, John?" Joe said.

"Yeah," John said. "I'm ready."

"I need to get a few things, Mr. Coleman," the man said, but Joe let off the brake and the truck moved. The man grabbed the outside mirror, printed the chrome with grease, and said, "Now wait a minute."

Joe put the brake on and shoved the shift into park.

"Let's go, Joe," the old man said. "Hell, he don't want to do nothing but charge something." He bent over and reached inside the cooler for a beer, and Joe saw something cross the black-haired man's face at the sight of the back of John Coleman's head.

"You better get them greasy goddamn fingers off my truck, boy," Joe said.

He acted as if he didn't even hear that, just kept holding onto the mirror and looking at John.

"All I want's five dollars worth of gas, Mr. Coleman. My wife told me she'd get paid next week, I promise you."

John Coleman leaned back in the seat and twisted off the top and turned the bottle of beer straight up in the middle of London Hill and took a good hit. He opened a bottle of the whiskey on the seat and did it the same way, then wiped his mouth. He didn't look at the man outside the truck when he spoke.

"You done promised me about twenty times. You ain't paid me nothing in three months and you just wasting your breath. Let's go, Joe."

The greasy hands went to the inside of the door as if to hold them from leaving, and Joe opened his door and walked around the back and right up to him.

"You get them hands off my truck."

The guy turned to him, looked him up and down.

"Fuck you," he said. "Who in the fuck are you?"

Joe didn't hit him but one time. The pickup wheels spun sand and gravel on him where he lay in front of the pumps.

They rode and drank. Joe sucked a cut knuckle and wished for his dog to lick it. John Coleman agreed that it would help.

"That boy," he said. "I've done him ever favor I could. Some folks you can't do nothing with. Just sorry. God knows I've done plenty of drinking and stuff in my time, but I be damn if I ever tried to cheat anybody out of any money."

It was late afternoon by then and they had the windows rolled down, the music turned down so they could talk. It surprised Joe that John Coleman would hear a song he recognized and, once in a while, turn the radio up, then turn it back down when the song was over. There were horses in pastures and hawks with their wings folded sitting high in the trees. One redtail hunted low over an overgrown field they passed, the land fallow, thick with cockle-burs. It floated along, turning, rising, passing again, wings flapping for a thermal.

"I'm glad they protected them hawks," John said.

"I sure like to watch em."

The sun waned and drew down between the clouds and put the land in a soft light, cooled the air. The hair riffled on their forearms where they held their elbows on the doors. They saw dead snakes here and there. Flattened rabbits and marsupials, awkward buzzards lifting from carcasses on long and laboring wings.

"You ever hear that thing about a possum having a forked dick?" said Joe.

"A possum breeds through his nose."

"I've heard if you put a split in one's tail and stick a stick through it and put him in the river, he'll just go around in circles till he sinks."

They stopped on the Lynch Creek bridge to take a leak and stood there drinking their beers while they pissed. John Coleman had a dick like a horse.

"Are y'all through working, Joe?"

"Yessir. We're finished for this year, I reckon. I could have made a lot more money if it hadn't rained so much."

They got back in and the black car was there suddenly, lights revolving, the door opening almost before it came to a stop.

"Well, I will be goddamn," Joe said. He'd started to pull off but he slammed on the brake and put the gearshift up in park and got out. He walked to the back of the truck. The deputy was mad, his chest heaving. He strangled something out and Joe said, "What?"

He looked back at John through the rear glass. All he saw was the back of his head.

"You been riding around drinking ever since I saw you?" the deputy said.

He saw then what was going on, loss of pride, the simple stupidity of youth, the weight of the badge. But he still wouldn't let anybody mess with him, he didn't care who. And he was drinking.

The deputy held out a little contraption made of plastic and metal. "You want to breathe in this?"

"Naw, I don't want to breathe in that."

He turned around and got back in his truck and asked John Coleman if he was ready for another beer. The deputy walked up beside the truck and held out the little thing. He had one hand on his gun.

"Are you gonna breathe in this or not?"

Joe didn't answer him. He pulled it into gear and mashed on the gas, being careful not to sling any gravel. The deputy stood in the road behind him growing smaller.

"I bet I pissed him off that time," he said.

John didn't answer. He was tracking the cruiser behind them in the fingerprinted mirror. The siren came on. Joe kept driving. They met several cars that nearly pulled over to the shoulders of the road but then went on past, the necks of the drivers craning to see. The car swung out behind him and came alongside. The deputy was motioning toward the ditch with his finger. He kept driving.

"What's the deal?" John said.

The car sped up and turned crossways in the road ahead of him, and Joe came to a stop this side of it. There wasn't any place to turn around. He put it up in reverse and hit the gas when he saw the deputy come out with his hand on his gun. He leaned out the window looking backwards and got it up to about forty, the rear end's high-speeded whining reminding him he'd never make it.

John Coleman sat sipping his whiskey and his beer. After a little bit he said, "I think he's gonna catch us."

Joe slammed on the brakes and the cruiser shot past, slewed sideways in the road with the tires barking. He started to take off again, keep him going like a runner between bases for a while, then said no.

He got out. He put his hands on the hood. The deputy walked up.

"I ain't done a goddamn thing," Joe said. "I ain't drunk. You better look for somebody else to mess with cause I ain't done nothing. You keep messing around with me and I'm gonna hurt you."

"Turn around," the deputy said. "Put your hands behind your back."

"You been watching too many goddamn TV shows, son."

The deputy came close with the cuffs in his hand.

Joe caught him by the neck and pushed him against the hood of the truck and got the pistol away from him without a shot being fired. All the while the boy's eyes watched him with a deep and maddened rage. Joe tossed the gun underhanded, lightly, saw it land in a clump of sagegrass on the other side of the ditch.

"I guess if I drive off now you're gonna get a shotgun out of the back and shoot my ass, ain't you?" he told him.

The deputy wouldn't say. They drove off and left him and he didn't follow them any more. Joe could see him in the rearview mirror, looking for the gun.

*

Later that night an unmarked Ford, a new dark blue one, was sitting beside his driveway, idling, when he pulled up. The sheriff himself. He stopped in the road for a moment and looked at the car and all it represented. Then he turned and pulled into his yard and killed the motor and got out and put the keys in his pocket. He was only a little drunk.

The sheriff had the window down and he was listening to country music on the radio. He turned the volume down and shook his head when Joe walked up beside his car.

"Get out and come on in, Earl," he said.

The sheriff picked up the microphone and spoke into it for a few moments and then he shut the car off. He opened the door and got out.

"You still got that badass dog?"

"Yeah, he's around here somewhere. Hold on a minute."

He walked across the yard and the dog came out from under the house. He caught him by the collar and pulled him over to the corner of the foundation and hooked him to a chain. Then they went in.

"I'd offer you a drink if I thought you'd take one," Joe said.

"I'll drink a Coke if you've got one."

"I've got one." He took it out of the icebox and handed it to him. "Have a seat. I'm gonna fix me a drink."

The sheriff settled himself on the couch and crossed his legs.

"How's your kids doing, Joe?"

"They all right, I guess."

"I heard you had a new grandbaby."

"Yeah. A boy. They didn't name him after me."

He finished mixing his drink and took it over to the table and pulled out a chair and sat down, lit a cigarette.

"All your kids about grown now, too, ain't they?"

"Yeah. One in college. The other one starts this fall. I reckon Johnny's thinking about getting married. I wish he'd wait. Get his degree."

"What's he going into, law enforcement?"

"Yeah."

"You got a new man working for you now, don't you?"

"Yeah I do," the sheriff said, and shook his head. He took a sip of his drink and waited a little, scratched the back of his hand. "I talked to the judge about you for a while the other day. He came to see me."

Joe picked up his drink and sloshed the ice around in the glass and took a good drink of it. "That fat sumbitch. What'd he 'low?"

"Well, I'll tell you. He 'lowed he was about tired of looking at you standing in front of him."

"Probation?"

"Aw naw. Hell naw. I had a little talk with my new man a while ago, too. I'm gonna let him shuffle some papers for a while. He was pretty hot. I asked him a few questions and pretty much figured everything out. He's a little gung ho, is all. A little overeager."

"Yeah, a little," Joe said.

"But he ain't what I'm worried about. Me and you been knowing each other a long time. I know how you are. He don't. He just made a mistake."

"He was just out looking for somebody to fuck with." The

sheriff looked at him for a few long slow seconds, and reached for cigarettes that were no longer in his pocket.

"Let me just ask you a question, Joe. Do you really want to go back to the goddamn penitentiary?"

He thought about it, shook his head. But he didn't answer.

"You can't go in people's houses and kill their dogs. It don't matter what else is going on. You can't fistfight with the Highway Patrol. Judge Foster won't put up with it. He don't have to put up with it. It's why they build prisons. He's wanting to give you three years with no parole for assault on a police officer. And I don't know if I can talk him out of it. He was mad as hell. And maybe I don't even need to talk him out of it."

The silence ticked by. They looked at each other in the little room and neither spoke for a while. The sheriff got off the couch and walked to the table and shook a cigarette out of the pack lying there and lit it.

"Now you done got me back smoking," he said. "Damn it. I been quit three weeks."

"I quit trying to quit. They's two cartons on top of the icebox if you want a pack."

The sheriff muttered something and walked over there and got a pack.

"There's some matches in the drawer."

The sheriff opened the drawer and got a box of them.

He pulled out a chair and sat down at the table beside him. Joe thought he looked old and tired. His hair was thinning, turning gray.

"How long you figure you and Willie Russell can keep shooting at one another before one of you winds up dead?"

Joe chuckled and picked up his drink.

"That bastard," he said. "Somebody ought to do the world a favor."

"I'm trying to do you one. You were thirty-five when you went to the pen the first time. What are you now, forty-two?"

"Forty-three. Fixing to be forty-four."

"You getting old, Joe. I ain't never mistreated you, have I? Tell the truth."

"Naw, you ain't, Earl. You've stuck up for me when you could."

"I used to be as wild as you."

"At one time you were worse."

"I can't tell you how to live. I ain't trying to. Charlotte never could do anything with you, it ain't no use in me trying. I've talked to her, too."

"I don't need you talking to her for me."

"She called me. I'm the sheriff. I had to go see her. She pays taxes in this county just like everybody else. She's got a right to talk to me. It ain't never too late till you're dead."

He didn't move, just looked at the cigarette smoking between his fingers, the brown nicotine stains.

"I been around for a while. I ain't dead yet."

The sheriff got up and clapped him softly on the shoulder, a reassuring pat between former friends.

"I'll see you, Joe. I hope you'll think about what I said."

Joe sat there while the lawman went out, while he went down the steps and started across the yard.

"Come back any time," he called out through the screen door, but the only answer was the car cranking and a brief squeal from a rear tire, the sound of the car rocketing down the road until it faded from hearing. The dog whined and he went out and unsnapped him from the chain.

There was no traffic on the road. The night lay hot and humid around him, and he considered going to town. Connie was gone, her clothes taken, only a broken comb left behind with a scribbled note he didn't bother to read. It was easier without her. He didn't have to listen to anything. But she'd made the bed feel better.

He went inside and changed his shirt and left again. The truck had plenty of gas left in it but he didn't want to go to town.

He backed out into the road and headed west, toward Paris and the Crocker Woods and the Big W, where there were dirt roads and big deer green-eyed in the night and no lawmen patrolling the old blacktopped roads. He got a beer from the cooler and opened it and rolled the window down and stuck his arm out. There was good music on the radio. The dark trees enveloped the road in a canopy of lush growth, and the headlights cut a bright swath through the night, exposing wandering possums, frozen rabbits, huge brown owls swooping low across the ditches.

He drove down from the hills and leveled out in the bottom where the young crops stood dark in their ordered rows and the smells of the night came fresh and welcome on the warm air.

He thought of the time the three blacks had hemmed him up and how someone had let them do it because his attitude was not good. Two of them were in for murder, but that didn't scare him and he didn't particularly respect that. Killings were different in that some were matters of honor and others simple acts of meanness committed during robberies against helpless victims and he didn't respect that. They came at him all at once and he broke one of the men's head against the side of a bunk and left the other two bleeding on the floor and kicked them a little as he talked to them and explained things and then fell on in line with the others in time for supper. That was the last time anybody messed with him. He'd done the rest of his time without incident.

It would be different now. He probably wouldn't know anybody in there, didn't want to know anybody in there. He hadn't made friends in there. He'd kept to himself and neither loaned nor borrowed. He didn't box. He read, slept, worked out with weights. He looked down now at the round ball of his stomach stretching the bottom of his shirt tight. But he couldn't argue with the man if he wanted to give him three years. And David Carson might not be so lucky this time. There was the matter of the dead Doberman. They'd have Duncan in court to testify, maybe. Duncan might listen to reason for enough money, or the right threat, or both. He smiled to himself, thinking of the look on the boy's face that night with the girl.

The figure struggling up out of the tunnels of night was overalled and walking like a person about to fall, his arms waving with some vague cadence and his legs slowly moving him along, the boy's daddy. Joe slowed and involuntarily moved the truck over when he turned and looked at what was coming toward him, as the old man cocked first a thumb and then moved toward the vehicle in an incoming rush with his arms out so that Joe had to wrench the wheel violently to keep from hitting him. He swept past him and slowed down even more, the figure in the brakelights' red glare receding behind him in the rearview mirror.

He drove very slowly and thought about walking home drunk in the dark for no telling how long and he wondered how it would be to be in that place.

He went another mile and then pulled into a driveway and turned around and went back up the road. The old man was about where he thought he'd be, plodding along with his head down and his arms swinging. He pulled across the road and slowed more and then stopped in front of him, the window down, his arm hanging out. The old man came closer, his steps heavy in the roadside grass, the crickets talking, a dead snake flattened in the road there in front of him. He walked beside the pickup window and never turned his head or gave any indication of anything and kept on walking and walked on past and Joe turned his head to see him growing darker as he stepped beyond the glare of the taillights. He knew he should let it go at that.

He went on up the road and threw the beer can into a ditch and got another one and smoked a cigarette. He hadn't been up around the old place where they lived in a long time, but there had been a time when seven coveys of birds could be stalked and shot at, a long time ago when he had good dogs, when the kids were little, before most of his troubles. There were Saturday afternoons when he could put the two dogs in the trunk and take his automatic and walk the fields in the stiff winter breeze and be one with the dogs, his eye steady on the barrel, the birds exploding from the cover on their dynamite wings, the brace, the shock of the shot, the birds dropping neatly, folding, the dogs already starting to move toward them. A long time ago, days he'd almost forgotten about. The house was in bad shape even then, the logs sagging in the middle and the vines climbing up their sides. It had been deserted for who knew how many years and was probably older than anybody he knew or had ever known. He couldn't imagine them living in it.

He thought about the boy's daddy taking the boy's money. A sorry motherfucker indeed.

He turned around in a churchyard and drove back down the road and turned the radio off. Wade was still going down the road when he pulled up beside him and stopped. The door opened immediately and he got in and placed his feet around the cooler and reached in nearly instantly and got himself a beer.

"Help yourself," Joe told him.

"Goddamn, I thought nobody never would stop."

"I tried to while ago and you just walked on past me. What are you doing out walking?"

"Well, I been flyin but my arms got tired. Damn that beer's good and cold. Can you take me home?"

"I don't know. I don't know if I can get up in there or not."

"Aw yeah, you can get up in there. Willie and them brought me home the other night."

"Willie?"

"Yeah. Willie and Flo. Aw, the sumbitches had been drunk, up at Memphis. Went up there and they had a bunch of money and they got off with some of them old stripper girls and went to this hotel in West Memphis, Willie said this old girl'd been rubbing his dick and everything so he said what the hell I'll fuck this son of a bitch, she went over there in the bathroom to do something and he passed out watching the television, come to she was going out the door, well, he jumped out of the bed and run grabbed her, had all her clothes on. Well, naturally she kicked him in the balls first thing and he grabbed her leg going out the door and she started in kicking him, him laying there hollering you mother-fucker and then she started slugging him with her damn purse in the head and liked to knocked him out again, so he grabbed her goddamn pants and pulled em off and said she took off out across the parking lot in her panties and he said she had a fine ass. Well, there was another son of a bitch in there he said done fucked and sucked everything in sight and she was passed out in the bed. Well, he said the old girl with his money was try-ing to get into a car out there and leave and his balls was about to kill him, so he runs out butt naked and she's cutting the top out of a convertible with a fingernail file and he just knocks the cold shit out of her with his fist and grabs her purse. The damn cops get there and one of em sticks a goddamn pistol right in his ear and says I'd love to see you breathe, and them cocksuckers take em to jail and it costs em twenty-four hundred dollars and he didn't even get a blowjob. I may go up there with em next weekend."

He turned his beer up and drained it with his throat pumping and rolled the window down and threw the can and puked down the outside of the door and rolled the window back up and got another beer. He opened it and started drinking it.

"Where you been?" Joe said.

"Over at some niggers'. They wouldn't give me no pussy. Black motherfuckin son of a bitches. Damn dog bit me."

He reached down and pulled up the leg of his overalls and ex-amined a wound there and let it fall back down over his wet shoes.

Joe could smell him, an odor of old sweat and puke and garbage. He turned the vent so that fresh air would blow in.

"Y'all still living up yonder where you were?"

"Yeah. We got it fixed up pretty good now. I won some money and bought some furniture. One of my girls run off, I reckon."

"One of your girls? How many girls you got?"

"I had about five at one time. I had three boys. Two of em's dead."

He never had heard the boy mention that. Or five sisters either. He guessed there were a lot of things about him he didn't know. Never would know. And might be better off not knowing.

"Aw, goddamn, she had to smartmouth everything I said. I got in a goddamn fistfight with her a while back. She stole some money from her mama and I tried to whip her ass and she picked up a goddamn board there bout long as your leg and hit me with it. I told her to get her ass out and she left. I don't know where she's at. Don't care, neither."

"How old's she?"

"Hell, I don't know. Seventeen or eighteen, I guess. You ain't got a bottle of schnapps in that cooler nowhere, have you?"

"Naw."

He was surprised that the old man had cigarettes, but he did, and his own lighter, and there was a bottle of something in a paper sack in his hip pocket, resting against the seat. They drove down through the bottom, and past the fields, and the cows stood behind fences or lay scattered over the pastureland in dark forms like black boulders against the emerald grass. He ran over a couple of snakes, lining the left front tire up with their heads and hearing the little pops when their heads exploded. Frantically writhing loops lashing the warm asphalt, left behind unseen in his wake.

"Your boy's a good worker," he said, finally.

"He'll probably grow up to be a smartass, too. That's the hardest fuckin work I ever done in my life."

"Give me one of them beers out of there," Joe said. "How many's in there?"

"I don't know," he said. He had his hand down in the cooler sloshing around. "How bout turning on the light?"

Joe reached up and turned the cab light on. The old man had a long scabbed cut down his jaw. Blood was caked on his chin. One sleeve of his shirt was torn nearly off.

"They's five or six in here, feels like."

"Well, hand me one."

The old man passed it over and put the top back on the cooler and reached for the bottle in his pocket. He opened it and Joe turned off the light and watched him out the corner of his eye turn the bottle up and pull steadily on it for a few seconds. He pulled it down and he heard his lungs rattle.

"Gadammmmmmmmmmm," he said.

"What are you drinking?"

"Damn if I know what it is. I thought it was schnapps when I bought it."

"Let me see it."

"I don't know what it is."

"Let me look at it."

He turned the light on again and the old man handed him the bottle. He looked at the label. It was a pint of Ron Rico 151.

"Goddamn," he said, and handed it back. "You could take a match and set that shit on fire."

"I believe you could."

He decided to drive down by the dirt road and see how far up it he could get. It was fairly dry now but he knew he'd never make it all the way. He turned off the highway and eased up the gravel road. The gravel was sparse and the fences were in bad shape. Small flash floods had swept over the road and it was rutted and washboarded. He hated to have his new truck on it. He went across a battered wooden bridge, and it creaked and moaned as he eased the weight of the truck over it. He looked down into the dark water where reptiles and amphibians lay unseen and where the coons walked and fed and listened for the hounds and lived their nocturnal lives.

"I heard that boy was going to buy that old truck off you," the old man said.

Joe glanced at him.

"Yeah. I reckon he is. I meant to get him today and help me bring it home but I never did get around to it."

"Where's it at?"

"Up at Oxford. Out there at Rebel."

"You gonna finance it for him?"

"He said he had the cash."

The old man was silent for a moment. A possum froze by the weeds and then trotted across the gravel with its tail high and went into a ditch and disappeared.

"I doubt if he's got enough money to buy a truck."

"He made plenty this spring. I think he saved a good bit. He supported your ass, didn't he?"

"I don't owe him *shit!*" the old man said, and Joe stopped the truck.

"What you stopping for? It's still a ways up there."

"This is far as I'm going. I'm turning around right here."

"Hell. Take me on up the road. I don't want to walk."

"Tough shit," Joe told him. He put it up in parking gear and looked at him. "That boy saved his money for a couple of months to buy that old truck. And let me tell you something. It's his. I could give a shit whether he pays me the money or not. I piss away that much gambling in one night. But he wants that truck. And if I find out something's happened to his money, I'm going to whip whoever's ass had something to do with it. Now get out. Before I knock your ass out."

The old man was silent. He opened the door and got out and shut it. He walked to the front of the truck and stood illuminated in the headlights, blinking like some huge grounded owl. He went on up the gravel road drinking the beer, stopping to look back once in a while, the wet legs of his overalls flopping around his legs. Joe watched him through the windshield, fading back into the darkness he had come out of, walking along with his head down like some draft animal strapped into a lifetime of hard work with no choice but to keep walking a row. The new truck hummed with precision, the clean dashboard, the bright dials and gauges. The wind lifted and moved a few strands of Joe's hair. He kept sitting there.

"You sorry son of a bitch," he said.

There was a dim light showing inside Henry's house and one vehicle was parked in the yard, an old Pontiac Tempest. The cot-

ton around the house was small and stunted and the whole place
looked as though it had settled into an era of decay. He pushed the
headlights off and sat with the parking lights on for several minutes but nobody came to the door. He was a little drunker now and
he wanted to gamble. Most of the beer was gone but there was
some whiskey under the seat. He lit a cigarette and pushed off the
parking lights and killed the engine. Henry didn't have a dog.
With the house so close to the road, his dogs kept getting run over.
He got out and went across the yard and mounted the steps and
knocked lightly on the door. No sound came from within, only the
soft murmur of a radio playing. He opened the screen door and
stuck his head in.

"Henry. Hey, Henry."

No answer. All asleep?

He stepped into the hall and opened the door on the right. The
room was dark and unoccupied. The door on the left was closed and
he knocked gently before he opened it. A wan blue light from a
silent television screen filled with snow cast the room in a shadowy
glow, a vague inconsistent light where sleeping figures sprawled.
There was an old army cot against one wall and Henry was piled up
in it naked but for his underwear, his arm over his face. Stacy was
in a battered recliner with a quilt thrown over him, his head back,
eyes closed, mouth wide open. And George, the blind brother, sat
in a straightback wooden chair with the 9MM in his hand and a
dead woman at his feet, whose blood had come out of her body
and made a dark rug on the floor around her. He held the pistol in
one hand and a glass of something in the other. His hair was
white, shaggy, disordered. The radio played country tunes softly.

He said one word: "Joe?"

But his visitor had no wish to be verified, and he did not answer. He let himself out as quietly as he had let himself in and got back in his truck and drove home through the black night, into oak hollows, past standing deer with eyes like bright green jewels, who raised their ears and stared as he passed by them and beyond.

There was a knock on the door the next morning and it took him a moment to realize and remember what he had seen, the milky blue opaque eyes dead and lifeless and unblinking and the woman undeniably dead, too, so still, so quiet.

He lay in the bed with the sheets twisted over him and stared at the ceiling until the knock came again. He looked at his watch and saw that it was nearly seven. Probably the boy.

His pants were lying on the floor and he got up and yelled that he was coming, then stepped into them and found his cigarettes and lit one and went up the hall to the kitchen and crossed to the door with just a little irritation toward the boy for waking him up so early. He unlocked it and swung it open and there stood Charlotte in her uniform, the dog fawning over her like a puppy.

"Well," he said. "Surprise, surprise."

She looked up at him and smiled that little smile. Then she stopped smiling.

"I ain't coming in if there's a woman here," she said. He stepped back from the door.

"Come on in. Ain't nobody here but me and the dog."

She came in and he closed the door behind her, wishing he'd combed his hair, and wanting the house to be a little cleaner. He saw her looking at the mess, clothes piled up, dirty socks on the floor. His muddy boots sitting in the kitchen, empty cans on the table.

"I didn't know if he'd remember me," she said.

"Shit. Him? Get you a chair and sit down. Let me go comb my hair. Why don't you make us some coffee? It's up there in the cabinet. I'll be right back."

"Okay. I can't stay but a little bit."

He went back to his bedroom and put on some clean blue jeans and a white shirt that he buttoned halfway up. He combed his hair and brushed his lower teeth and his denture, her asking him things, saying yeah or naw until he finished. When he went back into the living room she was sitting on the couch and she had folded some of the clothes.

"Don't worry about that stuff," he said. "I'll get it later. You put the water on?"

"Yeah."

He busied himself picking up cans on the table, pouring what was left in some of them down the drain, putting the cans in the overflowing garbage can inside the broom closet. He looked at her and she looked awfully good to him. She'd fixed her hair differently, and she'd gained a little weight.

"You look good, baby," he said.

"You don't."

"Well hell, I just woke up. What's the occasion?" She looked down at her fingers and moved a little ring with a red stone in it. She looked back up and she looked uncomfortable.

"I just wondered were you going to see the baby. He's been home for a couple of weeks now. Theresa would like for you to come see him." She waited a moment. "And I'd like for you to come see him. If you want to. I think he looks like you."

Years ago she would have broken and started crying. But that vulnerability in her eyes was gone now, all that cheerful hope. She was forty-seven now.

"I forgot your birthday," he said, and got down two cups from the cabinet, set out the sugar, got milk from the icebox.

"I don't want no coffee, Joe. I've got to get on to work anyway."

He got the coffee pot and poured two cups of water and then looked over his shoulder at her.

"Hell, you don't have to go to work till nine, do you? You got time to drink a cup of coffee I know."

He fixed it for her and carried it to her and retreated back to the kitchen table so that there was at least a barrier of distance between them. He didn't know what kind of thoughts she had about him now.

"Thanks," she said. She pulled out her cigarettes and he got up and got her an ashtray.

"I thought you quit," he said.

"I've cut way down. I don't know if I could quit completely. Working up there helps. We can't smoke inside the building any more. I don't smoke but five or six a day. I feel a lot better."

"You gained a little weight."

"A little."

"It looks good on you."

She didn't answer. For a while they sat in uneasy silence.

"I shouldn't have come over," she said. "I didn't call first. I didn't see no other vehicle outside. When did you get that new truck?"

"Yesterday."

"I like it."

"I do, too."

She smoked nervously, like someone who didn't know how to. After the first sip she didn't touch her coffee again, just set it back on the small table out of the way.

"He's got black hair."

"Oh. The baby."

"Who'd you think I was talking about?"

"I didn't know."

"Are you going to go see him? He's your grandson. It looks like you'd want to. He's cute as he can be."

He picked up his cigarette from the ashtray and sipped his coffee.

"Last time I saw Theresa she wasn't too happy with me."

"That don't mean she don't want you to see your grandson, for God's sake."

"I'd rather see the little fucker that got her pregnant. I'd still like to have a talk with him."

"And do what? Randy's done had a talk with him. That was bad enough. My God. It's a wonder I wasn't pregnant when we got married. You ain't forgot what it's like to be young that quick, have you?"

He didn't answer any of that. He sipped his coffee and looked out into the back yard, smoking his cigarette.

"All she wants is for you to go over sometime and see him."

"Well. I didn't know if she wanted me to or not. I didn't want to be in the way or nothing. Is she doing all right?"

"She's doing fine. She's going back to school to get her GED and then she's going to start out at Ole Miss part-time and work part-time."

"Who's gonna keep the baby?"

"Mama and Miss Inez. I'll keep him at night if she needs me to. I don't never go anywhere."

"You want some more coffee?"

"No."

"Well." He got up and fixed another one for himself, scratching his arm where the lead itched sometimes. He'd thought about seeing if he could have it taken out. He wondered if she'd heard about that.

"Are y'all working now?" she said.

"Naw. We through."

"How'd you do?"

"We did good. For all the bad weather we had."

"I guess you paid cash for the truck."

"Yep. That's usually the easiest." He stood at the sink with a fresh cigarette between his fingers, looking at the floor. "We've got plenty to do this winter. I got enough left to tide me over for once."

"If you don't lose it."

"I don't bet nothing but what I can afford to lose."

"You used to not worry about it."

"I'm more careful now. I don't bet the grocery money no more."

"That's nice to know after all them baloney sandwiches we used to eat."

"I had to eat em, too."

"Yeah. And the kids did, too."

The words seemed to hang in the air for a moment and he saw that she regretted them. After having to monitor him for so long it was a hard habit for her to break, he guessed. She looked at the door.

"I didn't come over here for this," she said.

"What did you come over here for, then?"

She got up from the couch and picked up her purse.

It had a long strap and she put it over her shoulder.

"I just wanted to tell you to come see that baby. Theresa ain't mad at you. She's just hurt because you ain't been over. We don't ask much no more."

"That's all you come over for?"

She turned her eyes to his face and said: "Not quite."

"You need some money?"

"No."

"What, then?"

She waited a long moment and then she walked to him, taking the coffee from his hand, undoing the top button of her blouse. He put his hand in there and touched her.

"You sure we ought to be doing this? We ain't married, you know."

He was smiling but she wasn't.

"I need it," she said.

"Okay."

He took her hand and led her down the hall.

The boy woke in the hot sunshiny hush of the old house and opened his eyes and looked upon his chest to see money piled there, looking as if it had just come out of a washing machine, all crinkled and twisted and perverted and jumbled into a wondrous pile of twenties and fifties and ones and fives.

He looked at it, with the happiness slowly growing on his face, and his hands moved up from his sides and captured it, lifting it above him, releasing it little by little, the crushed bills dropping and fluttering, caressing his face, brushing his eyelids, rustling softly in the air, like leaves in the fall that slip and twist and turn, dancing to the earth, dying in the light.

He was squatting on his haunches in the side yard painting a metal chair when the bossman came around a curve in the road, whistling, and put up his hand and waved. He'd been sitting there painting and thinking about the girl and thinking about going back to see her after he got the truck. He was the only one at home and he didn't know where the rest of them were. All their missions were of a certain furtive nature, like those of dope smugglers or bank robbers.

"Hey," he said loudly, and dipped his brush. He'd found the chairs at the dump and they were perfectly good, just rusted a little, and John Coleman had given him a small can of black paint and a tiny brush when he'd told him of his needs.

Joe walked up in the yard, stepping around the briers, looking in the grass for snakes. He was dressed as if he were ready for a dance or something, clean blue jeans and pale Tony Lama boots and a red striped shirt.

"So this is it, huh?" he said, and the boy grinned and kept painting.

"This is it. I'm painting me some chairs."

"I see that. Got em looking pretty good, too."

His friend squatted next to him and pulled out his smokes, looking all around.

"Damn, I ain't been up here in years. They ain't no telling how old that house is. Was that old tricycle still in there?"

"Yeah."

"Is it still in there?"

"Naw. Daddy sold it to somebody for a antique."

Joe smiled and sat down and leaned back, then stretched out on the grass and lit his cigarette.

"I got me some cigarettes inside," the boy said. He put the paintbrush on the lid of the can and got up. "Let me go in here and get em and I'll smoke one with you. You want a Dr. Pepper? But we ain't got no ice. We run out last night."

Joe held up a hand. "I'll pass. Here, smoke one of mine."

He was already headed in, going up the steps. After he got inside he poked his head out a paneless window and grinned again and said, "It ain't no need in me smoking yours when I got some in here. I just keep em hid so Daddy won't smoke em all up." He drew his head back in.

From where he lay Joe could see under the house and could see the sandstone foundation, the logs resting on strategic rocks maybe chipped flat by some pioneer with high boots and a muslin shirt. The logs had long cracks and they were huge and they bore on their sides many axe marks where the round sides had been hewed away. He couldn't imagine the weight of them, of how men had lifted them and put them into place, master builders turned to dust by now.

The boy came back out and sat down beside him and carefully pulled a cigarette from his pack and lit it with a gopher match, shaking the match out and taking a drag with his eyes closed. He smiled again.

"What you in such a good mood about today?" Joe said.

"I don't know. I just am. When we gonna go see them old girls again?"

"What old girls?"

"The ones we saw other night."

"Oh. Them? Boy, you better leave that old gal alone. She's liable to hurt you."

"Hurt me?"

"Hell yeah. She might squeeze you in two with them legs she's got. What are you doing today, anything?"

"Naw, I ain't doing nothing. You need me to help you?" The bossman sat up and crossed his legs.

"I thought we might go get that old pickup if you wanted to. I need to get it off their lot. I thought I'd drive you up there and you could drive it back home. You can drive it, can't you?"

"Sure," he said. He got up immediately and put the lid on the paint can. "Let's get out of here before they come back."

"Who? Your daddy and them?"

"Yeah."

"Where they at?"

"I don't know. I guess they left sometime last night. They was all gone when I got up this morning."

"What? They just take off and don't tell you where they going?"

"Yeah. It's always been like that."

Joe sat there for a moment longer and then he looked at the boy.

"I talked to your daddy a little while the other night. He said one of your sisters run off. Is that right?"

Gary was wiping the brush on a nearby pine tree. He nodded and stuck his cigarette in his mouth.

"Yeah. Fay took off. Shit, she's been gone for a good while."

"Where'd she go to, reckon?"

"No telling."

"Y'all didn't go look for her?"

"Naw."

"Why not?"

He gave Joe a little smile, lifted his shoulders in a small gesture of fatalism.

"I don't know."

He sat looking at the boy, watched him while he poured a little gas from a jug into a jar and put the brush in it and swished it around.

"She got mad at Daddy," he said. "She didn't like this place. Thought we's gonna get in trouble staying here. You the first one that's come around."

"What y'all gonna do if the owner comes around and runs you off?"

"Move, I guess. I'm ready to go if you are."

Joe waited just another moment.

"You ain't missing none of your money, are you?"

"Not a bit. I'm ready to go if you are."

The old truck was parked beside a new van, and Joe looked through the tinted windows, admiring the blue upholstery and the woodgrained paneling inside it.

"Boy, you could do you some crackin in this thing," he said. Gary was standing beside him with his hands cupped around his face, looking with him.

"Hell fire. I could live in this thing," he said. "Reckon how much it costs?"

Joe stood back and looked around.

"Shit. Probably about twenty thousand. You ready to go?"

"Yeah."

"Let me walk over here and crank it up and see how much gas it's got in it," Joe said, and he pulled the keys out of his pocket and opened the door and got in. The motor turned over slowly and caught, then died. He sat there pumping the gas pedal.

"Always give it a little gas before you try to crank it," he said.

The motor spun again and caught and he revved it up, little spurts of blue smoke coming from the tailpipe. The boy looked up and down the road in front of the auto dealership. Traffic was fairly heavy. He imagined the pedals under his feet and the wheel and the gearshift in his hands. Late afternoons of joyous tranquility on country roads with the radio playing, the girl beside him languishing on the seat, smoking a cigarette, her legs crossed, laughing with him. No more walking up and down the road.

Joe pulled on the handbrake and got out. The truck sat there shuddering and vibrating, idling with a rough stutter.

"You got plenty of gas to get home," he said. "You might want to stop at John's and put some more in it if you're going to ride around some, though."

The boy reached in his pocket and pulled out his money and held it out in a folded wad.

"Here," he said.

Joe looked at it. "What's that?"

"I got the money," he said. "Count out what's yours."

"Hell, I ain't worried about that. Just stick it back in your pocket. I got to find the title when I get home and sign it over to you anyway. You'll have to get you some insurance. You know that, don't you?"

"Insurance?"

"Yeah. It's a law in Mississippi. Can't drive without insurance. It's got insurance on it now. It's still in my name. After I sign it over to you it's yours. I'll show you what all you need to do sometime. Just come out to the house one day before long and we'll find the title and get it fixed up. I'm gonna go on. You gonna be all right?"

"Sure."

"You want me to follow you?"

"Naw. I'll be fine."

"All right, then. I'll see you later."

He walked over to his new truck and got in and cranked it up and pulled out. Gary put his money in his pocket and went to his truck. The door was open and he got in and sat down, looking at everything. He knew that certain pedals had to be pushed. He'd watched Joe drive it over and over. He closed the door. It sat there idling. He stomped the clutch and threw it violently into reverse and let out on the clutch and it died. He pulled it back down into neutral. It cranked easily now that it was warmed up, but he choked it off three times before he noticed the lever sticking out beside his left knee. He unlocked it and pushed it in and managed to back the truck up three inches before he choked it off that time.

By the time he managed to back it out of the parking space, two salesmen from inside had come out, maybe to make sure he didn't run over a new car on the lot. He could see them watching him and it made him nervous. He tested the brakes, jerking to a stop, then pulled it down into low and leaned far over the steering wheel and drove down the hill toward the road. He slammed it to a halt and let out on the clutch and it died again. He sat there cranking on it with one hand tight on the wheel. He looked both ways. Cars were coming both ways. He'd meant to watch Joe to see which way he went, but in all the excitement he'd forgotten to. He thought he might have gone left, so he turned his wheel to the left, too.

———

Cars were still whizzing by. He waited patiently for five minutes, until the road was completely clear, revved the engine up to a controlled screaming whine, and dumped the clutch. The truck shot out into the road and he cut the wheel so that the body slanted over on its springs and he missed second and then dropped it down into third, but it had plenty of torque by then and he went flying toward the first traffic light. Nobody had told him anything about that and he went through it on red. A new Firebird coming across squalled its tires and nosedived with smoke flying into a Volkswagen that had already been wrecked once. The boy weaved to the right and went around them, craning his neck to see. The drivers were looking at him and yelling inside their cars. He went on down the road. He made it through two yellows and one green, but at the next intersection cars were turning onto the street and he had to come to a complete stop. He wondered why the Firebird had come out of a side road like that and just plowed into another car. He felt a little better now, felt that he was starting to get the hang of it. He managed to glide to a fairly smooth halt and get it back down into low. As he sat there waiting and looking around, a police car with siren screaming and blue lights flashing came out of the pack of cars ahead and passed by him at fifty or so, gaining speed. The light turned green and he went on.

He turned the radio on low. The music was comforting, something low and sweet by a woman with a voice full of anguish. He had lots of plans, new clothes and a wash job for the truck, regular trips to the grocery store with his mother and sister in tow. No more walking to John Coleman's. Just drive up there and have a cold drink when he felt like it. Ice cream for little sister before it could melt.

He went halfway through town without incident and then, seeing a beer sign he recognized outside a store, he turned right suddenly without signaling. Somebody behind him blew a horn. He blew his in answer and drove on up to the store, parked and left it in neutral. He pulled out the handbrake, leaving the motor running.

Inside the store there was air-conditioned coolness. Five or six older black men were sitting around a table playing cards in the relative dimness of the rear of the building.

"Hey," he said to everybody. Another old man was almost asleep behind the counter, propped in a high chair with his jaw in his hand. The coolers were on the far wall and the boy walked over and stood looking through the glass. All kinds of brands, all of it cold. He picked a brand that had a colorful label and opened the door and reached in and got a six-pack. He walked back up to the counter with it and set it down.

"I need some cigarettes, too," he said, and started pulling his money out.

The black proprietor came awake groggily and looked at the beer and put his hand on it and looked at the register and blinked and yawned. He looked at the child standing before him and said: "What kind?"

"Winstons," the boy said. "I need me about two packs, I reckon. And some matches, too."

The storekeeper hit some buttons on the register and pulled the cigarettes out of a rack over his head and bent beneath the counter for the matches. He pulled out a sack and put the beer in it and dropped the other stuff in on top.

"You ain't workin for the man, is you?" he said. The boy stopped and looked at him.

"I used to," he said. "I just bought his truck." He pointed out the window. "See it out there? I got to wash it, though."

The man shook his head.

"I think you could use you a new fender, too. Seven eighty."

The police car went screaming back by as he walked out of the store with the sack in his hands. He wondered what all the excitement was about. Bank robbery maybe.

He drove out of town slowly, sipping happily on a cold beer, digging the music, the world as fine as he could remember it being in a lifetime.

There was a woman Joe saw sometimes who lived in a small community twenty miles south of London Hill, and he rode down there one Friday evening to see if she was home. She lived alone and she had a lot of money that she liked to spend on him. He never saw her out anywhere at all and she never mentioned other men, never called, never bothered him, was always glad to see him. Whenever he got with her they would drink for days and wind up in hotels in Nashville or Memphis or Jackson, Mississippi, ordering room service and driving her white Cadillac around and mixing drinks in the car.

The road to her house wound down through low hills and farms with ponds scattered throughout the green pastures. The evening he went, there were bats about and swifts coursing the coming night on their sharp-tailed wings. The earth lay doused in the cool of the approaching night and hay wagons with their loads of tiered green blocks churned slowly over the land with the helpers throwing the bales up. He breathed in the good scent of freshly mown fescue and slowly lifted a beer to his mouth.

The road was white stone and the tires sang slowly as he eased into the night. Silage barns stood in the distance and he saw a bobcat enter its run and disappear through the bordering bushes. Catfish ponds lay faintly green in the gloom, and on one bank, a farmer stood, throwing out feed by the handfuls.

The night moved in and he had to turn his parking lights on. He had to slow down once for a dog that was lying in the road. The dog got up grudgingly, it seemed, looking back over its shoulder as it walked to one side.

"That's a good way to get run over," he told the dog.

He sped up once he got on the state highway, his radio fading as he headed south. He changed to another station but it was no better. Finally he shut it off. He pulled his headlights on and the bugs swarmed in small knots ahead of him, blasting into the windshield and sticking there. The window was rolled down, his arm hanging out, and the wind was moving through his hair. The beer between his legs was empty so he pitched the bottle over the roof of the cab with a hard upward swing of his arm and looked back to see it sail into the ditch. He got another one from the cooler in the floor and twisted the top off, drank deeply and set it between his legs.

Near a small road sign that advertised a steak house he turned right and went slowly down a patched asphalt road where trailer homes and Jim Walter homes sat side by side, their yellow lights glowing, the people reduced to dim forms in the yards, tires hanging from scrubby trees with ropes. Just past this, kudzu lay solid on both sides of the road as far as the eye could see, claiming every hill, every light pole, every tree. Eventually it thinned away and there were trailers once again. A mile past the last one a fine brick home sat back from the road, a long low structure with a well-kept yard and a white wooden fence that ran around all four sides of the property. He slowed and turned into the driveway, a gravel lane between pine trees whose limbs nearly brushed the sides of the truck. He crept down the driveway with the rocks crunching under the wheels. When he came out of the trees there was no car in the carport and no lights on in the house. He stopped.

"Well shit," he said. He sat there looking for a moment, knowing he should have called first. It was nearly dark. He shoved the gearshift up in park and got out, walked up the little brick pathway, looking at the flowers she had planted there, and stepped up on the small stoop and knocked on the door. From somewhere came the faraway yap of dogs. He knocked again and then turned and went back to the truck and got in and turned around in front of the house and went back out the driveway. A car was coming down the road, slowing as it passed him. A man was driving, with a woman sitting beside him, and they looked him over as they went past. He didn't wave. He turned the wheel and lifted the beer to his lips and drove quickly back to the state highway and turned the wheel east, toward Lee County, toward Tupelo and a bigger city and more bars and more policemen available to get after him. Knowing it as he sped that way, not really caring.

Full darkness descended and he kept drinking, tossing the bottles out over the roof and reaching for fresh ones in the floor. Later he stopped at a liquor store just inside Tupelo and bought a bottle of Crown Royal and checked in at the Trace Hall and pocketed the key without going to the room and got back in the truck and drove to a honky-tonk a few miles away. He hid his pistol under the seat and locked his truck. A sign outside the door promised the appearance of George Jones but he doubted it.

There was a long bar inside, and of all the faces reflected in the glass, there was not one he knew. He took a stool and ordered whiskey and Coke and drank the first one within three minutes. When he motioned for a refill the bartender shrugged and poured.

A hefty bouncer with a black shirt and cold eyes watched him from a corner. Joe looked up and saw him watching and locked eyes with him until the bouncer looked away. The bar was dark and country music floated through the smoky air. Couples danced to the slow ones under turning lights. He saw a woman down the bar looking at him, smiling at him, whispering to her friend, turning back to smile again. He picked up his drink and moved that way.

He woke in a strange bed, in a room filled with daylight. He rolled over and rubbed his eyes, his tongue like a thick pad of cotton. He was naked under satin sheets, his clothes hung carefully over a chair. His shoes were on the floor together, neatly, beside the chair. His wallet and keys and change and comb and pocketknife were on a table beside the bed. He dozed, slept again. Settling in peace he dreamed of the cotton fields of his youth, the shimmering rows spread out before him as he worked, the little plants falling away cleanly from the sharp blade of the hoe as he thinned them and dragged out the grass, the brown dirt turning darker as he chopped and stroked with the hoe, working his way toward the end of the row and the shade where the water bottle and his lunch waited. He worked an endless row in his dream and his mouth was dry in the dream and he came awake with a great thirst and sat up and rubbed his face and reached for his underwear and pants.

When he opened the bedroom door, there were some framed pictures of teenaged children in a paneled hall and he knew none of them. The house he stood in was quiet. He could hear a lawnmower running somewhere. To the right was what looked like a kitchen and he had orange juice on his mind if there was any to be had.

There were three plates smeared with the remains of eggs sitting on a bar, before three stools lined up next to the refrigerator. He moved to a double glass door and looked out into a back yard with lawn chairs and a gas grill and an above-ground swimming pool where children's rings with the heads of horses and ducks floated on the bright water. There seemed to be nobody about. He went back to the refrigerator and opened the door, then shut it and read the note addressed to him: *Joe, I had to go to the airport. Fix yourself some breakfast if you want it. I'll be back by eleven, Sue*

The night came back in a rush and he looked at his watch. It was ten-thirty. He opened the door again and pulled out a quart bottle of Tropicana and rummaged through the cabinets until he found a glass and poured it full. He stood at the bar and drank it down quickly and immediately felt better. He couldn't remember exactly what she looked like, and he hated to stick around any longer.

He was buttoning his shirt in the bedroom when he heard the

front door slam. An unfamiliar voice called his name. He heard the sound of her heels clicking on the parquet flooring in the kitchen, then the muffled sound of her footsteps on the carpet of the hall. He turned toward the door. The steps paused. A vision of loveliness there at the door, an approving grin which he returned.

"Hey," he said.

"Hey yourself." She put her purse down and walked over to him and put her arms around him. She kissed him, a small good fragrance in his nose. Her breasts flattened against him and he held her by the shoulders. She kicked her shoes off and moved her hands down the front of him, reaching, touching. He kissed her neck. She pushed him backwards toward the bed. He didn't protest.

That afternoon they lay in the sun on chaise longues with a small cooler of beer beside them, rising to slip into the pool and float on air mattresses, bumping into each other with the warm rays on their bodies. She'd found an old pair of pants with a waist that fit him and she'd cut them off with pinking shears. Her body was tanned in a black one-piece, her brown hair just turning to gray. She was forty-one and she'd been divorced for two years. He learned that her two children had just left that morning for a two-week visit with their father in Orlando.

There was a high wooden fence around her back yard and she lay with her eyes closed, floating on the air mattress with a small smile on her face. Joe watched her in wonder and kissed the tiny freckles at the tops of her breasts. When the sun went straight overhead she took him back to the cool sheets of her bedroom and rocked and swayed over him, that dreamy smile growing to a shuddering twitch of lips with her breath catching harshly in her throat, their bodies in total harmony with each other, the only one ever except Charlotte. She folded herself over him and kissed the side of his throat and stroked his arms and chest with fingers soft and sure. They talked in low voices and when the sun started down she drove him back to the bar for his truck.

That night they had drinks on a patio she and the children had built themselves, porterhouses sputtering while small yellow flames leaped in the gas grill. She kept a careful eye on the steaks and cooked them just the way he liked them, bleeding red juices when she cut them with the knife. He held hands with her at times, something he hadn't done in a long time, and had thought he'd never do again.

Long after midnight he held her in the bed while her head rested on his chest. He listened to the slow measured sound of her breathing and wondered how any man could give up something like her. The sculpted ivory of her torso where the sun had not touched it made her legs and arms look black in the darkness of the room. Her lacquered fingernails rested lightly on his stomach. He dreamed again, but not of childhood fields. He dreamed of the prison yard and of clearing the roadside grass with sickles and the horses the guards rode standing over him drooling their slobber down on his bare back and of enduring it all, watching the days tick off the calendar one by one and the hot Mississippi sun bearing down on the truck patches, him on his knees pulling tomatoes and beans and peas, of the heavy wire mesh fences that fenced in the inmates, of the smoky lights that loomed in the darkness outside the camps, where in the black towers the unseen guards with their rifles sat watching for movement in the packed dirt beside the buildings. He twisted in his sleep, his legs moving. Near dawn he got up and put on his clothes and gathered up his things and let himself out of the house quietly, locking the door firmly behind him, not looking back, getting in his truck and turning on the parking lights, backing out of the driveway slowly, easing into the street, pulling the headlights on and reaching down for the last lukewarm beer in the cooler, eyeing the whiskey that was still on the seat. The gas tank was half full, more than enough to get home.

The old GMC with the battered fender was parked near a wooden bridge on a gravel road three miles from London Hill, and the old man was sitting on a downed tree with his shoes and socks off, paring his toenails with a pocketknife. From time to time he looked over the lip of the creek and watched a big perch that was riffling over the shallow water, flitting here and there above the sand bottom on feathery fins. Once in a while he rubbed his swollen knuckles.

He could see the youngest girl moving in the back beneath the camper bed, the truck rocking slightly each time she moved on the cot and turned uneasily. There was a good breeze easing the heat underneath the massive oaks and he fanned at his opened shirt with his hat. From time to time he lifted a bottle in a paper sack and drank from it, watching up the road, waiting.

After a while a slowly growing noise began to creep its way into the uncertain realm of his bad hearing, and he cocked his head to determine from which direction it was coming. He saw it round the curve, a plume of dust rising close behind it like a small brown tornado that was content to stay in the middle of the road. It was a white Ford pickup. Soon he could hear the rocks speaking beneath the tires.

The girl sat up on the cot.

The old man nodded, putting his hat back on his head, getting up with studied slowness and crossing the ditch to lean against the fender.

The truck slowed, pulled up behind and stopped. Willie Russell was driving and another man was with him. They didn't get out. They sat there on the seat like mutes or idiots, looking back and forth at one another and at him leaning on the fender.

"Hell," the old man said. "Cut your motor off."

Russell cut it off. Wade walked over to the Ford and put his hand on the side mirror.

"Where's she at?" said the driver.

The old man motioned with a cocked thumb over his shoulder.

"Thirty dollars," he said. "Apiece." The one on the passenger side already had his money out. The mutilated driver bent forward in the seat, struggled with his back pocket for a moment, and drew out a cracked brown billfold. He pulled money from it, worn bills greasy and soft as chamois. They paid the old man the combined sixty dollars and he counted it and nodded and pocketed the money. He turned without speaking and walked up the road to sit on the roots of a big tree in the shade about a hundred and fifty feet away.

They got out of the truck together and looked both ways up the road. They entered through the back door of the camper. The door came down. It closed with a rattle, rattled again, then slammed hard.

The old man fanned himself with his hat, lifted his whiskey from a pocket, and looked off into the distant fields burning under the sun.

After a while the truck began rocking, the worn springs creaking mildly as if in some weak protest or outrage.

Gary was in the woods, by the spring. He held his knees and rocked there, back and forth, the wet rag he had soaked in the spring water pressed to the eye already swollen shut. The day was hot and the sun lanced down between the trees and he felt it on the back of his neck like a warm hand. The spring bubbled gently and the leaves whispered quietly and he saw before him not unlike a dream the *seven states they had lived in, transient, rootless, no more mired to one spot of territory than fish in the sea, Oklahoma, Georgia, California, Florida with tall and black-haired Tom falling off the truck and the truck behind them running over his head. That was in 1980. He could see other states, other days, mild ones, mountains in the distance, the little tarpaper shacks where they had once lived. Miles and miles of blacktop highway, the bundled clothes, the mildewed quilts after a night of sleeping on the side of the road. All his life he'd been hungry, all his life waiting behind the old man for whatever scraps of food were left, watching the quick champ of his stubbled jaws, the food disappearing rapidly from the plate, the lowered eyes of his mother as if she hadn't noticed that something was wrong. They'd never furnished an answer for Calvin but he remembered him clearly because he had carried him. He had white hair, white as cotton. They had been living in a camp outside Oklahoma City. There were tents pitched everywhere, and everybody did their cooking outside over fires. But they had little to cook. His father stayed gone most of the time, and when he came in, it was late at night, and there was always trouble, and arguing, and Calvin crying for something to eat, sucking at the meager breasts of his mother even after there was no more milk, and she would shush him, rocking him, both of them crying together in their emptiness. He remembered all that. Finally there was no work for them. The Mexicans had come in a flood and the old man cursed about them, saying how they'd taken all the jobs to where a white man couldn't get work.*

There was a city they walked into one day. They went to a park and located a water fountain, sat down in the shade that Fourth of July. Children raced over the grass, chasing balloons, and people were sitting on the ground eating from picnic baskets. His mother went among the happy people, stooping and bending, saying things to them, getting something here, pointing back to them, getting something there, and he sat with his father and the girls and Calvin in the shade until she returned bringing them chicken legs and biscuits and sandwiches. He took a chicken salad sandwich and broke off little pieces of it, pinched small bits off and fed them to his little brother, watching him gum the bread and meat. He found a cup and filled it with water and gave him small sips.

He ate a little himself. He made sure his little brother got all he wanted. He rocked him in his lap, mopped the sweat from his forehead with his shirttail, crooned him to sleep. And when he slept, he laid him on the soft grass and turned him on his side.

One couple kept watching them. An older couple, white haired, with nice clothes and diamond rings. They came closer finally.

The man pulled at the crease of his trousers before he sat down. His wife lingered nearby.

"That's a beautiful baby you have," the man said.

His father turned and frowned. "Hey," he said.

The man came forward in a parody of a duckwalk, inching along. He had steelrimmed glasses that flashed and caught the dying sun. They began talking. The woman eased herself down on the grass and smiled and smiled. On a plywood stage a band had formed to play bluegrass, boys and men made up in western shirts and jeans and boots, scarves knotted around their necks. There was a fiddler among them and he stepped up and bent to the microphone, bending his arm and keeping his chin tucked. They started playing.

He sat in the grass and heard them and watched them and it seemed like everything would be better in his world if they could find one place to stay. He knew even then that they were different, his people, this family that traveled all night sometimes. The sky grew darker and the lights came up and the people sat on the hillsides and watched the bands come up and make their introductions and then take the stage and do their numbers. There were four bands that played that night, and when the last band ended its final set it appeared that something had been arranged.

He had never ridden in such an automobile. He sat in the back seat of the Lincoln with the girls and his mother, Calvin asleep in his lap. His father was in front, with the man and his wife. There was whiskey. He could smell it. He'd learned the smell of it early. His father and his mother passed the bottle back and forth and she drank heavily, the only time he ever saw her do that. They talked like old friends, his father in his torn overalls and the man and the woman in their nice clothes.

They drove for miles in the night through strange country, some of it barren, flat, gray as stone. Later there were oaks and beeches and river bottoms, plowed dirt black as night. He slept some. And when he woke they were still talking, still passing the whiskey bottle, but his mother and the girls were asleep. And Calvin. By leaning up over the seat he could see him cupped in the woman's arms, his bland face and closed eyes a picture he wouldn't forget. There was a look of radiance on the woman's face such as he had never seen on the face of anybody. There was joy there, the purest sort of happiness. He could see his little brother's face blue in the dashlights, the crown of hair around the woman's head shot through with light. It had been puffed up, made to look thicker than it was. He could see her scalp.

When he woke again it was to early morning darkness. The woman and the man and Calvin were not with them. There was a Greyhound bus parked at the curb, gouts of smoke curling from the tailpipe. His mother was having some kind of fit. She had her face in her hands, clawing at it, backing away from the car, and his father was talking to her from behind the wheel. Then he got out of the car and took her roughly by the arm and tried to fling her in through the open door, but she caught herself against the frame and pushed back with her arms, saying no in a high chant. His father wrenched her around by one arm and doubled his fist and hit her in the face and she sat down in the seat. He bent over and caught up her legs and put them inside the car. He started to slam the door but she came back out. He kicked her and she flew back, moaned, and fell half over in the floorboard. His father slammed the door on her and walked around and got in. The boy he was then looked out the window, saying nothing, watching the huge trembling bus idling at the curb with the dark figures of sleeping passengers inside. And the car began to slide away. Window by window they left it, the long gray dog emblazoned on the side moving backward, the nose and the outstretched feet, then lamp posts and storefronts and closed shops and sidewalks and finally empty streets, ghostly intersections where red lights slowly blinked and no people stood. He turned around in the seat on his knees and felt of the rich upholstery of the car and felt the quiet power that began to pick up speed and bear them nearly noiselessly through the night. He watched the town grow smaller behind them until it was only a dim blaze of lights at the end of two black lanes of highway marked on each side with a white strip, the dots and dashes of centerline emerging ever quicker from beneath the trunk, the red glow of the taillights skimming and a yellow sign receding to a small bright dot.

The morning was only a few hours old but the whiskey bottle was half empty. He wasn't weaving badly, and he almost made it to his house. But then he saw the boy going down the road walking, and he pulled over. The boy stood there a moment, looking away with his hands in his pockets, then turned his head to face him with the big purple bruise over an eyelid that was completely closed, the lid stretched tight like the skin of a ripe plum.

"Get in," Joe said.

The boy shook his head. A car came up the road, slowed, and drove between them. The boy stood there looking with one eye across the short distance that separated them.

"Get in, Gary."

He seemed to hold back from taking some final step. Whatever there was in his face was something he hadn't shown before. But finally he walked across the little asphalt road and stepped down into the ditch briefly and opened the door and got in.

"Look here."

The boy turned and showed it to him. It looked even worse up close.

"Your daddy's left-handed, I see," he said, and the boy drew back before he could touch him and eased back against the seat. He looked like a joke but he wasn't a joke.

"How you know he did it?" he said.

"Who else would? Where's your truck?"

The boy said nothing. Joe looked up in the rearview mirror and saw something coming and sat there until it went past. Then he pulled out.

"I should have done give you a boxing lesson."

"I don't need no boxing lesson. I'm gonna bust his damn head open is what I'm gonna do."

"That might cure it. I ain't going to ask you if it hurts. Why don't we stop by the house and get some ice for it? It might take some of the swelling down."

"I had some cold water on it. I don't guess it done no good."

"Ice is about the only thing that'll help it. It's probably too late to help it much."

"Where you been?" the boy said. "You all dressed up."

"I been over at Tupelo. I just got in a while ago. Here, take you a drink of this whiskey. That'll make your head feel better. It always does mine."

The boy picked it up and twisted the top off slowly, tilted the neck toward his nose and sniffed and moved it to his mouth all in one motion, taking just a tiny sip, then another, then he took a full swallow while Joe watched him and drove at the same time. He didn't make that bad a face.

"Get you a Coke out of the floor there. I put two quarters in a Coke machine at a gas station in Pontotoc a while ago and three of them son of a bitches come out."

338

The boy reached for one of the cans in the floor and held the bottle up.

"You done drank all this this morning?"

"Yeah. I started early today. Listen, you got any idea where your truck might be? When did he get in it?"

"Early this morning. I was asleep and heard him crank it up."

"You didn't hide the keys?"

"Naw. I didn't think to."

Joe slowed the truck as they came within sight of his house, and he reached and got the whiskey. He put on his blinker and pulled into his driveway and parked the truck. The dog watched from under the house. Joe lifted the whiskey and pulled hard on it, took it down, and turned to face the boy for a moment.

"You want another drink?"

"Might as well," he said. They sat there in the truck with the sun steadily climbing. "I don't guess it matters what time of day you drink, does it?"

Joe gave him a little wave of his hand.

"It don't to me. I reckon one time's good as another."

The boy opened the Coke and took a drink of the whiskey, then turned up the Coke. He did that twice.

"Damn, you need to quit hanging around me, boy. Give me that bottle back."

He was grinning when he said it. He nearly tousled the boy's hair, but turned instead and looked at the house. It looked like they might as well go find the old man and see if they could untangle things.

"I reckon he's got Dorothy with him."

"Who's Dorothy?"

"That's my little sister. The one that can't talk."

"Can't talk?"

"Won't. She used to would. She just quit one day and ain't never said another word."

"You shittin me."

"Naw."

"How old's Dorothy?"

"I don't know. I guess about twelve or thirteen."

"He ever took her off before?"

"Not that I know of."

A dark thought moved in his mind and he looked at the boy carefully. He put the top back on the whiskey.

"Tell you what," he said. "I'll run in here and grab some ice and a towel. You had anything to eat?"

"I don't want nothing to eat."

"All right. Just hold on and we'll ride down the road and see if we can see your truck anywhere, okay?"

"What if we find it?"

"I hope we do," he said, and got out. He lit a cigarette, said something to the dog, and went on in. He was back out in a few minutes with a towel and some ice. The boy watched him while he laid the towel out on the seat and started cracking the ice in the tray, not saying anything else.

When they backed out into the road, Gary had a large wad of towel pressed against his eye. Joe drank some more of the whiskey and then ran one hand through his hair. Part of his shirttail was hanging out of his pants and the truck was low on gas.

"I come by other day and I didn't see your truck," the boy said. "I was gonna see about that title or whatever."

Joe was mostly looking out the window while he was driving. Somebody was building an addition on Jim Sharp's house and a concrete truck was backed up against the house, the huge cylinder turning, men working in high rubber boots.

"Yeah," he said absently. "Yeah, we got to get that fixed up one of these days."

He turned off onto the first gravel road and reached for the whiskey again.

"You ought to just move in with me is what you ought to do," he said. "Hell. At least you wouldn't have to worry about him stealing your goddamn truck."

He took a drink and passed the whiskey back to the boy. The road was dry but spotted here and there with mud holes and he splashed through most of them. The cows stood back from the road like statues as they passed. The sun was bright, the pastures laden with dew shining in the early morning light. Bobwhites dusted themselves in the road before running single file into the weeds.

"Move in with you?"

"Hell yeah. You could find something to do this summer. Shit, paint houses or something. I know you could find you a job. You could probably get on a crew and do some carpenter work or something. It's lots of stuff to do, you just got to get out and find it."

"What would I do about them?"

"What do you mean?"

"Well. I'd kind of hate to just go off and leave em."

"Why? What in the fuck have they ever done for you?"

"I just kind of hate to go off and leave em."

"Stay with em, then."

They went across the first bridge and it rattled underneath the truck as they rolled over it. He could see the old GMC from there, parked beneath the oaks that shaded the next bridge. The other truck was parked beside it, the white Ford, but he already knew what they would find. He slowed the truck. The sun was climbing higher. He thought about the old cons in the pen who would take the young and pretty boys down and how they would muffle their screams while they raped them. How everyone turned their heads and looked away because it didn't concern them and it wasn't them.

"Listen. If anything starts happening, you get your little ass out of the way. You hear?"

"What do you mean?"

"I mean get out of the goddamn way. Put the cap on that whiskey."

A man was leaning against the fender of Willie Russell's truck. He'd seen him before, but he didn't know his name. He hung around the Dumpsters sometimes, driving a wrecked car full of feral children.

"Stay in the truck," he said, and stopped and reached under the seat for the pistol. He saw Wade stand up quickly and walk across the road and climb with a wild and pawing energy the brier-infested opposite bank, look back once and pile headlong over the fence to vanish in the tangled growth there. When he had the gun in his hand, he stomped on the gas and sped across the bridge and slammed on the brakes, and was out the door with the pistol almost before the truck had stopped moving. The man on the fender started backing away with his hands out in front of him, then he turned and started running. Joe let him go.

When he stepped around the end of the GMC and looked inside and saw what was back there, saw the blood on the little girl's legs, he backed up a step and waited. She was putting her clothes back on. Russell was fastening his pants and trying to talk to him. Joe didn't answer him. Gary had gotten out and was suddenly standing beside him, looking in.

"Dorothy," he said, the only word he said.

"Get her out, Gary. Get her out and get her in my truck and you go home."

She pulled her dress down and quickly got off the cot, and slid out over the top of the tailgate. Gary took her hand and led her away. She wasn't crying. She wasn't making any noise at all. Gary put her in the truck and went around and got behind the wheel, and Joe looked at him for a moment. Their eyes met for the last time and then the boy looked down at the gearshift. After a few seconds he pulled the lever down and took his foot off the brake and they went rolling past. Joe realized too late they'd taken his whiskey. The truck went on down the road and when the sound of it finally faded away, he walked close with the little gun out in front of him and pushed the safety off with his thumb. It made a tiny click and Russell closed his eyes and covered those eyes with his hands. Waiting. Joe started to tell him a few things first, then decided there was no need of that.

EPILOGUE

That winter the trees stood nearly barren of their leaves and the cold seemed to settle into the old log house deep in the woods. The old woman felt it seep into her bones. Each morning the floors seemed colder, each day it was harder to crank the truck. The boy piled wood for colder days to come. At odd times of the day they'd hear the faint honking, and they'd hurry out into the yard to see overhead, and far beyond the range of men's guns the geese spread out over the sky in a distant brotherhood, the birds screaming to each other in happy voices for the bad weather they were leaving behind, the southlands always ahead of their wings, warm marshes and green plants beckoning them to their ancient primeval nesting lands.

They'd stand looking up until the geese diminished and fled crying out over the heavens and away into the smoking clouds, their voices dying slowly, one last note the only sound and proof of their passing, that and the final wink of motion that swallowed them up into the sky and the earth that met it and the pine trees always green and constant against the great blue wildness that lay forever beyond.

Printed in the United States
6577

9 780446 394383